Danger *at* *the* Cove

Also by Hannah Dennison

ISLAND SISTERS

Death at High Tide

HONEYCHURCH HALL

Death of a Diva at Honeychurch Hall
Tidings of Death at Honeychurch Hall
Dangerous Deception at Honeychurch Hall
Murderous Mayhem at Honeychurch Hall
A Killer Ball at Honeychurch Hall
Deadly Desires at Honeychurch Hall
Murder at Honeychurch Hall

VICKY HILL

Accused!
Thieves!
Exposé!
Scoop!
A Vicky Hill Exclusive!

Danger *at* *the* Cove

An Island Sisters
Mystery

Hannah Dennison

MINOTAUR
BOOKS
NEW YORK

First published in the United States by Minotaur Books,
an imprint of St. Martin's Publishing Group

www.minotaurbooks.com

Map illustration by Rhys Davies

Library of Congress Cataloging-in-Publication Data

Names: Dennison, Hannah, author.
Title: Danger at the cove : a mystery / Hannah Dennison.
Description: First Edition. | New York : Minotaur Books, 2021. | Series: The Island sisters ; 2
Identifiers: LCCN 2021008172 | ISBN 9781250194503 (hardcover) | ISBN 9781250194527 (ebook)
Subjects: GSAFD: Mystery fiction.
Classification: LCC PS3604.E5867 D36 2021 | DDC 813/.6--dc23
LC record available at https://lccn.loc.gov/2021008172

Our books may be purchased in bulk for promotional, educational, or business use. Please contact your local bookseller or the Macmillan Corporate and Premium Sales Department at 1-800-221-7945, extension 5442, or by email at MacmillanSpecialMarkets@macmillan.com.

First Edition: 2021

10 9 8 7 6 5 4 3 2 1

To Mark Durel
With affection and gratitude

WINDWARD POINT

SHIPWRECKS

WHISTLE BUOY

RUINED WATCHTOWER

WILLIAM'S BENCH

WILLIAM'S QUAY

CAVE

TREGARRICK
ROCK

LAKE

BIRD HIDE

TO BRYHER

TERRACE

THE DELL

WILLIAM'S WOOD

GALLEON
GARDEN

TREGARRICK ROCK HOTEL

SEA TRACTOR

MERMAID LAGOON

SKIFF

CAUSEWAY

TO ST. MARY'S
3 miles

TO PENZANCE (CORNWALL)
28 miles

RHYS DAVIES

Danger *at* *the* Cove

Chapter One

"Do you mind moving those plants into the potting shed before you run my errand, Ollie?" I pointed to the flimsy trays of plastic pots filled with geraniums, begonias and lavender that stood next to the empty cast-iron urns along the flagstone terrace. "There's another storm forecast for early evening and I don't want them to blow away."

I put down my fork and trowel and got to my feet, dismayed at the stiffness in my legs from kneeling. For the past two hours I had been weeding the flower borders in preparation for the upcoming grand reopening of the Tregarrick Rock hotel.

"Anything for you." Ollie, our newest hire, gave me a gold-capped smile. "I'll get the wheelbarrow."

It was a crisp spring day in March with a light breeze. Birdsong mingled with the muffled sound of waves breaking against the distant rocks below. White clouds drifted across a blue sky, but far away on the horizon, toward the Atlantic Ocean, an ominous band of dark clouds was building.

Over the past few months, the Isles of Scilly had been struck by a number of ferocious storms that were working their way through the alphabet. Tonight we were promised Storm Iona. Though all the islands had taken a battering, nature had given Tregarrick in particular one extraordinary surprise. The violence of the weather, coupled with extreme spring tides, had shifted the seabed, and three days ago the wooden ribs of what remained of a nineteenth-century schooner had surfaced from the deep in Tregarrick Sound.

Shipwrecks were not uncommon around Scilly. In fact there were over eight hundred wrecks scattered all over the ocean floor. Still, it was impossible not to get caught up in the mystery of what had happened to the old schooner and what treasures might emerge from the deep. Unfortunately, Cador Ferris, the one person who would really know, was off the grid in the Bahamas on a marine salvage expedition himself. As heir to the Tregarrick island estate, Cador was our landlord. He'd already left for Nassau when Margot and I moved in three months ago, and despite repeated attempts to get ahold of him to discuss repairs to the hotel, we'd not heard from him for weeks.

In the meantime, thanks to a supermoon, combined with a phenomenon called syzygy and the vernal equinox, we were eagerly awaiting tomorrow's once-every-eighteen-years chance to actually walk on the seabed out to the wreck at low tide.

"You mentioned you were seeing your girlfriend after you've picked up my package from the courier," I said to Ollie.

"Yeah, that's the plan."

"Just be mindful of the time and the tide. Don't leave heading back to the last minute like you usually do. And yes," I added firmly as Ollie gave me an eye roll, "I know you're an excellent skipper and I know that the crossing only takes twenty-five minutes from St. Mary's, but I'm serious. Can't you meet Becky another day when there isn't a storm forecast?"

"Nope," said Ollie. "Her dad has finally agreed to see me. It's time to talk to him man-to-man."

"Well, good luck," I said. He was going to need it.

Ollie's infatuation with young Becky Godolphin, the only daughter of one of the founding families on Scilly, seemed to be all consuming.

"Just because I don't wear a suit, old Cyril thinks I'm not good enough for his only daughter," Ollie went on. "Idiot."

I regarded our twentysomething handyman-cum-gardener with amusement. With his dark shoulder-length hair tied back into a ponytail, gold-capped front tooth, body piercings and both arms heavily tattooed with skulls and mermaids, Ollie could easily pass for a pirate.

My sister, Margot, and I had yet to meet Becky, who by all accounts was classy and intelligent and just as obsessed with him—enough to change her mind about going off to study medicine at the Imperial College London so that she could stay close by Ollie.

Margot sided with Becky's father. Even though we'd never met him, we'd heard that Becky was the center of his world. I could understand Becky's fascination with Ollie, though. He had an insatiable curiosity, committing to memory everything about the history of the Isles of Scilly, including where to catch the best sunset or watch for a rare migrating whale. He had a wicked sense of humor and was the epitome of a bad boy with a heart. He was also an excellent seaman.

"You'll have to ask Dennis for the boat key to the *Sandpiper*," I said.

The *Sandpiper* was a twenty-four-foot cabin cruiser. Margot and I had bought her secondhand from Cador and had her repainted a vibrant turquoise. It was our latest in a rather long line of acquisitions—including new laptops and new appliances—that Margot had insisted were necessary to make running our fifteen-bedroom boutique hotel smooth and efficient.

Although we would continue to use the trademark "sea tractor" to ferry visitors across from Tregarrick at low tide, having the cruiser gave us the freedom to get off the tidal islet whenever we chose.

"On second thought, I'll be fine in my old dinghy," Ollie said suddenly.

"You told me the dinghy had a slow puncture," I said. "I really don't want my new camera equipment sinking to the bottom of the ocean and you with it. Take the *Sandpiper*."

"I didn't know you cared." Ollie grinned. "Okay. I will. Do you need anything else while I'm on St. Mary's?"

This was another thing Margot and I had rapidly discovered as we'd adjusted to life in the Isles of Scilly. Apart from a general store and a post office, the Salty Boatman pub, St. Paul's church and a cute little gift shop on Tregarrick itself, all the shops and social services were on the main island.

"Thanks, but there's no need. We've got a grocery shipment from Tesco tomorrow." Then I thought again. "Actually, there is one more thing. Would you mind checking our PO Box at the post office?"

When Margot and I first moved to Tregarrick Rock, we decided to rent a postbox on St. Mary's. We rarely used it, since it turned out that the inter-island postal service was surprisingly efficient for regular mail, so we often forgot to check it.

"Dennis can give you the key for that, too," I said.

Ollie pulled a face.

I regarded him with dismay. "I thought you and Dennis were getting along better now."

Ollie shrugged. "Sort of. He's just so . . . particular about everything. He lives by his watch."

It was true. As a former marine, our hotel manager, Dennis Simmonds, was obsessed with punctuality and dependable to a fault. He was the complete opposite of Ollie, who preferred to "go with the flow" and had a propensity to tell Dennis to "lighten up."

Ollie picked up the handles of the wheelbarrow and, with me following, set off for the potting shed.

"No point unloading the plants," I said as Ollie maneuvered the wheelbarrow inside the small space. I closed the old wooden door behind us on our way out and looped the padlock through the hasp, but as usual I didn't lock it.

"Don't forget to take your waterproofs," I reminded Ollie. I pointed to a mug with a pirate on the front that he'd set down on the fence post. "And please take your mug back to the annex."

He rolled his eyes again. "Anything else?"

"Make sure your phone is charged in case I have to call you."

"Yes, Mum."

I laughed. "You bring out the maternal instinct in me." It was true, he did. Ollie didn't like to talk about his past—I knew he had grown up in care somewhere in Cornwall—and I never pressed him. He seemed happy to be working for us and I was pleased when he said he felt he was part of our little family.

Behind the potting shed was a narrow path flanked by a laurel hedge that led to an ugly green prefab annex. Accessed down a short flight of steps, it was used to house six seasonal staff. At the moment it was home to Ollie, and temporary accommodation for Sam Quick, one of the two electricians who were currently rewiring part of the hotel.

Ollie picked up his pirate mug and headed for the annex, reappearing five minutes later dressed in waterproofs. He brandished his iPhone. "Call me if you think of anything else." He hesitated, then took a deep breath. "Any chance I can have an advance on my paycheck this week?" He gave a sheepish grin. "Becky's twenty-first birthday is coming up and she's seen a bracelet she really likes."

I wished he hadn't asked. Ollie was lucky we paid him weekly—and in cash—but he'd asked Margot already for an advance this week and she'd said no.

"Ollie, I'm sorry, but not this time," I said.

The problem was that Margot and I were strapped for cash, too. My sister's divorce settlement was still not final and the small life insurance policy from my deceased husband, Robert, had all but gone. I'd even had to sell a Rolex Comex Submariner from the watch collection that he had—by sheer luck—transferred into my name before he died and that thankfully his creditors couldn't touch. Perhaps it was just as well that Robert had died before he knew the full extent of the damage his business manager had done to all his hard-earned savings.

Then, just two weeks ago, an electrical fire had started in the kitchen. Fortunately, Dennis had put it out before it had taken hold. We subsequently discovered that the hotel wiring hadn't been updated for over forty years and that it couldn't support most of our new appliances.

By some miracle, we managed to find a local electrical company, Quick & Sons, who agreed to rewire the one branch circuit that mattered until we could afford to do the rest, but the process had been incredibly disruptive. Right now the kitchen, reception area and Residents' Lounge resembled a building site and, with the open house just over a week away, I was worried we'd never be ready in time.

"Speak of the devil," muttered Ollie just as Dennis, a burly man in his fifties with closely cropped hair and a military bearing, strode toward us. He was wearing his civvy street uniform of formal black jacket and red polka-dot tie.

Dennis had worked at the hotel for years and stayed on when Margot and I took over. He had been fiercely loyal to Cador's father, Jago, and it was only during these past few weeks that he had warmed to us as he realized we weren't planning on making drastic changes to the spirit of the hotel.

"I thought you'd like to know that I just got a call from Cador Ferris," said Dennis. "He received my email about the wreck and is on his way back. If he makes all his connections, his ETA will be between sixteen and seventeen hundred hours on Sunday afternoon."

"That's great news." I was pleased, as the list of things to discuss with Cador was growing longer by the day. Gesturing to Ollie, I added, "Ollie needs the keys for the *Sandpiper* and PO Box. He's running an errand for me."

Dennis's hazel eyes narrowed. "But I gave him the key two days ago."

"Oh right, yeah. You did." Ollie flashed a smile. "I think I left it in the glove box on the boat—"

"Then you'd better go and check," said Dennis.

"Can't you just give me the spare?" Ollie demanded. "I'm in a bit of a hurry and by the time I've gone down to the causeway and—"

"Just give him the spare, Dennis," I said. "Ollie will give both boat keys back to you when he returns. Right, Ollie?"

"Cross my heart and hope to die," said Ollie with a grin.

Dennis gave a grunt that implied he was not amused. "Margot is looking for you. She's in reception."

"Will you let her know I'm out here?"

Dennis nodded and strode away, with Ollie hurrying to keep up with his long strides.

My thoughts automatically turned to Cador.

Following Jago's death and the decision of his mother, Tegan, to live in Germany with her first love, who was undergoing treatment for cancer, Cador had inherited the island of Tregarrick. Luckily for us, he wasn't interested in running the hotel, which was why Margot and I had been able to lease it for a peppercorn rent with the proviso that we handled the miscellaneous "repairs." Unfortunately, those repairs were proving to be far more expensive than either of us had predicted.

The enormity of what Margot and I had taken on hit me afresh. We had jumped at the opportunity for a new start far away from her old life in Hollywood and mine in Kent. Although we still loved this corner of paradise and were determined to make it work, I knew that Margot had been having second thoughts, and I'd be lying if I said I hadn't had them, too.

We were no strangers to the hospitality trade. Our parents had run a guesthouse in Hove for years before they both died; I had worked at the Red Fox art gallery in Soho until I married Robert, and Margot had moved to Los Angeles with her producer husband, Brian, where she'd run an independent film production company and rubbed shoulders with Hollywood celebrities.

And then, all of a sudden, everything changed. Robert died and Brian divorced Margot and a few months later, here we were running a crumbling Art Deco hotel twenty-eight miles off the southwest Cornish peninsula.

We must have been mad, I thought. But then, as I perched on the edge of a stone planter, I took in the magnificent views and remembered why I had fallen in love with Tregarrick Rock in the first place.

It was no more than an islet, connected to the island of Tregarrick by a tidal causeway that took about fifteen minutes to cross on foot or by sea tractor. For an islet so small, the topography couldn't be more diverse.

On one side, broad terraces of subtropical plants, lofty California pines and holm oaks crept up the hillside to meet William's Wood, a dense forest of evergreens that provided a shelterbelt to the eastern elements. There was also a Bronze Age burial chamber set into the hillside.

William's Wood overlooked Tregarrick Sound toward the neighboring island of Bryher. Below was Seal Cove, aptly named for the seals that loved to bask on the rocky outcrops. On the same side was the Mermaid Lagoon, a saltwater swimming pool cradled in a natural rock formation and accessed down a steep flight of stone steps from the rear of the hotel.

Moving to the center of the island was a dell, or grassy basin. Enclosed by lush plants, it was laid to lawn and dotted with a handful of topiaries in exotic shapes. A box hedge archway opened onto one of my favorite places—the Galleon Garden of ships' figureheads. Many of them had been salvaged from the surrounding ocean floor.

Beyond the dell was a lake, bordered by tall pampas grass and reeds that hid a wooden bird hide. Scilly was a well-known stopping place for migrating birds and a paradise for bird-watching—something I had recently discovered and loved to do.

To the west stretched a rugged coastline blanketed with gorse and bracken that reminded me of the Scottish Highlands, complete with a ruined watchtower that perched majestically on the bluff. It had been a place of refuge for the Royalists seeking sanctuary during the English Civil War.

Finally, there was Windward Point Lighthouse right on the northernmost tip of the island—the perfect logo for our hotel stationery.

The beauty of our new home, and all the renovations we had made so far, had helped diminish the harrowing events of the past few months. The loss of my adored Robert was becoming more bearable.

For the first time in years I had taken out my camera again. It was one of the many things I had enjoyed doing before I had married, and had willingly—though unconsciously—put aside in favor of spending time with Robert. Now I was on a voyage of self-rediscovery and although there were times when my sadness was overwhelming, the magic of Tregarrick Rock had become my sanctuary, too.

Unfortunately, the same wasn't true for my sister. She was impulsive and headstrong, and I'd been worried about her abrupt decision to quit Hollywood and move here. I knew that she missed her life in Los Angeles, and any day I expected her to announce that she was going back to California.

"Hey, sis. There you are!"

I hadn't heard Margot's footsteps as she approached. Wrapped in a cherry-red cashmere shawl, she waved a clear plastic folder at me. "Kim's magic checklist!" Margot picked up the kneeler, carefully balanced it on the planter next to mine and took a seat.

"You shouldn't sit on a cold surface," she scolded. "You'll get hemorrhoids."

"That's an old wives' tale," I said.

"Maybe." She grinned. "But is it worth the risk?"

I regarded my big sister with relief. Her eyes sparkled and she actually seemed cheerful.

Margot had evidently spent the morning touching up her roots—she was not a natural blonde. I had wondered what she had been up to and was pleased at this display of vanity. Margot—usually high-maintenance—hadn't bothered with her appearance for weeks.

"Good job with the hair," I said. "That explains what you were doing."

"Well, that, and finalizing the plans with Kim for our open house." Kim Winters was our new super-efficient cook-cum-housekeeper-cum-marketing guru. With her obsessive attention to detail, she and Dennis had turned out to be the perfect team to manage the hotel. "Take a look."

Under the heading *Open House, Saturday, March 28th, ten a.m. to six p.m.* was a long list of items, including hiring a calligrapher, writing the labels for the arts and crafts exhibition, setting up the garden furniture on the terrace and confirming local sponsorships for the finger foods and beverages. Most items had been ticked off as completed, except for three major jobs—sorting out the flower beds and planters on the terrace; rewiring and repainting the kitchen, ground-floor reception area and Residents' Lounge; and hanging the art we'd sourced from local artists.

"I think we're nearly there," Margot declared.

"I think 'nearly there' is rather optimistic," I said gloomily. "Have you been in the Residents' Lounge today? You can't just slap on new paint. It will need to be completely replastered first. Quick & Sons are definitely not living up to their name. They're so slow!"

"Well, Kim suggested a painting party," said Margot. "What do you think?"

"A painting party?" I regarded her with amusement. "I don't think I've ever seen you hold a paintbrush."

"There's a first time for everything," she said. "And I know that Louise won't mind."

"Louise?" I said. "Who is Louise?"

Margot looked uncomfortable. "Now, before you freak out, let me explain . . ."

Chapter Two

I regarded my big sister with a mixture of dismay and annoyance as she finished explaining. "When is this Louise person coming?"

"She was going to email me her dates, but the Wi-Fi keeps going down every time there's a power cut," said Margot. "I assume it could be any day."

"But . . . we aren't ready for guests!" I exclaimed. "We don't even have a serviceable kitchen!"

"I told you not to freak out!"

"I'm not freaking out!"

"You should hear yourself." Margot thrust out her jaw. I knew that look. She was not going to budge on this. "Louise is a friend. She won't mind the mess."

"Mess?" I said with scorn. "That's a bit of an understatement."

I thought of the gaping holes in the walls that spewed old Romex wiring and the torn-up shag pile carpets that exposed the rough floorboards underneath the mountains of rubble and dust. Thankfully, the gorgeous Art Deco dining room had escaped the electricians' sledgehammer because it was on a different branch circuit.

"Can't she come when we're ready?" I begged.

"Evie, I want to help her," Margot said. "Her husband, Chester, has just died, and she's devastated. They were besotted with each other. You of all people should know what that feels like. Don't you have any compassion?"

"That's not fair," I said, but Margot's arrow had hit its mark. Of course I knew what it felt like. "I just don't remember you ever talking about her to me, that's all."

Margot sighed. "That's because she's an L.A. friend. Remember? I don't know the names of all your friends and I hardly expect you to know the names of all mine. Besides, you and I were barely in touch."

"That's an exaggeration," I said, though it wasn't far from the truth.

Margot and I had been very close growing up—best friends, in fact. At one time, we had both worked in London. But when she met Brian and moved to Los Angeles and I married Robert, we just drifted apart.

"Louise was the very first friend I made in L.A. Actually, she's British," said Margot. "She was very good to me. She took me under her wing. She was like a sister."

"Thanks," I said wryly.

"You know what I mean. She looked after me as an older sister. You're my younger sister. It's not the same."

I smiled. "I was teasing you."

"She sounded so upset on the phone," Margot went on. "To be honest, she sounded a bit suicidal. No exaggeration. Do you want that on your conscience?"

"Of course I don't," I said. "But she'll have to take us how she finds us."

"She will," Margot said eagerly. "She just wants to be left alone to grieve, and I can't think of a better place to do that than here."

"Where do you think we should put her?" I asked.

"The Agatha Christie suite," Margot declared. "But don't tell her about Lily."

It was the best suite in the entire hotel, but it was also where a longtime resident, Lily Travis, had died just a few months earlier.

"Do you know if Vicar Bill cleared out Lily's stuff?" Margot went on.

"He told me he was going to do it after the funeral." I felt a pang of guilt. I should have followed up, not just to find out if Lily's brother needed my help, but to check on his welfare. I'd been too busy with other things.

"Good," said Margot. "So all it needs is a quick vacuum, fresh linens and towels. Maybe put in a bunch of daffs and some fruit? Perhaps a bottle of bubbly? And don't worry, Louise is really low-maintenance."

"Like you?" I teased again.

"Lower than me," said Margot. "It will be lovely to catch up with her. Hear all the latest gossip and read the trades. I'm *desperate* to read the trades!"

I glanced at my watch—a Rolex Lady-Datejust 28, a

thirtieth-birthday present from Robert. "Let's go inside and check the Agatha Christie suite now. I could do with a break."

As we headed for the kitchen entrance, we found Sam, shovel in hand, digging a deep hole a few feet away from the outside wall that housed the exterior electrical panel.

It had been Vicar Bill who recommended we hire Jerry Quick of Quick & Sons, an electrical contractor from St. Mary's. We'd been so desperate to find an electrician immediately following the fire that we didn't interview anyone else. As it turned out, Jerry's cousin Sam had come back to Scilly for his mother's funeral and agreed to stay an extra two weeks to help him out. They both seemed only too happy to live at the hotel, which solved the logistical problem of working around the tide to get them on-site every day.

Sam's uniform of black holster trousers and red company sweatshirt—*Quick by Name, Quick by Nature*, read the slogan— seemed incongruous with his sun-bleached thatch of hair, dark blue eyes and surfer-boy demeanor. It came as no surprise to either of us when he told us his primary job was working as a dive instructor for tourists out in Chuuk Lagoon in Micronesia. Like Margot, he'd been living overseas for years.

"That looks like hot work, Sam," I said. "How far down do you have to go?"

Sam gestured to a thin metal pole that had to be at least eight feet long. "Deep enough to put this ground rod in. I'm surprised that no one has been electrocuted."

"It's so infuriating losing the Internet every time you have to switch the power off," Margot grumbled.

He gave an apologetic smile. "Yeah, I know."

"I really need to check my email," Margot went on. "I'm expecting something very important."

"It should be up and running now," said Sam. "I'll text Jerry and ask him to go to the turret to reset the modem. Hang on a mo." We waited while he did, and then he looked up from his phone. "I need to pick something up from Pegasus Couriers this afternoon. Can I borrow the *Sandpiper*?"

"It's so annoying that they can't deliver to Tregarrick," Margot grumbled again.

"Ollie's just left," I said.

"Ollie's done what? Gone to St. Mary's?" Margot's eyes widened. "Doesn't he know there's a storm forecast?"

"He'll be back way before then," I said. "He can collect your package, too, Sam."

"Oh, that's alright," said Sam.

"But he's going to Pegasus, too," I insisted. "He's picking up some camera stuff for me for my new darkroom."

"Don't bother him. It's not important," said Sam. "It's just for my godson's birthday."

"How old is he?" Margot asked.

Sam seemed taken aback. "Um. Eight. Why?"

"My godson is eight and I never know what to buy him," said Margot.

"It's a Bazooka water-blast pistol," said Sam. "Top-of-the-line."

Margot smiled. "Sounds fancy."

Sam frowned. "Oh wait. What's the date today?"

"The twenty-first," Margot said.

"Sorry. It's arriving on Monday." Sam gave a sheepish grin.

"That's the thing about living on an island. It's easy to lose track of time."

We left him to finish his digging and headed inside, where my concern about getting ready for our open house hit me afresh.

"Don't worry." Margot gave me a nudge. "It'll get done!"

Kim was waiting for us in reception. "There you are." She brandished her ever-present spiral notepad. "Did you have a chance to look at my report?"

She was immaculately turned out in her usual navy shift dress, along with a jaunty floral scarf—she owned a gazillion different scarves—and kitten heels. Kim wore her hair in a chin-length bob and was never seen without her dark red lipstick.

"Yes," I said. "Very thorough. Thank you."

"I just spoke to St. Austell Brewery and they've agreed to give us four kegs of their best," Kim continued. "I went ahead and ordered the wine from Holy Vale Wines, so, per our discussion on March second about showing support for the community, we're able to focus one hundred percent on local vendors."

"Brilliant," Margot enthused.

"Great job," I agreed.

When we interviewed Kim for the role of housekeeper and chef through West Country Recruiters, she came highly recommended. She'd held down a high-powered job with Top Flight, a sporting event management company in London, and was super-efficient. When we offered her the position, Kim didn't seem to be bothered about the cut in her salary, because she'd received a generous severance package from her previous employer. We couldn't believe our luck, especially when Kim enthusiastically took on the extra roles of handling our marketing and social media needs—even posting about Mister Tig, the hotel cat, on Instagram.

"Now, I hate to add more to your to-do list," said Margot. "But we need to get the Agatha Christie suite ready."

"Upstairs?" Kim looked surprised. "But . . . we agreed the event was just going to be restricted to the ground floor and, if weather permits, on the terrace. No one should be going upstairs."

"No, it's for a close friend of mine, Louise Vanderhoven," said Margot. "She lives in Los Angeles. Unfortunately, she has just lost her husband. It was very sudden and very public."

"Oh, I'm so sorry to hear that." Kim frowned. "Vanderhoven. I feel I should know that name."

"You probably read about it in the papers," said Margot. "Chester died right in front of her at a charity event jammed with celebrities at the Beverly Hills Hotel."

"Oh God. Yes." Kim nodded. "Didn't he get a fishbone stuck in his throat?"

I was appalled. "How awful."

"When is Mrs. Vanderhoven coming?" Kim asked.

"That's the thing," Margot said. "It could be any day. I haven't been able to get ahold of her, so I assume she must be in transit."

"Of course," said Kim. "I'll get to it right away."

"We can do the suite together," I said to Kim. "It'll be quicker."

"Thanks." Margot shot us grateful smiles. "And meanwhile, I'll try to track Louise down." She brought out her iPhone and stared at the screen. "I thought Jerry was supposed to be resetting the modem."

"We only saw Sam a few minutes ago," I reminded her. "Jerry has to go up to the turret. Maybe when this is over, we can get the modem moved to the office. I have no idea why it wasn't put there in the first place."

"We can't have this happen when Louise is here," said Margot. "She'll still be working virtually and will need the Internet."

"What does she do?" Kim asked.

Margot filled Kim in on Louise's glamorous life and all the celebrities she knew. "And with any luck, she'll help us with the open house," she said.

"Evie! Margot!" Dennis hurried over, looking worried. "I've just had a phone call from Vicar Bill. He's left the quay on Tregarrick and they're on their way. Do you know anything about an expected guest—a Mrs. Vanderhoven?"

I gasped. "She's *here* already?"

"And she's had to endure the sea tractor," said Margot. "How infuriating! We could have coordinated with Ollie and brought her over in the *Sandpiper* if we'd known sooner."

"Why don't we put her in the Margery Allingham suite instead?" I suggested. "It's smaller and we can get it ready much more quickly. She's bound to be exhausted."

Margot shook her head. "I promised her the Agatha Christie suite. But don't worry, she and I have loads to catch up on. While you're cleaning, I can take her into the Residents' Lounge—"

"Jerry's working in there," Kim pointed out. "All the furniture is in the middle of the room under dust sheets."

"The office, then," said Margot. "Just call me there when the suite is ready. Oh!" Her face fell. "But what about dinner tonight? The Tesco delivery doesn't arrive until tomorrow, does it?"

The weekly order from Tesco was put on the *Scillonian* from Penzance in Cornwall, twenty-eight miles from the Isles of Scilly. From there, the groceries arrived at St. Mary's and from there another boat would ferry them to Tregarrick . . . and from *there* they either came across on the *Sandpiper* or by sea tractor. It was quite the military operation, but Kim did a brilliant job of managing it.

"I could call Ollie and he could pick up a few things from the co-op on his way back to the harbor," I suggested. "Louise will probably be hungry and want some lunch, though."

"She's from L.A.," said Margot. "She doesn't eat."

"No worries." Kim smiled. "I have some meals in the freezer that I made for these kinds of emergencies. Although, actually, yes, Ollie should pick up some fresh vegetables. I can make a salad. I'll give you a list."

"Wonderful!" Margot and I chorused.

Kim scribbled half a dozen items on a scrap of paper and handed it to me. It was usual salad fare—romaine lettuce, cucumber, avocado—*must be ripe*—Belgian endive, radishes and cherry tomatoes.

"I'll go and get the cleaning supplies and meet you in the Agatha Christie suite," said Kim, and left.

"Kim's in a good mood today," Margot remarked.

"Chelsea won last night," I said.

Margot looked blank.

"The football team," I said. "It seems that Kim and Jerry Quick are die-hard Chelsea fans."

"I'd never have taken her for a football supporter." Margot sounded surprised. "Why am I always the last to know these things?" She gave a yelp of alarm. "Louise is going to be here any minute. I must go and change."

I took a photo of the shopping list and sent it in a text to Ollie. He called me back immediately.

"I don't have any money on me," said Ollie.

"Just tell the co-op we have an account," I said. "Oh, and Sam is expecting a package at Pegasus, too. Just in case it's there."

"Jeez. I'm not sure I'll be able to carry everything," Ollie grumbled.

"My package won't be heavy and Sam's will definitely be light," I said. "It's a fancy water pistol for his godson's birthday."

"Lucky kid," said Ollie. "I always wanted one of those."

Promising he would see me in a couple of hours, Ollie rang off.

Chapter Three

I took the main staircase and stepped onto the first-floor landing, where fifteen suites flanked the long corridor. A large picture window stood at one end, looking east to William's Wood, across Tregarrick Sound and over to the neighboring island of Bryher.

At the other end, a narrow flight of stairs went up to Margot's and my self-contained two-bedroom flat on the top floor, and the three bedrooms that were currently used by Dennis, Kim and Jerry.

Each main suite was named after a mystery writer from the Golden Age of mystery and detective fiction. During the twenties and thirties, the hotel had been very popular as a writers' retreat. It was even rumored that Agatha Christie herself had stayed there many times.

Cador's great-grandmother had been an avid reader and used to hold salons in the Residents' Lounge, where shelves of first editions were available for guests to borrow. It was my hope that we would revive her salons as well as offer creative writing and artist retreats. We'd inherited the built-in clientele of repeat guests, many of whom had stayed here as children themselves and now had grandchildren of their own. Their annual vacations had become family traditions. When we first announced we were taking over, we'd received many emails begging us to keep things exactly as they had always been.

Unfortunately, Margot didn't share my vision. She was obsessed with the idea of putting in a helipad and wanted to focus on corporate retreats, add a spa and a five-star restaurant. It was a touchy subject and one we both kept shelving.

Kim and I reached the Agatha Christie suite at the same time. She had donned an old-fashioned blue floral pinafore. She carried a caddy of cleaning supplies in one hand, and our shiny new Miele vacuum cleaner with all the attachments in a blue cloth bag was slung over her shoulder.

The moment we walked in, my heart sank.

"Oh no!" Kim wailed. "What's all this stuff doing in here?"

It was still full of Lily Travis's possessions. In all the chaos of my move from Kent and Margot's from Los Angeles, we'd just assumed that Vicar Bill had done what we'd asked and packed up all his sister's things. I kicked myself for not making sure.

Vicar Bill had obviously made a start. It looked like most of the silver-framed photographs, porcelain figurines and cut-glass paperweights that had lined the many bookshelves had been put into cardboard boxes ready to be taken away, but everything else stood in random piles on the floor. Lily's bedroom and her clothing hadn't been touched.

I pointed to a connecting door. "We'll move everything into the Margery Allingham suite. It'll be quicker."

The Agatha Christie suite was one of the few rooms that was furnished exclusively with the original Art Deco furniture. There were credenzas, armchairs, a gorgeous Bergère three-seater sofa, Tiffany lamps and a walnut veneer demi-lune cocktail cabinet tucked in one corner. A pair of frosted-glass French doors opened into the master bedroom, which housed a huge king-size bed with a walnut veneer sunray headboard. As well as an en suite bathroom, there was an additional powder room next to the entryway.

Three enormous floor-to-ceiling windows fronted a circular balcony that followed the line of the building and wrapped around a green-topped turret—the inconvenient location of the dreaded modem. Access to the turret was by a spiral staircase that was neatly hidden behind a trompe l'oeil panel painted in blue geraniums.

Kim opened the wardrobe doors. "Wow, do you think we might be able to hang on to these—especially the 1930s stuff?"

Lily's wardrobe held a surprising number of vintage dresses from the 1930s, '40s and '50s, as well as an assortment of fascinators, and a couple of ostrich feather boas.

"They're beautiful!" I enthused. "I'll ask Vicar Bill."

As we worked together, Kim eagerly outlined her vision for the open house and art exhibition. She had persuaded a jazz trio from Penzance to perform 1930s songs for free, with the idea of making them a regular act. As Kim chattered away, it was obvious how much she loved event planning.

Almost an hour later, what remained of Lily's life had been

packed away in boxes—neatly labeled with Sharpie—and black dustbin liners, her clothes and chests of drawers cleared out and moved next door. Lily's vast quantities of magazines had been put into recycling bags, every imaginable surface had been wiped down and I had cleaned the picture windows inside and out with white vinegar. All that remained to be done was to vacuum, and clear out the powder room.

"What about this?" Kim presented a parquetry jewelry box made of walnut. "I've looked inside and it definitely shouldn't stay here. Most of the contents are vintage costume jewelry, but there are a couple of nice pieces—two pearl necklaces and several gold chains."

"Vicar Bill might still be around to ask. He always scrounges a cup of tea."

"I'll pop downstairs right now," said Kim.

"Thanks," I said. "No need to come back. I can finish up in here."

Kim left and I headed for the powder room.

The room was painted baby pink, with a faceted vanity mirror on one wall and double cupboard doors above a washbasin on the other. Lily's toothbrush was still on the countertop and all her makeup pots and brushes were laid out on a white linen cloth. There was a faint smell of perfume. On the hook behind the door was a pink silk robe and sash. I felt as if she would walk in at any minute. It was a little creepy.

I doubted if Vicar Bill would want to keep any of Lily's toiletries, but I put them in the box all the same to sift through later. Not so with Lily's personal pharmacy.

As well as Tregarrick's postmistress, Lily had been the resident midwife. With the nearest hospital on St. Mary's, she had naturally kept a well-stocked medicine cabinet. There were over-the-counter bottles from aspirin to ibuprofen, prescription pills from Vicodin to Ambien—many well past their expiration dates, an assortment of homeopathic creams, a handful of EpiPens, packets of syringes in sterilized sleeves and gauzes and bandages all neatly organized by size.

I labeled this box, too, and put it with the others next door. Returning for one last look, I remembered that Jerry had been working on the modem in the turret and was notorious for leaving his coffee mug up there.

I headed over to the trompe l'oeil and pressed the smallest blue geranium, which triggered the door catch. The panel popped open.

A draught of cold air struck me as I entered the small circular tower room with its navy ceiling painted like a starry night sky. Built-in seats with cushion pads ran around the perimeter. One of the windows was open, so I closed it. Sure enough, an empty coffee mug emblazoned with the Chelsea Football Club trademark sat on the table, along with one of our hotel stationery pads bearing the Windward Point Lighthouse logo. I noticed a cryptic jumble of letters had been scribbled in pen, presumably computer coding or an I.P. address.

The modem was wedged among a sea of long cables that spilled out of a bank of rectangular built-in wall units. Those needed to be shut, too. It was then that I saw the phone on the floor under the cables, a cheap pay-as-you-go mobile. I'd seen Jerry's own phone before, so I had no idea why he'd need a second one up here.

The rotary dial telephone rang from below. Grabbing the coffee cup, I slipped the pad and the phone into my back pocket and clattered down the steps to answer.

It was Margot calling. "How much longer are you going to be?"

"Is she here already?" I said.

"Yes!" Margot trilled. "We're in the office."

"I just have to give the turret a quick vacuum," I said. "I'll be down ASAP." Fifteen minutes later, with Jerry's mug and burner phone in hand, I gave the Agatha Christie suite a satisfied glance-over and went to meet Margot's friend.

. . .

If I had been expecting a grieving widow, I couldn't have been more off.

Louise seemed anything but heartbroken. When I stepped into the office, the friends were talking animatedly and didn't notice me at first. I caught snatches of Johnny this, Orlando that, Nicole and Meryl.

I guessed that Louise was somewhere in her mid-forties, but it was hard to tell because her face was completely wrinkle-free. She had definitely had work done. She wore her long blond hair loose, and severe, heavy eyebrows and scarlet lips made her striking rather than beautiful. I could see why she would be a good publicist, though—she exuded confidence and self-assurance.

Louise was dressed in a Burberry trench coat, black turtle-neck, leather trousers and red suede pixie boots. In fact, her outfit was eerily similar to the one my sister had evidently donned to greet her, although Margot wore Louboutin ankle boots. I hadn't seen those for some time. Margot had also slathered on the makeup—another thing she'd toned down these past few weeks.

I hung back, feeling somewhat self-conscious in my jeans and sweater, but reminded myself that I'd spent most of the day gardening and cleaning.

Margot spotted me and beamed, and I realized she'd put in her Linda Blair emerald-green contact lenses. Margot hadn't worn those in months.

"Here is my baby sister, Evie Mead. Evie, this is Louise Vanderhoven." Margot was clutching two magazines to her chest—the *Hollywood Reporter* and *Variety*. She grinned. "Louise brought them just for me. I am *starved* of industry gossip."

Louise greeted me with a hug, keeping hold of her iPhone. "So lovely to meet you Evie. Gosh. I would never have taken you for sisters!" She stepped back. "You look so different."

"She doesn't usually look like something the cat dragged in," Margot teased.

"I've been gardening," I protested.

"Louise, you're going to love the Agatha Christie suite," gushed Margot.

"That's the one with the turret, right?" said Louise.

"Yes, it's the perfect place to meditate," Margot went on. "And you should see the Art Deco furniture! Of course it looks a little shabby, but that's what makes this hotel so special. It's not sterile like any of the Four Seasons hotels you are used to. I mean, you could be anywhere in a Four Seasons hotel."

"But you don't have a spa," Louise reminded her.

"Not *yet*," Margot declared. "But soon."

Louise turned to me. "Margot tells me that you're an art dealer and professional photographer."

"Art dealer?" I said. "Well, I worked in a gallery once upon a time. As for photography—"

"Evie gave all that up when she married," said Margot.

"It was my decision," I said. "And I was happy to."

"As you well know, she had to take care of him," said Margot.

"Tell me about it," Louise said dryly. "We have to look after the old husbands. But it's worth it in the end. Love them and they'll show you their appreciation." She grinned. "Especially when they're dead!"

Margot exploded with laughter. "God, you are so funny! I'd forgotten how funny you are."

I didn't think she was funny at all.

Louise glanced down at her iPhone.

"She's joking, Evie!" Margot rolled her eyes. "My sister can be so serious."

"Oh. Right. Very funny," I said.

"You're young!" said Louise. "You'll meet someone else, just you wait and see."

"I don't want to meet anyone else." To my dismay, I felt a lump form in my throat.

"Of course you feel that way." Margot looked contrite and hurried to my side. "Louise didn't mean anything by it, Evie," she said gently. "She's just as devastated as you. She's only putting on a brave face—aren't you, Louise?"

"That's me. Brave," said Louise, looking at her iPhone

again. She lifted a finger—"Wait—hold that thought"—and deftly tapped the keypad with astonishing speed.

As we waited for Louise to finish—presumably sending an important text—I took in our newly decorated office. We'd got rid of all the 1970s horror furniture and burned the shag pile carpet. The floorboards underneath had been in surprisingly good condition and had buffed up beautifully. We'd put down a large oriental rug, bought two new desks and oak filing cabinets. Perhaps we shouldn't have splashed out so much on the office, but as Margot had pointed out, we worked in here all the time.

"Sorry," said Louise. "Where were we?"

"How was your crossing from Penzance?" I asked, eager to change the subject. "The locals call it the Great White Stomach Pump."

"I got ample warning," said Louise. "I was fine thanks to Avomine and . . . wait for it—" She delved into her voluminous Birkin bag and took out a pair of motion-sickness cruise goggles, which she put on. "Do they suit me?"

Margot burst out laughing and I couldn't help laughing, too. Louise looked hilarious. I felt myself relax. Maybe I was too serious. Just because Louise seemed flippant didn't mean she wasn't suffering inside. I decided to make a conscious effort to cut her some slack.

"I hope you have an elevator," said Louise. "I fell off my shoes back in the summer and my ankle never healed properly. Those steps up from the causeway nearly killed me and I practically broke my ankle again on that top step. You need to fix it."

"I know," I agreed. "It's on our list."

"I wondered why you were wearing flats. Cute boots, though," said Margot. "Does your ankle still hurt?"

"A little, but luckily there is a pill for that," she said. "There are pills for everything. But seriously, sweetie, you need a helipad or an elevator from the beach. If you want to attract Angelina, you can't expect her to climb Mount Everest."

"Actually, I disagree," I said lightly. "Isn't that the kind of challenge Angelina Jolie likes?"

Louise's eyes widened. "Margot didn't tell me you knew Angie."

"Of course she doesn't," said Margot. "I totally agree about the elevator and the helipad. But Evie won't have it. She wants to keep the old-fashioned charm."

"There is a limit to old-fashioned charm when—" Louise glanced at her iPhone *again*. "I can't access my e-mails. That's weird. I had a signal a minute ago."

"The Wi-Fi can be unpredictable here," I said.

"Now that will definitely be a problem," said Louise. "The kind of guest you want to attract is intravenously connected to the Internet."

"Not necessarily," I said. "Some people just want to switch off from all that."

"Evie loves being contrary," said Margot.

"No, I don't," I said.

"You see!" said Margot. "I rest my case."

"I can tell you now that any talent who claims that they want to detach themselves from twenty-first-century living doesn't mean it," said Louise. "I know a lot of social media influencers and the Internet is their livelihood."

"The goal of this hotel is to escape modern technology," I said. "We want our guests to detach themselves and step back in time. No television in the rooms, board games, cards, plenty of reading, painting, lots of fresh air and dressing formally for dinner, 1930s attire preferred."

Margot gave an exaggerated shudder. "Ugh. Don't you think that sounds awful, Louise?"

Louise thought for a moment. "Oh. Actually, hmm. I quite like that direction. Let me give it some thought and we can talk branding when we meet later to go over your marketing plan."

"Does Kim know?" I asked.

Margot nodded. "She's fine with it."

"I don't want to tread on anyone's toes," Louise declared. "I did have a quick look at your online presence on my way over, however. Who is Mister Tig?"

"He's the hotel cat," I said. "A former resident created an Instagram account just for him. Since Kim took over, Mister Tig has become so popular that his followers have trebled."

Margot sniggered. "She's our cat influencer."

Louise laughed, too.

"It's always helpful to have a fresh pair of eyes, Evie," said Margot.

"And you've certainly got those," I teased.

Louise walked to the window and looked out at the view. "It's so beautiful here. I can see why you love it. Even that weird tractor contraption across the causeway is charming— although I felt I was riding a camel—and the old boy with the dog collar and the parrot—"

"It's a macaw," I said.

"They're like something out of a Disney movie," said Louise. "Hilarious."

"We do have a hotel cabin cruiser," Margot cut in. "But it's being used today—"

"Yes," Louise mused. "I see great things for this place. It's definitely got potential. Put in a spa, a five-star restaurant . . . and who wouldn't want to come here? Richard Branson, eat your heart out!"

"Exactly," Margot enthused.

"You're attracting the superrich," Louise went on. "Not the day-trippers coming to the Scilly Isles."

"It's not called the Scilly Isles," I said. "It's either Scilly or the Isles of Scilly." Now I *was* being contrary, but I couldn't help myself.

"Whatever. Potay-to, potaarr-to, tomay-to, tomarr-to," said Louise. "Pure semantics."

"Not if you want to keep the locals happy," I persisted.

Louise gave a dismissive wave. "What's your budget? I mean, you have to be looking at at least a mill. Dollars, that is."

I gasped. A *million*? Right this minute we were down to our last few thousand pounds.

I waited for Margot to contradict her, but to my astonishment she said, "Yes. That's what we thought, too."

"Luckily, you *have* millions, sweetie," said Louise. "And of course let's not forget Evie's hefty life insurance policy."

"That's very funny," I said. "See? I do have a sense of humor."

But Louise didn't seem to hear. "Don't spend all your alimony, though, Margot," she ran on. "Keep some back for yourself. Having been married three times, I don't want you to make the same mistakes I did. I didn't get much from my first, and completely blew through the second settlement. But the third . . . believe me, I'm very conscious of getting older and building a nest egg for my future."

I waited for Margot to contradict that, too, but she just said, "Exactly!"

Louise pointed to a suspicious-looking brown circular stain in the corner above the window. "That does not look good."

"Yes. We'll need a new roof," Margot agreed.

"Sometimes you have to spend a lot to make a lot," said Louise. "But let's face it, you're sitting on a gold mine."

"I keep telling Evie that," said Margot.

"When I arrived on Tregarrick, I felt as if I had stepped into paradise," said Louise. "All those flowers! And the smell—the air is so clean! This place totally reminds me of the South of France or even Hawaii. It really has an island feel."

"That's because it is an island," I said.

Louise regarded my sister with a huge smile. I could see deep affection there.

"Margot, I am so happy to see you thriving." Louise's smile grew broader. "I was going to wait until we opened a bottle of bubbly, but I don't think I can wait any longer."

"Wait for what?" Margot said.

Louise strode to the sofa, where she had left her Birkin bag, and swiftly pulled out a small package wrapped in tissue paper and tied with a red bow.

She handed it to Margot. "Happy birthday, sweetie."

Margot frowned. "But it's not my birthday."

"Margot's birthday was in January," I pointed out.

"Belated, then. Who cares, just open it," Louise exclaimed. "To hell with that old fart of an ex-husband. We'll show him!"

Mystified, Margot pulled off the bow and unwrapped the tissue paper.

Louise beamed. "Guess what, Margot. We're going to make your movie."

Chapter Four

Margot sat there staring at the hardback book with a tattered dust jacket in her hands. Her face was flushed and she looked confused. "I don't understand."

On the cover I could see a lighthouse, and what looked like a submarine lurking in the dark seas beyond.

"I'm giving up all that PR stuff," said Louise. "All those high-maintenance celebrities. You know how I've talked about wanting to executive produce movies and walk the red carpet wearing Armani? Well, I did it. I got it. I took the plunge."

"What is *it* exactly?" I said, but Margot seemed too shocked to say anything.

"*It*, Evie," said Louise, barely able to contain her excitement, "is a book called *Lighthouse of Sorrow* by Ernest Potter. For years all I heard Margot talk about was this book she and Brian were trying to get made into a movie."

"This is one of your jokes, isn't it?" said Margot. "The option expired ages ago."

"After Chester died, it got me thinking about what I really wanted in my life," Louise said. "So I picked up the phone and contacted the author myself. Even though he's ninety, he's as sharp as a tack. Money sure does talk and, well . . . the book is ours!"

"Louise, I . . . I . . ." Margot began. "I just don't know what to say."

"Can someone tell me what's going on?" I demanded.

"It's the story of a lighthouse keeper out in the North Sea during the Second World War," said Louise. "This is Academy Award material. I can't wait to see Brian's face when we win Best Picture. You know what they say: Success is the best form of revenge!"

Margot nodded but she didn't look happy. If anything, she looked as if she were going to cry.

"Your sister was obsessed with this story for years," Louise explained. "Brian refused to option it for a fourth time and I thought . . . well . . . why do you need Brian? I mean, now you can make whatever movies you want. We'll start our own production company. I've got money. You've got money, and best of all"—she took a deep breath—"we have an investor who is totally loaded."

Finally, my sister spoke. "This is unbelievably thoughtful, Louise, but—"

"I know, I know." Louise was all smiles. "It's a lot to take in." She turned to me. "You really should read this book, Evie. It was a bestseller in 1975."

"I don't think I can go through all that again," Margot said slowly, but even as the words came out of her mouth, she started leafing through the book. "Brian and I got so close to a green light so many times—"

"I know, sweetie." Louise gave a sympathetic nod. "But that was because you didn't have the big bucks to play with the big boys."

"And she still doesn't," I put in.

"To be honest, Louise, I'm taking . . . I'm taking a sabbatical from Hollywood." But Margot continued to turn the pages.

"Because of *Brian*?" Louise seemed incredulous.

Margot shot me an anguished look. I sprang to her rescue. "She's just not ready yet," I said firmly. "She's, er . . . healing."

Louise didn't seem remotely discouraged. "I can tell you that, from personal experience, the only thing to do is throw yourself into your work. It'll take your mind off things," she said. "But I get it. It's all still a bit raw, especially now he's going to be a father."

The color drained out of Margot's face. I was shocked. Margot and Brian had only been apart for a few months.

"She's pregnant?" Margot whispered.

"Oh God." Louise gasped. "You didn't know?"

Margot straightened her shoulders. "Of course I knew," she said lightly. "I'm happy for him—for both of them."

"And when Brian said he'd never been happier, I got so angry. I mean . . . how dare he!" Louise seemed genuinely outraged for my sister. "So that's when I came up with this idea. I talked to my financial advisor . . . and here we are!"

Margot wore a fake smile on her face, but I could tell she was barely holding herself together.

"Your room has been ready for ages, Louise," I said quickly. "Let's go and collect the key and pick up your luggage."

Margot shot me a look of gratitude. "I'll be there in a moment. Oh—and you can give me that," she said, nodding at the coffee mug in my hand. "I can take it to the kitchen."

Suddenly, there was a click and all the lights went out.

"Oh no!" wailed Louise. "This is ridiculous!"

As we descended the main staircase to reception, I noticed that Louise had to hold on to the bannister to navigate the stairs.

"Are you sure your ankle is okay?" I asked.

"I just need to pop a couple more Advil," she said. "I'll be fine."

When we entered the reception, it was empty.

I hit the old-fashioned bell on the wooden counter. "Dennis! Hello?"

Behind the counter was a very small back office with a swing door that led to the kitchen beyond. We'd put an old Olympia typewriter in full view for a bit of period atmosphere, but had splashed out on a computer for Dennis.

Usually the Art Deco bronze lady lamp was enough, but not today. It was very gloomy.

On the wall next to the counter was an information chalkboard showing the times for high and low tides, sunrise and sunset.

Louise gestured to the chalkboard and said, "What the hell is a . . . sz . . . sz . . . szzz—?"

"It's pronounced *s-i-zz-er-gyy*," I said. "It's to do with the alignment of the sun, moon and earth and it doesn't happen very often. It means that once or twice a year, at the vernal and autumnal equinoxes, the tides are super-high and super-low. And tonight you're in for an even bigger treat," I went on. "There will be a supermoon. To have that coincide with the vernal equinox is really rare. It only happens once every eighteen or nineteen years. It means that the tide will be so low that we will be able to walk out to the wreck tomorrow."

"Oh," said Louise. "So that's what Vicar Bill was talking about when he brought me over. I thought he had a problem with his false teeth or something."

"It'll be high tide early evening, then low tide around three in the morning," I said. "So accessible roughly tomorrow at lunchtime."

"Count me in," Louise enthused. "I'm definitely up for a bit of treasure hunting."

"Aren't we all?" I laughed. "At the moment the identity of the ship is a mystery."

"The schooner in the sound is called the *Virago*." Sam emerged from the short open hallway that led to the basement. "I've been doing a bit of research and I'm pretty sure it's her." He wiped a hand on his trousers before offering it to Louise to shake. "Sam Quick. Pleased to meet you."

I hastily jumped in with the introductions, rather surprised by Sam's familiarity.

"Yeah," said Sam. "I'm helping my cousin Jerry out, but if anyone knows about shipwrecks, it's me. I grew up here. Allow me to be your guide."

"That would be great!" Louise exclaimed.

"And you've picked a good time for your visit," Sam went on. "The best time to beachcomb is after a storm and we'll be in for a big one tonight." He gave a gracious bow and with exaggerated chivalry added, "Ladies, excuse me," and left.

Louise raised her an eyebrows. "Well, he's cute."

It was true, Sam was attractive and charming, but neither Margot nor I were in the right frame of mind for romance at the moment and my face must have shown it.

Louise grinned. "There's nothing wrong with a bit of window-shopping. Is he single?"

"I have no idea," I said. "Sam lives overseas."

I hit the bell on the countertop again.

Louise frowned. "*When* did you say your opening was?"

"The twenty-eighth," I said.

Louise looked over the reception area with a critical eye. The spectacular floor-to-ceiling windows had the most stunning views of the lighthouse in the distance, but it was hard to ignore the current state of affairs. The space looked like a construction site. The walls had been stripped of their geometric brown, orange and cream wallpaper and were waiting to be replastered, primed and painted.

"We had an electrical fire, so rewiring had to be a priority," I said.

Louise raised an eyebrow again. "Define 'electrical fire.'"

"Half the kitchen went up in flames," I said. "If it hadn't been for Dennis having the presence of mind to grab the fire extinguisher, I dread to think what would have happened."

"You've certainly got your work cut out for you," said Louise. "Where is your staff? Won't they be able to pitch in?"

"They'll be starting the week after the open house," I said. "The hotel always closes for the winter, then we rehire for the season that runs from April to October. I'll get your room key."

I lifted up the hinged countertop and stepped into the alcove. The brass keys were stored in a pigeonhole cabinet. I pulled out the key to the Agatha Christie suite and went to join Louise, who had drifted over to the picture window. She stared out over the terrace.

"That lighthouse couldn't be more perfect for our movie," Louise said dreamily. "It's as if this island were made for *Lighthouse of Sorrow*. Will we be able to look inside?"

"Sadly, no," I said. "The footbridge has been washed away and even with the low tide, it's just too dangerous."

Suddenly, there was a loud click and buzz and the lights came back on.

Louise immediately looked at her iPhone. "Thank God for that!"

Dennis and Jerry Quick emerged from the short open hallway. In his mid-forties, Jerry wasn't an unattractive man, but he was a bit odd. Blue eyes loomed behind heavy-lensed black-framed glasses, and an unusual streak of white stood out in his short-cropped dark hair. His uniform hung loosely on his skinny frame, cinched in place by a tool belt.

"I keep telling them not to overload the system," grumbled Jerry to Dennis. "But they don't listen."

I pulled out the burner phone from my back pocket and handed it to Jerry. "You'll want this. You left it in the turret."

Jerry looked startled. "That's not mine." He pointed to an

iPhone tucked in his tool belt. "This is mine. But I'll take it. It must be Sam's." He took the burner and left.

"I'll get your luggage." Dennis ducked under the countertop and retrieved a Gucci Globe-Trotter from the corner of the back office.

"But . . . where is my other suitcase?" Louise demanded.

"This was all there was on the sea tractor," Dennis said. "When the water taxi dropped you off outside the Salty Boatman, didn't you check to see if all of your bags were there?"

"Me? Why should I have to do that?" said Louise. "I tagged the bags before I boarded the ferry and was told that the crew members would make sure they would arrive at Tregarrick Rock." Louise's voice was growing shrill, and the friendly tone had vanished. "What if my bag has been stolen?"

"Don't worry," said Dennis. "It won't have got far. Leave it to me."

"Was there something important inside?" I said anxiously.

"Important?" Louise said with scorn. "You could say that. I need my medication. I can't sleep without my Ambien."

"We've got some herbal nighttime tea," I suggested.

"Don't be stupid. That stuff never works!" Louise must have realized how she sounded because she added, "Sorry, Evie. With the jet lag—"

"Dennis will ring the boat people at St. Mary's," I said.

"Can't he go back and get it?" Louise asked.

"That won't be possible this afternoon," I said. "The tide is coming in—"

"What do you mean, not possible?" Louise's voice rose again. "Don't be ridiculous. Of course it's possible."

"Don't worry," said Dennis smoothly. "The folks on the *Scillonian* will soon realize what has happened. In which case your suitcase will arrive here at approximately eleven hundred hours tomorrow."

"Trust me, if I were Angelina Jolie and had lost my luggage, I would expect you to swim the Atlantic for me. So, wait"— Louise's eyes widened—"are you telling me that *no one* can get here this afternoon? No one at all?"

"Unless they have their own boat, but even then, it's not wise," I said. "It would take a very experienced sailor to dock at the floating pontoon at high tide."

"And we're not sure when exactly the storm will hit," Dennis pointed out. "Current atmospheric conditions are unpredictable."

Louise's face fell. "Then . . . we're *stranded*?"

"That's part of the charm," I said lightly.

"Why don't we start by phoning the *Scillonian* luggage office?" said Dennis calmly. "We should be able to track your suitcase down that way."

"I'll speak to them," said Louise. "I know how to deal with customer service. I'm not going to be fobbed off with pathetic excuses."

"And while you do that, I'll call Ollie," I said. "If your suitcase is still on St. Mary's, maybe he can go and get it."

Dennis lifted the hinged countertop and gestured for Louise to come into the back office.

Ollie's mobile rang and rang. I was just about to give up when there was a click and a female voice came on the line. It was Becky.

"He's talking to Dad behind closed doors." She sounded nervous. "I don't want to interrupt them."

"Is everything okay?"

"I don't know," she said. "It's . . . you know what Ollie's like. Sorry . . . can I give him a message?"

I filled her in on Louise's missing suitcase. "I wanted to catch Ollie and give him a heads-up. Will you ask him to call me please?"

Becky having assured me that she would, I disconnected the line just as I heard a hiss. I turned around to see Margot cowering behind a potted palm, gesturing for me to come over.

"Louise has lost some of her luggage," I said, expecting Margot to fly into a panic. But to my surprise, she pointed in the direction of our office.

"I have to talk to you," she said urgently. "In private."

Chapter Five

My sister's face was riddled with anxiety. She continued to pace the office.

"I know Louise means well," Margot exclaimed. "But jeez . . . I can't believe she suddenly wants to be a producer! And not only that, she's even found an investor!" She stopped by the sofa and sank down. "I just don't know what to do. You're always so sensible. What do you think I should do?"

"Well, the book obviously means a lot to you," I said.

Margot nodded. "It's a fantastic story and with the right talent attached it could be an amazing movie, but believe me, it's a long shot. I mean, my heart wants to do it, but I've got to be realistic. Louise genuinely thinks she'll make a fortune, but Hollywood doesn't work that way. Brian and I tried to get *Lighthouse of Sorrow* off the ground several times. It's so hard being an independent producer without the backing of a major studio. That's why Chandler Productions struggled so much." She gave a heavy sigh. "The thing is, even though

Louise inherited a lot of money from Chester's estate, it won't be enough to finance this kind of movie. We're talking millions and millions of dollars, Evie."

"And she seems to think we have millions and millions of dollars," I said. "Something I noticed you didn't even attempt to deny."

Margot gave a rueful smile. "True. But she wouldn't have believed me anyway."

I hesitated to say what needed to be said. "Margot, I will honestly understand if you want to go back to L.A. and try to make this work."

"I don't," said Margot. "Not really. But I'd be lying if I said I wouldn't hate Louise for doing it without me. And what if . . . I mean . . . what if the movie got made after all?"

"What are the chances?" I said.

"On a par with winning the lottery," she said. "The thing is, I know Louise. She won't take no for an answer." Margot groaned. "I hate myself for getting dragged back into this world again, but I just can't help it! Fred Allen said, 'You can take all of the sincerity in Hollywood and put it into a mosquito's navel and still have room for two caraway seeds and a producer's heart.'"

"I have no idea who Fred Allen is, but it sounds as if it's highly unlikely that anything will come of your book anyway," I said. "Investor or not."

"You're right." Margot nodded. "Until there is money on the table, it's just on a wing and a prayer. Isn't that what Dad used to say?"

"If I were you, I'd just humor Louise and make sure you

don't sign anything," I said. "Nothing is going to happen this weekend anyway."

"Okay. And don't worry, I know what I'm doing." Margot stood up and gave me a hug. "I feel so much better now! Thank you, sis. I guess we should go and find out what has happened to Louise's luggage."

"Louise mentioned her medication was in the lost suitcase," I said.

"Oh dear," said Margot. "We definitely have to find that bag."

"Does she have a life-threatening condition or something?" I asked.

Margot shook her head. "Her doctor prescribed antidepressants and sleeping pills. As you can imagine, she was distraught over Chester's death."

I didn't comment. Perhaps the antidepressants explained Louise's apparent lack of grief.

Margot and I returned to reception. Louise was standing next to her Globe-Trotter. She looked annoyed. "Oh, there you are."

"Any luck?" I asked.

"It's on St. Mary's," Dennis said. "They'll take it to the ticket office so that Ollie can pick it up."

"Great," I said. "Problem solved."

"Don't forget that the ticket office closes at sixteen-thirty hours," said Dennis. "He had better get a move on."

"Let's go up to your room," said Margot. "Dennis can bring your luggage."

"You go on ahead," I said. "I'll catch you both up."

The trio headed for the stairs. My call to Ollie went unanswered and eventually to voice mail, so I left a message about picking up the suitcase and sent him a text asking him to call me to make sure he actually listened to it.

I then called Godolphin Court and told Becky about the suitcase, too. Finally, I rang the ticket office and spoke to Sandra, who confirmed that she could still see the *Sandpiper*, tied up at the dock, from her window.

Since there was nothing more that I could do, I hurried to the Agatha Christie suite to find Louise in raptures over the room, but no Margot.

"I'm so glad you like it," I said to Louise. "Where is Margot?"

"She's gone to get the bottle opener," said Louise. "I hate the corkscrew kind."

Kim had done a great job. She had filled three Art Deco cranberry-colored vases with daffodils and tulips, and had magically rustled up a hospitality basket filled with fruit and Scilly Maid chocolates and a bottle of chardonnay from Holy Vale Wines. The latter sat on ice in a silver bucket alongside two wineglasses and a corkscrew bottle opener.

"Where is this famous turret?" Louise asked. "Margot says it has a three-hundred-and-sixty-degree view."

I showed her how to open the panel and she clattered up the spiral steps. When she returned, she was beaming happily. She roamed around the suite, touching the furniture and opening and closing the drawers. "I *love* it. This is what I miss about England—a real sense of history. You just don't get that in the States. Especially in California, where anything older than five years is torn down."

Louise drifted over to the balcony door and opened it. I followed her outside. The views were spectacular.

A low dividing wall split the balcony in two at the curve. There was an iron fire escape at the far end. Empty planters lined the brick wall. I'd be planting them up with geraniums soon. Tarpaulins covered two sets of tables and chairs and a patio swing that we were going to move downstairs and out onto the terrace below for the open house.

"Where is the shipwreck?" Louise asked.

I gestured to the neighboring island of Bryher, on my far right. "You can't see it from here. You can from the turret but only at low tide. Don't get too excited. It's just some wooden ribs. It's not a galleon from a film set."

"It really is lovely here." Louise took in a deep breath and slowly exhaled. "I won't get tired of the fresh air." She pointed to the lake. "Is that wooden shed a boathouse?"

"It's a bird hide," I said. "We get a lot of bird-watchers here. Every room has a set of binoculars"—another expense that for some reason we'd thought was a priority—"and an illustrated booklet on birds is in the top desk drawer. It's full of anecdotes and fun facts."

"About . . . *birds*? Seriously?" She gave an indulgent chuckle. "Like, what's a robin's favorite worm?"

"Take the Manx shearwaters for example." I went on to tell her about the black-and-white seabird that could be traced back to 2,000 BC on Scilly. "By the thirteenth century, the birds were actually used as currency," I told her. "Annual rents were paid in birds to the Duchy of Cornwall."

"The Duchy of *Cornwall*?" Louise said. "You mean Prince Charles?"

"Other than Tresco and Tregarrick, the Isles of Scilly are still owned by the Duchy of Cornwall."

"Ah, now you're talking." Louise nodded. "Americans love Royalty." Louise took in another deep breath. "I can see why Margot loves it here. And now with her millions and your millions, she can do whatever she likes! Maybe you'd like to invest in our movie, too. We could make you an executive producer."

I knew I had to say something. "Louise, Margot will be annoyed with me for telling you, but I feel I must. Brian had massive debts. Margot and I do not have millions of pounds."

Louise rolled her eyes. "Yeah, right. You'd be surprised at how many times I've heard that story. Mark Zuckerberg is down to his last billion, blah blah blah."

Margot was right when she'd said that Louise wouldn't have believed her. I was wasting my breath.

Louise paused to think. "What you need is a business manager to handle your money. I think you should talk to Randy."

I frowned. "Randy?"

"He's my financial advisor and the investor for our movie," said Louise. "I just hope he can get here before the storm."

I stopped in my tracks. "You mean . . . he's coming here tonight?" Margot hadn't said anything about another guest and I wondered if she knew.

"Yes. Although I suppose it depends on the tide and the weather." She hesitated for a moment before blurting out, "It's a bit awkward, actually."

A peculiar feeling started to form in the pit of my stomach. "Awkward. Why?"

Louise took a deep breath and looked me straight in the eye. "The thing is . . . for the first time in my life, I am in love!"

I was so surprised, I just stood there gawking.

"His name is Randolph Campbell," gushed Louise. "He's Australian but he lives in Hong Kong and is incredibly rich!"

So much for Louise being suicidal over her husband's awful death.

"I honestly don't know what to say." And I didn't. It was the last thing I ever expected from a widow of just a few weeks.

"I know it seems a bit fast, but it's not like he and I are strangers," Louise babbled on. "I met Randy two months before Chester died—"

"A whole two months?"

Louise didn't seem to catch my sarcasm. She was too excited. "He's amazing! So talented! So fit! So gorgeous! So young!"

I still couldn't believe it. "And he's coming here."

"It was love at first sight for both of us, but he refused to have anything to do with me because I was married," she said in earnest. "It's not that I was having an affair with Randy—far from it. He's not like that. He's very respectful. You have to believe me."

Much as I didn't want to believe her, I found that I did. My relationship with Robert had started off with a spark that we had both ignored. It was only after his wife had run off with a musician and wanted a divorce that we acknowledged our feelings for each other.

"You'll adore him," Louise ran on. "And I know Margot

will, too. It was actually his idea that Margot and I form a production company. He'll be our silent partner."

My heart sank. How would Margot get out of this?

"Randy and I met Brian at the gala—"

"The one where your husband choked to death on a fishbone?" I couldn't help but say.

Louise was unfazed. "No, another one." She chattered on, oblivious to the dig. "Randy does the charity circuit, too, and he got to talking to Brian about gap financing. I thought, if Randy is going to bankroll any production company, it's not going to be Brian's. It's going to be Margot's. Honestly, Brian's smugness made my blood boil. So here we are."

"I know that Margot is touched," I said carefully. "Especially with you coming all this way in person."

"Well, it sort of killed two birds with one stone, really." Seeing my puzzled expression, Louise continued. "Randy is a triathlete and it turns out that something called the Ötillö Swimrun is going to be held in the Isles of Scilly this summer. He suggested we just pop in and take a peep at the terrain."

Pop in?

The only people who popped in to Tregarrick would have sailed on galleons full of Peruvian gold or slave trader ships on their way to the New World.

"I've never heard of the Ötillö Swimrun," I said.

"I know, I hadn't heard about it, either," said Louise. "It all started in Sweden after a drunken bet between four friends as to whether they could swim and run seventy-five kilometers—that's nearly forty-seven miles—unaided across the Stockholm archipelago. It was such a success that there are now about five hundred events that take place all over the world. You should definitely mention that on your website, by the way."

"Um. Right, okay," I said.

"Randy is obsessed with running, swimming, competing in marathons." She gave a wistful sigh. "He's one of the world's most eligible bachelors, but he doesn't want people to gossip about his private life. He's the Australian equivalent of John F. Kennedy Jr." She paused to take in the Agatha Christie suite again. "And frankly, I can't think of a more romantic place to take my relationship with Randy to the next level."

"I feel that I must warn you that Margot won't be happy about this at all," I said. "She thought you were devastated by your husband's death, especially given the horror of it." In fact, my sister was surprisingly old-fashioned when it came to relationships. It had made Brian's humiliating betrayal all the more difficult for her to bear.

"Oh yes. The fishbone thing was awful," Louise said quickly. "But everyone has been so kind. Especially Margot. Speaking of Margot, I thought you could pave the way."

"Pave the way?" I said. "What do you mean by 'pave the way'?"

"Do you think that Margot will get weird about us sharing a room?"

"Sorry, but I'm staying out of that."

"She's not changed then." Louise laughed. "Margot always was a bit of a prude."

"She's not a prude," I said defensively, though I sort of agreed. "Margot's a bit of a romantic, that's all, and I'm quite sure she'll agree that mixing business with pleasure is a bad idea. What happens if your blossoming relationship falls apart and Randy pulls out of the financing?"

"He won't," said Louise. "I'm all about contracts. I've been around the block a few times. You don't need to worry about that."

I wasn't so sure.

"Once Margot meets Randy, she'll love him," Louise declared. "You will, too. Everyone loves Randy. Oh Evie, this is the first time in my life that I have truly felt in love."

"Yes. You already told me. But I thought you'd been married three times," I said bluntly.

"Which is why I know this is different!" Louise gave a rueful smile. "I'll admit that my first marriage was one of convenience. My second was—to be honest—for his Hollywood connections. My third, well, it was a mutual arrangement. Chester wanted a trophy wife and I wanted an Aston Martin." She laughed again. "Just kidding. We did respect each other. Honestly."

The door opened and Margot walked in with the bottle opener.

"What do you think of the Agatha Christie suite, Louise?" Margot enthused. "Don't you just love it?"

"I adore the retro vibe." Louise shot me an anxious look. "And I know that Randy will, too."

"Randy?" Margot frowned. "Who is Randy?"

"He's the investor I was telling you about," said Louise. "Oh Margot, please be happy for me." She hurried to Margot's side and reached for her hand. "I'm in love! His name is Randolph Campbell. He is six feet tall with the most gorgeous blue eyes and incredible body and—"

Margot's jaw dropped. "Your husband just died and you're in love with someone else? *Already?*"

"Of course I loved Chester," said Louise desperately. "But actually, Chester would have given me his blessing. I'm sure of it."

Margot snatched her hand away, appalled.

"You'll really like him when you meet him," said Louise.

"Meet him," Margo repeated. "He's coming *here*? When?"

"Well . . . he was supposed to be coming t-t-today," Louise stammered. "But—with the weather, and the tide—"

"Today? With the weather and the tide?" Margot echoed.

"You sound like Roger the parrot," Louise said nervously.

"Roger is not a parrot," Margot snapped. "He's a *macaw*!" She headed for the door, muttering about having left the iron on.

"Where are you going?" Louise shouted after her. "He's going to finance our movie. Margot! Do you realize what that means—?"

But Margot had vanished.

"Iron? What iron?" Louise seemed bewildered. "I hope Margot's not having second thoughts. Randy never finances movies and he's only doing this for us."

"I'll go and talk to her and leave you to settle in," I said hastily.

"Evie—wait—one more thing," said Louise. "Do you have a portable radiator or something? It's really cold in here."

Chapter Six

I found Margot staring out of the kitchen window in our flat. Her entire body was rigid with tension.

"Iron?" I teased. "I don't think I've ever seen you with an iron."

She spun around, seething with indignation. "I just had to get away before I said something that I'd later regret. You know how I am."

"Ah," I said. "Yes, I do."

"I thought Louise was suicidal over Chester's death," Margot exclaimed. "And now she's got a new boyfriend!"

"I know," I said.

"I swear I thought she'd overdose, Evie, and suddenly, she arrives like the Queen of Sheba, bearing gifts and *my* book." Margot shook her head with seeming disbelief. "You know, I tried to stop Louise from coming. I even told her it was a bad time for us, but she sounded so miserable that I gave in."

"I'm sure she meant well," I said cautiously.

"And who the hell is this Randy person anyway?"

I relayed what I knew from my earlier conversation with Louise. "And apparently, he's one of the world's most eligible bachelors."

"Is that supposed to make everything better?" Margot fumed.

"He could have been a pirate with a gold-capped tooth," I said. "Speaking of pirates, I couldn't reach Ollie." But Margot didn't seem to be listening.

"It's going to be horribly awkward with this Randy person," she said. "I feel so manipulated."

"Look, no one can force you to agree to anything," I said.

"No, I suppose not," said Margot. "But I'll tell you one thing, there is *no* way that Louise and Mr. Perfect are going to share a bedroom."

"Oh, Margot—they're adults!"

"No. I really liked Chester," said Margot. "He was a nice man and he only died a few weeks ago. You have to admit this seems very fast. What if he's after her money?"

"Good question," I said.

Margot gave a mischievous grin. "We'll put him in the George Goodchild suite. It's at the other end of the hotel from the Agatha Christie suite. I'll lay trip wire or something just in case they decide to sneak around in the middle of the night."

I laughed. "I don't think you need to. George Goodchild is underneath us."

"Well, she's not getting underneath Randy."

"You know that room hasn't been touched for months," I reminded her.

Margot reached for the set of master keys that we kept on a

hook in the kitchen. "Then we'd better get cracking. Remember what Mum used to say? There's nothing like a bit of elbow grease to soothe the soul."

. . .

The George Goodchild suite was one of my favorite rooms. It was light and sunny, with gorgeous western views over the Atlantic Ocean. The next land mass was America.

I'd only just discovered Goodchild's work, but I was thoroughly enjoying it. Born in 1888, Goodchild had enjoyed a career that spanned sixty years. He had over two hundred written works published under a variety of pseudonyms. My favorites were his Inspector McLean stories, and his lesser-known romance novels, which he wrote under a variety of female pseudonyms. It was unusual to find a male author from that era writing from a woman's perspective—and writing well.

For nearly an hour, Margot and I worked in companionable silence. We checked all the light bulbs, wiped down all the surfaces, meticulously cleaned the bathroom, replaced the linens and towels and polished every bit of furniture with beeswax. All that was left was a thorough vacuum.

"I do *love* our new Miele," I said as I plugged in our latest purchase.

There was a flash of sparks and a loud bang. I leapt back with a yelp of pain. "Jeez! This is getting ridiculous!"

"Ssh! Quiet!" Margot cried. "Wait . . . is that . . . can you hear . . . is that screaming?"

We listened. And it was. Not only that, the screaming was getting louder and louder.

"Oh my God!" Margot shrieked. "It's Louise!"

We tore out of the room and raced along the landing, but just as we reached the door to the Agatha Christie suite, the screaming abruptly stopped.

The door was locked, but luckily I had the master set of keys in my pocket. We burst inside, but Louise wasn't in the sitting room. To my dismay I spied a blackened power strip where the portable radiator, a lamp and the television had all been plugged in. The extension cord disappeared into the master suite.

"Bedroom," I exclaimed.

We dashed through the double doors.

"Oh no!" Margot cried. "Look!"

Louise, dressed in a hotel-issued white toweling robe, lay on the bathroom floor, her eyes closed. Her hair surrounded her head like a halo. There was an awful smell of burning and plastic.

Margot pulled me back. "Is she dead?"

For a moment I was struck by how much younger Louise looked without makeup on, but then I noticed her outstretched arm and the livid red weal across her open palm.

On the tiled floor, a few feet away, were the remains of Louise's hair dryer. It had been plugged into an adaptor that was connected to the extension cord that snaked from the sitting room.

"Don't touch her yet!" I assessed the situation and double-checked that the lights still weren't working. "Okay. I think it's safe now."

Margot dropped to her knees, hastily rearranging the toweling robe that had begun to creep open, revealing Louise's naked body. Margot reached for Louise's wrist to check her pulse.

I held my breath and waited for what seemed like ages.

"She's alive!" Margot said. "Thank God!"

Louise's eyelids began to flutter and then popped open. She seemed confused. "Where am I?"

"You've had a bit of a shock, but you're going to be okay," said Margot.

Louise's eyes focused on Margot. "And who are you?"

"It's Margot. You're going to be okay, Louise," she said again. "Can you try to sit up?"

Louise whimpered. "I don't think so."

Margot and I eased her upright until her back was resting against the bath—which was still full of water. The enormity of what could have happened had the hair dryer fallen in filled me with horror.

Louise began to shiver. "What happened?"

"You've had an electric shock," I said.

"My hand hurts." She inspected it. "I'm injured. Scarred. I'm going to be scarred for life."

"It's just a burn," I said. "It will heal. Margot, I saw some calendula cream in Lily's medical supplies. Can you go and get it?"

Margot needed no encouragement. She hurried away.

"I'm cold," said Louise.

"Let's get you into the sitting room," I said.

I helped her to the Bergère sofa, then grabbed a pale blue chenille throw from the master bedroom to drape around her shoulders. She pulled it close.

"I was drying my hair," said Louise. "And then . . . there was a loud pop and a flash. It knocked me off my feet." She touched the back of her head and winced. "I think I must have hit the edge of the bath."

"Thank heavens you let go of the hair dryer. Otherwise . . ." I couldn't finish that sentence. "You were lucky, Louise. You can't use a hair dryer in a British bathroom—that's why there aren't any sockets."

"You can in America," she said.

"Where did you find the extension cord anyway?" I asked.

"It was in the bottom of the wardrobe."

Of course it was. I'd noticed it there when Kim and I were cleaning, but never thought I'd need to remove it. "The voltage is so much higher here," I said. "Your hair dryer blew the fuse and nearly took you with it."

"You should have a warning sign about the voltage." Louise seemed to be rallying. "That hair dryer cost me three hundred dollars."

"There was a hair dryer provided for guests in the vanity unit." I pulled open the top drawer. It was full of all kinds of potions and a lot of products with the brand name Goop. "Oh. I could have sworn it was in here."

Louise pulled a face. "Cheap ones can ruin your hair. I stuck it in a desk drawer. Mine is a ghd hair dryer, so I'm afraid you'll have to replace it."

"Of course," I said. "I'm so sorry."

Margot returned with a tube of calendula and gave it to Louise. "It doesn't expire until 2022."

Louise made no move to apply the ointment. She just sat there, seemingly deep in thought. "I think I should see a doctor," she said slowly. "Just to make sure that everything is okay."

Margot and I looked at each other knowing full well that wouldn't happen—at least, not anytime soon.

"There isn't a doctor on the island," Margot said. "So . . . it won't be today."

"You've got to be kidding me," said Louise.

"It's part of the old-fashioned charm," I said, in a poor attempt to diffuse the tension.

"Isn't there an air ambulance or something?"

"There is," said Margot. "But that's usually for emergencies."

"This *is* an emergency," said Louise. "I was electrocuted. I need to see a doctor. I have A.F."

"What's that?" Margot said.

"Atrial fibrillation," I explained. "It's an irregular heartbeat." Thanks to Robert, I knew all about heart conditions and, although A.F. was fairly common, it could have been fatal in this instance. Maybe Louise was right. She should see a doctor.

"Oh." Margot shot me an anxious look. "But you're feeling better now, Louise, aren't you?"

"You don't understand," Louise whined. "Medical bills in California are thousands of dollars and if there's a problem later on—especially with a preexisting condition—I won't be covered by my insurance."

"It's true," Margot admitted. "Brian had a panic attack once and we had to go to the E.R. We didn't even call an ambulance.

I drove him myself. He was there for six hours and it cost nine thousand dollars because we didn't have medical insurance."

Louise turned to me. "You see. We've got no choice." She pulled the chenille throw even closer as she seemed to be hit by another wave of shivering. "I hate to do this because we're friends, but if that happened and my insurance was rejected, I'd have to ask you to pay for my medical bills in California. And *then* the insurance company would insist that I sue *you* for negligence."

I was appalled. "Us? Why?"

"But it wouldn't matter," said Louise. "After all, you must have insurance for your guests, covering accidents and that kind of thing."

"Of course we do," Margot said brightly. Only, this was yet another item on our to-do list that we hadn't got to yet.

"So it wouldn't come out of your own pocket, would it?" said Louise.

I had an idea. "Louise, I'm so sorry none of this is working out for you. With the power cuts and the state of the hotel, and now this horrible accident, perhaps it's better if we get you back to St. Mary's first thing in the morning. There's a doctor there. And there's also a really lovely sixteenth-century hotel called Godolphin Court. It has a spa. You and Randy could go and stay there."

Then, suddenly, came the sound of male voices outside the room. I recognized Dennis's but not the other.

"The door's open," I heard Dennis say. "I'll leave you to it, sir."

"Thanks, mate."

"It's *Randy!*" Louise cried. Her transformation was astonishing. She sprang to her feet, tossing aside the chenille throw, and quickly primped her hair. "Randy! Randy!"

And at that moment there was a whir and flicker and all the lights came back on to perfectly illuminate the tall bronzed Adonis standing in the doorway.

Louise burst into tears.

Chapter Seven

We watched in astonishment as Randy enveloped Louise's small frame and held her tight.

Dressed in neat beige trousers, a neat beige open-necked shirt and a neat navy sports jacket, everything about him was . . . neat. He was devastatingly handsome, so handsome that Margot, who had sworn off men forever, muttered, "Is he for real?"

Louise's eyes shone with adoration, her hand injury soon forgotten. "Oh God, I've missed you so much."

"I'm here now, babe," he said softly, stroking her damp hair. "Everything is going to be all right. I told you I'd come."

Margot seemed too mesmerized to speak, but I recovered my manners. "Welcome to Tregarrick Rock, Mr. Campbell."

"I'd shake hands but"—he nodded to Louise, nestled in his embrace—"they're otherwise occupied. But please, call me Randy."

"I'm Evie Mead," I said. "And this is my sister, Margot Chandler."

Louise was positively glowing with happiness. "I can't believe you're really here."

"You know me," said Randy. "Where there's a will, there's a way." He gave a broad smile that revealed a chipped bottom tooth that only added to his charm.

I couldn't make out his accent. It sounded Australian, as Louise said he was, but there was something else—a slight twang that I couldn't quite identify.

"I can't place your accent," I said.

"Born in Australia," said Randy. "But I spent a lot of time in South Africa prospecting for gold."

"Gold!" I exclaimed. "Seriously?"

Louise grinned. "That's how he made his fortune."

"Ssh." said Randy.

"But it's true!" she insisted.

"That was a long time ago," he said.

Not that long ago, I thought. He was definitely younger than I was, and probably a decade younger than Louise. Margot didn't say a word.

"Look. Poor me." Louise stepped back to show him her injured hand. "The hair dryer exploded. I told them that I'll be scarred for life."

Randy gently kissed her palm. "Do you think you'll live?"

"I want to see a doctor, but they said there isn't one here." Louise gave a childish pout. "Make them get me a doctor."

Randy frowned. "Let me see." He studied her hand again

and looked up to wink at me. "Hmm—will it drop off? No, I don't think so," he teased. "Is it going to be a bit sore? Yes, probably. Now go and get dressed, dry your hair and then you can tell me all about it."

Louise grabbed Randy's hand and tried to pull him with her into the master bedroom. "Come with me."

"Whoa, steady, babe." He extricated his hand. "I'll be waiting right out here. I'm not going anywhere."

Yet again, I was astonished at the whole situation and a little repulsed if I was really honest. Louise was so infatuated, it was embarrassing. Although I had to admit, Randy really was gorgeous and—on the surface—not what I'd expected at all. He actually seemed nice.

Margot still hadn't uttered a syllable.

Louise practically skipped to the master bedroom and made sure to leave the double doors ajar so she wouldn't miss a second of our conversation.

Randy scanned the sitting room and gave an appreciative whistle. "Your website doesn't do this justice." He strode to the window. "Do all the bedrooms have such an incredible view?"

"Yes, it's amazing, isn't it?" I said.

Margot finally spoke. "And yours does, too. You're going to love staying in the George Goodchild suite. It's at the other end of the landing."

"It's okay, Margot," Louise called out from the bedroom. "Randy is going to stay here with me."

Margot pretended not to hear. "George Goodchild was a writer in the Golden Age of mystery and—"

"Cool." Randy nodded. "I bet he knew Agatha Christie."

"Um. Yes, he probably did," said Margot. "I think you'll be *very* happy in that room."

"If it's as lovely as this suite, then I know I will," said Randy cheerfully.

"We don't want to put you to any more trouble, Margot." Louise peered through the gap between the doors—in lacy black underwear—her disappointment plain. "We can share this suite. It's huge."

"But since I'm working odd hours," said Randy, "I'd keep you awake, babe. I'm finalizing a big deal at the moment for my Hong Kong client. I wasn't sure if I could come at all, but then I figured they'd have the Internet here. We're not on the moon."

"As I was telling Louise," I said, "we're in the process of rewiring part of the hotel and redecorating for our open house. If you are in the middle of something important that relies on the Internet, you might be happier staying at Godolphin Court on St. Mary's."

"It's very private up in the turret." Louise was still peering through the gap in the doorway. "You can work up there."

Randy laughed. "I'm sure it is, but George is good enough for me, especially as I'm a bit of an insomniac—"

"But so am I!" Louise exclaimed.

"When I can't sleep," said Randy, "I like to go running."

"At *night*?" Margot said.

"I told you, Randy is a triathlete," Louise said happily.

"Speaking of being an insomniac," I cut in. "Did Ollie bring Louise's missing suitcase?"

"Ollie?" Randy frowned.

"The skipper," I said. "Gold tooth, ponytail, lots of tattoos?"

Randy shook his head. "No, the bloke who brought me over was one of the local fishermen. He wasn't happy, because he says there is a storm coming in, but I made it worth his while!"

I stifled a surge of annoyance. A quick glance at my watch confirmed that Sandra's ticket office would be closed by now.

"Interesting bloke," Randy went on. "He also told me about your upcoming open house."

Dennis had once said that the boatmen know all the gossip, and it would seem that he was right.

"It looks like you've still got quite a bit of work to do," said Randy. "No offense, but I used to be a brickie—built my own place on the Gold Coast—so if you need an extra pair of hands this weekend, you've only got to ask."

This was not what I'd been expecting, and judging from Margot's expression, neither had she.

"We couldn't possibly ask you to do that," Margot said. But then she looked at me and shrugged. "Well, we are a bit short-handed—"

"Then consider it a way to repay your hospitality," said Randy.

But at this moment I was more preoccupied with Ollie. "Did you happen to see a turquoise cabin cruiser down at the harbor? Or even at the floating pontoon when you arrived?"

"Sorry, no," said Randy. "There was a dinghy pulled up onto the rocks but no other boat. "Why? Is there a problem?"

"Wait. Are you telling me that Ollie forgot to pick up my suitcase?" Louise emerged from the bedroom, having obviously caught the tail end of our conversation. She was dressed in tight-fitting jeans and a hip-length turtleneck sweater in dove gray. Her hair was still damp, but she had swept it back to the nape of her neck and coiled it into a tight knot. With scarlet lipstick and large silver hoop earrings, she reminded me of a flamenco dancer.

"We're just finding out," said Margot.

"Come here, you." Randy raised his left arm as an invitation and Louise hurried to his side, burrowing into his shoulder. He gently pushed her back so he could reach into his jacket pocket to withdraw an envelope. "I've got something for you."

"Oooh!" she squealed. "Is it what I think it is?"

"Open it and see," he said.

Louise pulled out what looked like a check. Her eyes widened with surprise as she gave it a cursory glance before throwing her arms around Randy's neck. "You are a magician!"

There was a knock on the door.

"Come on in!" Louise shouted.

Dennis appeared with a cabin-sized holdall made of soft brown leather. "Where would you like this, sir?"

"Mr. Campbell is in the George Goodchild suite," said Margot. "The door is unlocked."

Dennis's expression remained neutral. "Certainly."

"Lead the way, Dennis," said Randy.

Louise, still clinging to Randy's hand, followed him.

Margot and I stepped onto the landing.

"I'll go and tell Kim we have one more for dinner," said Margot. "Are we going to do the dress code thing? I doubt if they've come prepared."

When Kim had launched our new website, she'd stipulated

that in keeping with the age of the hotel, there would be a formal dress code—preferably in period—with cocktails at six-thirty p.m. and dinner at seven-thirty p.m.

"I haven't thought about it," I said. "We need to track down Ollie."

"Oh God, yes." Margot bit her lip. "Louise's medication—"

"And the salad ingredients for Kim," I reminded her.

"Louise loves salad," Margot declared.

I called Ollie's mobile. It went straight to voice mail. Surely he wouldn't have switched the phone off? Next, I called Godolphin Court. Becky didn't even give me a chance to speak.

"I'm so sorry I forgot to give Ollie the message about the suitcase." Becky's voice cracked with emotion. "He left in a huff and now he's not answering his phone."

I glanced at my watch. It would be dark soon, to say nothing of the approaching storm.

"Dad is hopelessly old-fashioned," Becky went on tearfully. "He doesn't understand that we're in love. I don't want to go to uni. It's a waste of time. Ollie and I just want to be together."

"Of course you do," I said, but I was more interested in what Ollie was doing right this minute. "Do you know if Ollie picked up my camera equipment from Pegasus Couriers?"

"Yes. He brought the packages here," said Becky. "There were two."

Sam's package must have arrived after all. "What about the groceries?"

"Ollie told me he was going to stop at the co-op last.

It's close to the harbor. I'm so sorry about forgetting to give him the message. Will you ask him to call me when you see him?"

Promising I would do just that, I disconnected the line and called the harbormaster who told me that Ollie had left St. Mary's at five forty-five. Although there was a bit of a swell building, Ollie should easily get back before the storm.

That still didn't solve the problem of Louise's medication, but then I had an idea.

I found Margot in our office, working on her computer, and quickly filled her in on Ollie's movements.

"How infuriating!" Margot exclaimed. "Louise has already asked me three times when her suitcase is coming."

"I was thinking," I said slowly. "You might not like it, but . . . when Kim and I were clearing out Lily's room, she still had all her medical stuff in the powder room."

"Wait . . . are you suggesting—?"

"I am pretty sure I saw sleeping pills," I said. "But I know what you're like with expiration dates."

"We won't give Louise the bottle," said Margot. "We'll just give her a handful to tide her over. She won't care."

I regarded my sister with surprise. "Seriously?"

"Seriously," Margot repeated. "We often shared a room at film festivals and she gets paranoid if she doesn't get her sleep. Where did you put them?"

"In the Margery Allingham suite with the medical supplies," I said. "I left them on the desk in a box labeled Medical Supplies."

Margot beamed. "Brilliant. I'll go and get them."

"I'm going to meet Ollie down at the causeway," I said. "He may need a hand to carry everything."

"You're a glutton for punishment, Evie," Margot teased. "Those steps are killer. I'm sure one of the guys will go if you ask them."

"Good idea," I said.

Chapter Eight

When I entered reception, it was empty. A sudden roar of laughter erupted from the basement below. I went to investigate, thinking that Ollie must be back.

Instead, it was Randy, Jerry, Sam and Dennis. They were standing around the wall unit that housed the fuse box and circuit breakers, engaged in lively conversation.

The basement was huge and stretched the length of the hotel. When we first took over, Margot and I were thrilled to discover a load of Art Deco furniture that presumably had been moved down there when the hotel was "modernized" in the 1970s. As we revamped each room, we switched it back. Unfortunately, we couldn't get rid of the 1970s furniture because it didn't belong to us, but at least it was kept out of sight.

At the far end were two doors. One opened into a wine cellar and the other was my new—almost finished—darkroom.

Randy saw me first and waved a greeting. The four of them were grinning—even Jerry.

"I heard you laughing from upstairs," I said as I joined them. "Care to share the joke?"

The men exchanged furtive looks and it was obvious that the answer was no.

"It's a guy thing." Randy grinned.

"I need a volunteer to go down to the causeway and help Ollie," I said.

"Did he bring Mrs. Vanderhoven's suitcase?" Dennis asked.

"No. The ticket office closed before he could get there," I said.

"I'll go," said Sam. "I think I've heard enough about well-rooted ground rods for today." There was another roar of laughter as Sam left the basement, along with Dennis, who said he had to get back to reception.

Randy pointed to the archaic fuse box. "Seriously, though," he said. "I was saying to Jerry that until you rewire the whole hotel, you're just going to run into the same problem every time the system is overloaded."

"Yeah, I told them that already," said Jerry. "It's a miracle that no one has been electrocuted yet."

I immediately thought of Louise and her hair dryer—a miracle indeed.

"And they will set the timer so that all the appliances come on at the same time and blow the fuse," Jerry grumbled on. "And I'm the one who has to get out of bed to fix it."

"That happened once, Jerry," I said firmly. "And as Margot and I told you, we didn't expect you to come downstairs in the middle of the night. It could easily have waited until the morning."

"She says that now," said Jerry to Randy. "But then I'd get

it in the neck from Kim about no power to make the morning tea."

Randy clapped his hand on Jerry's shoulder. "You went above and beyond the call of duty, mate."

The two of them went on to discuss the differences between a 15-ampere branch circuit with a 1,500 wattage, and a 20-ampere branch circuit with a 2,000 wattage. It all went over my head. It was clear that Randy seemed to know what he was talking about.

"And they only want me to rewire half of the hotel," Jerry went on. "They don't understand it's not in neat sections. This place has been partially rewired many times over the decades and, to be honest, it's a total headache. As it is, I'm working at a loss."

"You helped out two sheilas in distress, mate," said Randy to Jerry. "That's an honorable thing to do."

"Well . . . yeah," Jerry agreed. "Vicar Bill told us they were in a bit of a bind but then suddenly, she wants a darkroom!"

"Which you are being paid for," I pointed out.

Randy chuckled. "I hear you. Always happens, doesn't it? But you did it anyway. You didn't want to let them down. So when do you think you'll be finished?"

"I reckon three more days for the wiring," said Jerry. "And three for painting—so yeah, let's say six to be on the safe side."

I felt sick. That left just two days to get all the art on the walls before the open house.

Randy must have sensed my dismay, because he smiled broadly and said, "Hey! Don't worry, Evie. We'll all pitch in."

I shot him a grateful look. Louise was right. It was hard not to like Randy.

The three of us returned to reception, where Louise and Kim were admiring Mister Tig, who was sitting on the countertop.

Louise rubbed his ears. "He's such a handsome cat. He really looks like he's wearing a tuxedo." She picked him up and buried her face into his fur.

"Mister Tig likes you," I said.

"That's because I have kitties in L.A. I do miss them." She saw Randy and her eyes lit up. "Don't you think he's handsome?"

Randy smirked. "Are you talking about me or the cat?"

Kim brought out her iPhone from her pocket. "Can I take a few photos of you guys for Mister Tig's Instagram account?"

"Of course!" Louise beamed. "Will you tag me, too?"

Louise posed for the camera.

"Let's have Randy holding Mister Tig now," said Kim.

"Sure thing," said Randy. "I happen to like cats."

Louise passed Mister Tig to Randy, and I held my breath. This would be the ultimate test, I thought. Part of me half hoped that Mister Tig would resist Randy's charms, but it was not to be. He lounged happily on his back in Randy's arms, purring loudly.

Kim was surprised. "Gosh. He loves you!"

"I told you, everyone loves Randy." Louise moved in to snuggle with the love of her life. "Will you take a photo of the three of us?"

More photos were posed for and taken until finally, the cat—and Randy—had had enough and broke free.

"I'll post these on Instagram right now," said Kim, all

business. "Is it okay to mention your names and your connection with Hollywood with hashtags?"

"Yes, of course," Louise said. "And Randy is a triathlete. He's registered for the Ötillö Swimrun in June, too, so maybe add that? Good publicity for the hotel."

"Got it." Kim's fingers tapped her iPhone and flashed a smile. "Thanks."

Randy checked his watch. "I need to freshen up. I'll come and fetch you in twenty minutes, babe."

"Twenty!" Louise yelped. "I'll never be ready in twenty minutes."

"Then you'd better get your bum into gear," he said.

And with that, the pair of them headed for the main staircase.

"How's dinner coming along?" I asked Kim.

"Everything is under control," she said. "Just waiting for the salad stuff."

"Oh—did you give Vicar Bill the jewelry box?" I asked.

"Yes." She nodded.

"Thanks for being so organized," I said. "We're happy you're here."

"Me too." Kim smiled and headed back to the kitchen.

I was glad that she seemed to be settling in so well.

I found Margot in our flat, sitting at the kitchen table and scribbling in a notepad. The *Lighthouse of Sorrow* was splayed open next to a stack of Post-it notes, many of which had already been stuck on random pages.

Following our earlier conversation about Louise and the book, I was surprised.

Margot looked up and sat back in her chair. "I thought I would take another peep," she said, as if reading my mind.

"Well? What do you think?" I asked. "Is it still as good as you remembered?"

"I'll be honest," she said. "Yes, it is. And now that we have the money, we can afford to attract A-list talent. Can you imagine having Meryl Streep sitting in the Residents' Lounge?"

I forced a smile. "Wow. That would be amazing."

Margot laughed. "You are so transparent! You are horrified by the idea."

"Of course I'm not," I lied.

"It'll be excellent publicity for the hotel," she enthused. "Other film companies will be desperate to use Tregarrick as a location. What with the shipwrecks and the castles—I mean . . . Louise's hairdresser knows one of the producers who worked on *Game of Thrones*—"

"*Game of Thrones!*" I exclaimed in horror.

"Tregarrick could be the new Dubrovnik," Margot burbled on happily. "That was where Cersei did her walk of shame. Fans will beg to stay on the island. We'll soon put this place on the global map."

"But it already is," I protested. "We're eighty percent booked for the summer already."

Margot looked puzzled. "How can we have bookings already?"

"Of course we have!" I was exasperated. "Tregarrick Rock has repeat guests. They come here year after year. They booked last year for this year. Kim sent out a newsletter and told them that although the management was new, nothing else had changed."

Margot seemed surprised. "Oh."

"We discussed this before you went back to Los Angeles to get all your stuff," I said. "Remember?"

Margot shook her head. "No. I don't remember agreeing to any of this."

I distinctly remembered telling her, but she had been consumed with organizing her transatlantic move and had been very distracted.

"Well, we won't be shooting this year anyway," she said dismissively. "We'll just block out the weeks we'll need next year. Don't worry. We'll figure something out."

I nodded, fighting a sea of conflicting emotions. Margot seemed the happiest I'd seen her in weeks and I didn't want to put a damper on things.

"I'm going to get ready for dinner," I said.

"Evie—wait a minute. Sit down." She pointed to the chair across from her. So I did.

"Nothing has changed, you know," she said. "I'm not going to move back to L.A., whatever Louise might think. This movie is a one-off. I'll probably have to go to the States occasionally, though. Evie?" I could tell she was trying to reassure me, but it wasn't working. "Louise is right. Success is the best form of revenge."

"So you're doing this to prove something to Brian," I said.

Margot bit her lip and looked away.

"Margot?"

When she looked back, her expression of desperation surprised me. "I just need to do this. It's important to me. I can't explain, because I don't really know why, but . . . I'd really like your blessing."

I jumped up and hurried to her side, throwing my arms around her tiny shoulders, and gave her a hug. "Of course you have my blessing, silly."

"Argh, I can't breathe!" She laughed and pushed me away. "What? You really thought I was going to abandon you?"

"You said you missed L.A., remember?"

"I miss the idea of L.A., that's all." She grinned. "Let's just see what this Randy is all about. You seem to forget this is not my first rodeo."

"Okay. I'm going to change and you should, too." I thought for a moment. "Are you dressing up?"

"As in, am I donning 1930s attire? No. Are you?"

"I thought I might make an effort," I said.

"Okay," was all Margot said, and turned her attention back to *Lighthouse of Sorrow*.

After showering, I swept my shoulder-length hair into a knot at the nape of my neck, and donned a simple, fitted mid-calf-length black dress, adding some vintage paste jewelry—dangling earrings, a matching tight bangle and a long necklace—which I'd bought on eBay. It seemed a good compromise between modern dress and 1930s period attire.

Margot took one look at me and said, "You look lovely, but I fear that you will be the only one who's changed for dinner."

We left the flat and took the stairs down to the landing just as Randy was exiting the George Goodchild suite.

"Gosh," Margot gasped.

Dressed in a white tuxedo and pristine spats, Randy had even oiled back his hair to look like a 1930s gentleman. "Kim told me it was compulsory."

"You actually brought that with you?" I was amazed.

"It was on your website," he said. "Formal period attire preferred."

Margot's face fell. "Is Louise going to dress up?"

"I'm afraid so," said Randy. "She told me she bought a vintage full-length satin gown."

Randy offered an arm each. "Shall we go downstairs?"

"No. I'm going to change," Margot said suddenly.

"We'll wait for you," said Randy. "Louise is nowhere near ready."

"No, you both go on ahead." Margot hurried back up to the flat.

Randy offered me his arm again. I linked it in his and we made our way to the main staircase.

"Louise tells me that you're a widow," Randy said.

"Oh—yes." His remark took me by surprise. "It was . . . a few months . . . just last November, in fact."

I really didn't want to talk about Robert with a stranger, as well-intentioned as Randy might be.

"I'm sorry. That sounded crass," Randy said apologetically. "I just wanted to let you know that I understand how you must be feeling."

Of course he couldn't possibly know, but all I said was, "Thank you."

"There's no shame in grief, you know," Randy went on

gently. "You Brits are so messed up—all that stiff-upper-lip bullshit. I keep telling Louise to let it all out, but she won't."

I didn't quite know how to respond to that comment. From what I'd seen of Louise, she hadn't seemed able to keep it all in.

"I still have moments when I want to cry," said Randy. "And my sister, Carrie, died so long ago."

"I'm sorry." I felt terrible. "I didn't know that you had lost someone, too."

"Why would you? We've only just met." Randy slipped his hand inside his tux, pulled out a crumpled photograph and gave it to me.

I stared at a beautiful girl with sun-bleached blond hair, wearing a red bathing suit. She was posing on a sandy beach, holding a surfboard, with dramatic waves in the background. Carrie could have been a poster child for *Baywatch*.

"She's stunning," I said.

"Carrie was seventeen when this was taken, and six months later she was dead," Randy said quietly.

"Oh. Gosh. I . . . I'm so sorry," I said again.

"She was an excellent surfer—she could have turned professional—and a strong swimmer. She knew the beach well, but she got caught in a freak riptide."

"I'm sorry," I said yet again.

"I was there." Randy swallowed hard and blinked several times, as if holding back his tears. "I grabbed my paddleboard and went in after her, but . . ." He shook his head, unable to speak for a moment. "So yeah, I know all about grief."

I gave the photograph back. He stared at Carrie's image a little longer before slipping it back inside his pocket.

"My parents never got over it," Randy went on. "Mum died shortly after that and then my dad just wasted away. It's true that you can die of a broken heart."

"I believe you can," I said.

He mustered a brave smile. "Sorry. That sounds so maudlin! We can't turn back the clock. We have to make the most of what we have because, if we don't, somehow it's a betrayal of their memory—don't you think?"

"I hadn't seen it that way." And I hadn't.

"Wouldn't your husband want you to be happy?" Randy went on. "You're so young. He wouldn't want you to pine away. He'd want you to go and live your life. I know Carrie would have wanted me to live the life that she wasn't able to have. So that's what I do. Everything I do is for her. I run for her, I swim for her—everything."

To my surprise, I felt my eyes sting. Randy seemed so sincere and so earnest.

He offered me his arm yet again. "Let's go downstairs and have a good time."

As we made our way to the dining room, I asked, "Have you read *Lighthouse of Sorrow?*"

Randy shook his head. "No, I don't get a lot of time to read fiction. I prefer biographies."

"It's been a pet project of Margot's for years," I said.

"I know. Louise has spoken of nothing else," he said. "She's very fond of Margot."

I was glad to hear it.

"Have you financed many films?" I asked. "I don't know the first thing about Hollywood."

"I stay out of the politics," said Randy. "I'm just the money-man."

"So how does it all work?" I said.

Randy laughed. "There are so many different options. You really want to know?"

"Yes," I said. "I'm interested."

"Well, when a production company is funding a project independently—meaning without the backing of a studio—there's gap and super-gap financing," said Randy. "It's a form of mezzanine debt financing where the producer will complete their film finance package by procuring a loan. That loan is generally secured against the film's unsold territories and rights or some other form of collateral."

"I have absolutely no idea what you're talking about." I grinned. "Margot had told me it was complicated."

"If you really are interested, I'll give you a lesson tomorrow."

"I'll be honest, no. Not really," I said. "But as my dad used to say, there's no such thing as a free lunch. I'm just curious as to how it all works."

"Your father sounds like a wise man," said Randy.

"He was," I said. "And Margot is very savvy about this kind of thing."

Louise might well be a novice, but my sister was definitely not. Trustworthy as Randy seemed to be, I felt it important to point this out.

"She would have to be," said Randy mildly. "I'll be honest, I don't have many clients willing to invest in movies, but I can see how much this book means to both of them, so . . ." He stopped and looked me straight in the eye. "I'll do whatever I can to make it happen. Your sister is in good hands."

We reached reception to find Kim, dressed in a Pic-Wic black-and-white maid's uniform and lace cap. She looked worried and beckoned me over.

"You go on ahead," I said to Randy, and pointed him in the direction of the dining room, where the strains of the Dorsey Brothers playing "By Heck" could be heard. I was pleased. Dennis must have got the vintage tabletop phonograph to work.

"What's wrong?" I asked.

"I know it's only salad," said Kim. "But where the hell is Ollie?"

Chapter Nine

I was annoyed. "What do you mean? He's not back yet?"

"Sam said he waited for an hour down at the causeway," she said. "This is typical of Ollie. He's unreliable and forgetful. I know you want to give him a chance, but how many chances is he going to get?"

I knew that Kim had a point. "Let me find out what's going on," I said.

"And let me know when you do. I'm going back to the kitchen," Kim said, and left.

I lifted the counter and headed for the phone. Even though the harbormaster had seen Ollie leave out, he wouldn't have known for sure where he was going. Maybe Ollie doubled back?

Becky answered on the first ring. "Ollie?"

My stomach flipped over. "You mean Ollie's not there?"

When I told her the reason for my call, she burst into tears. "This is all Dad's fault," she wailed.

"Is there somewhere else Ollie could have gone?" I suggested. "He must have friends. Perhaps on another island?"

"I suppose so," she whispered. "Yes. I can call around."

"And please let me know," I said. "Tell Ollie to call me and if I don't answer, he's to leave a message saying where he is. I definitely don't want him attempting to come home tonight."

I hung up the phone and tore back upstairs to grab my iPhone, which I'd left on the kitchen counter. It only just fit into my tiny evening purse. The only rational explanation I could think of was that he had gone back to St. Mary's and not contacted Becky, or gone on to another island, but he still would have called. Unless the battery on his phone was flat, which was possible.

I took a deep breath and forced myself to put Ollie to the back of my mind. It was time to join our guests.

Shabby by daylight, the dining room looked incredible at night. The ornate stained glass ceiling with its peacock motifs and beveled mirrored walls dazzled with the light from the waterfall chandeliers and beaded wall lights.

Floor-to-ceiling pale blue curtains cascaded from the scalloped pelmets and were held by tasseled tiebacks that overlooked the flagstone terrace and grounds. Octagonal tables and barrel-backed chairs were set around a small parquet dance floor. A white grand piano sat in one corner and in another was a stunning mirrored Art Deco bar, where Dennis, dressed—to my delight—in 1930s butler garb, was mixing cocktails.

Thankfully, Jerry and Sam had not had to touch this room, because it was on a different electrical branch circuit, though of course at some point the rewiring and the headache that went with it would have to be done.

I felt a twinge of excitement. Even though there would be just the four of us dining here tonight, it was easy to imagine how the place would look with a full house—especially if Kim's jazz trio idea became a regular feature.

I joined Randy at the bar where Dennis was shaking a silver Art Deco cocktail shaker. He poured the pale liquid into a green-stemmed glass, added a twist of lemon zest and handed it to me.

"I hope you like it," said Dennis.

I noticed that Randy was nursing a crystal glass of fizzy clear liquid. "Dennis couldn't tempt you?"

Randy shook his head. "This is Perrier. No ice, no lemon. I'm in training. The Boston Marathon is coming up soon, but trust me, once it's all over, I'll be first in line at the bar."

I took a sip of my drink. "Gosh. It's delicious, Dennis. What is it?"

"A White Lady," said Dennis. "In keeping with the period, of course."

"Lemon juice, Cointreau and dry gin, right?" said Randy.

Just then, I spotted Jerry standing at the entrance to the dining room. He had changed into jeans and a white button-down shirt. It looked like he'd even had a shave.

"I hope you don't mind," said Randy. "But I asked the boys to join us tonight."

I was a little surprised—we'd never shared a meal with Jerry and Sam. In fact, I hardly knew either of them. Sometimes we ate in the kitchen with Kim, Dennis and Ollie; at other times we cooked for ourselves in our flat. Although Jerry was staying in the hotel, he joined Sam in the small kitchen in the annex for meals. Often we found out that Ollie had eaten twice.

Randy waved Jerry over. "Come and have a cocktail."

Dennis mixed another White Lady. "Tonight's specialty."

Jerry accepted the cocktail, took a sip and gave an appreciative nod. "I ran into Kim. She said that Ollie never came back. Sam waited down at the causeway for over an hour."

I noticed Dennis's jaw harden. "So Mrs. Vanderhoven's suitcase is still on St. Mary's."

"It would seem so." I mustered a smile, not wanting to discuss staff business in front of Randy—or even Jerry, for that matter.

Randy must have sensed my unease because he changed the subject, asking Jerry about the family business. Jerry told us that his great-grandfather started Quick & Sons in 1911. "Now Dad's gone," he said, "I've taken over. Kept the name going."

Randy nodded. "Not many family businesses like that anymore. I'll drink to that." He raised his Perrier and we all clinked glasses.

"And you and Sam are cousins?" Randy asked.

"Through my uncle's marriage to his first wife," said Jerry. "But up until Aunt Marie's funeral, I hadn't seen him for years."

I glanced over and saw Sam framed in the doorway. He waved and came over. His hair was wet and though he had made an effort to wear clean jeans and had even located a red-and-white striped tie, his shirt needed a good iron.

"Sorry," he said sheepishly. "This is all I have. Have you heard from Ollie?"

"No," I said. "I was hoping you might have. I heard you waited down at the causeway for ages."

"Don't worry, Evie," he said. "Ollie's a good sailor. He'll show up eventually."

Dennis handed Sam a cocktail. He tried it, but pulled a face and asked for a beer. "Just the bottle," he said. "No glass."

"He's a peasant," said Jerry. "Doesn't appreciate the finer qualities of life."

"Louise tells me that she's going to ask you to be a consultant for their movie," said Randy to Sam. "Apparently you know a lot about shipwrecks."

"I run a wreck diving business out in Micronesia," said Sam. "Ever heard of Truk Lagoon—or Chuuk Lagoon as it's called now—and the Japanese Ghost Fleet?"

Randy shook his head. "Not my area of expertise."

"During 1944 and 1945 the U.S. and its allies sank more than fifty ships and destroyed over four hundred aircraft," said Sam.

I found it hard to imagine such a bloodbath and said so.

"Everything is still down there," Sam went on. "Jeeps, boxes of supplies . . . and what remains of the bodies. Every time I dive, I see something new. It certainly puts life in perspective."

"What about the wreck out in the sound?" Randy asked.

"As I already told the girls, I think it could be what's left of the *Virago*," Sam said. "Immaculate records were kept of the fates of the one hundred and sixty-seven vessels that were built on Scilly between 1774 and 1896. The *Virago* went down in 1851 in the straits. We might get lucky and find stuff belonging to her, but to be honest, she wasn't carrying anything of real value—not like the *Isadora*. Now, she's the real prize. She's the Holy Grail of ships."

Randy nodded. "But you're saying the wreck isn't the *Isadora*?"

"If only she was! To be able to walk out to a wreck is golden," Sam enthused. "You've timed your visit well."

"It sounds like we have," Randy said.

"And within a week or two, she'll be off-limits to anyone without a permit," said Sam.

"What permit?" I asked. "And why off-limits?"

"She'll be declared a protected wreck so that no one can excavate her without permission from the government."

"Is that normal around here?" Randy asked.

"Pretty normal everywhere." Sam took a swig of beer. "It's because of looting. Selling artifacts on the black market."

"I didn't know that," I said.

"There are sixty-two protected wrecks designated under Section 1 of the Protection of Wrecks Act 1973," Sam continued. "Five of those protected wrecks are around Scilly and that's not counting the hundreds of other vessels that went down."

"That's a huge number," I exclaimed.

"These islands served as the thoroughfare to the New World," said Sam. "We're talking schooners, barques and cutters, some as heavy as four hundred tons. When steam and steel came along, manpower just couldn't launch that kind of weight off the beaches."

"Have you always been interested in wrecks?" Randy asked.

"Who wouldn't be, growing up around here?" said Sam.

"Then you obviously know Cador Ferris," I said.

"Of course I do," said Sam. "We were at school together."

"They were the best of friends," Jerry put in.

"Well, yeah. Back then we were. We were kids," said Sam. "We spent many hours fantasizing about finding the *Isadora* and spending all her gold."

"Say the word *gold* and you've got my attention," said Randy. "What's the *Isadora*?"

Sam filled him in. I knew a little about the seventeenth-century galleon that sank north of Windward Point Lighthouse because Dennis had told me. But I was a little surprised at the depth of Sam's knowledge given that he'd been out of the country for so many years.

"One of my clients invested in the expedition to find the *San José*," said Randy suddenly.

"Are you kidding me?" Sam stopped dead, disbelief etched on his face. "He invested in the *San José*?"

"What's the *San José*?" I asked.

"A Spanish galleon that sank off the coast of Cartagena on the eighth of June in 1708 with six hundred people on board and twenty *billion* dollars' worth of silver, gold and jewels," Sam said. "*Billion*, Evie, not million."

"Twenty billion!" I exclaimed. "I can't even imagine what that amount would look like."

"Come on, give me his name, man," said Sam.

"I'm afraid I can't—client confidentiality—but . . ." Randy thought for a moment. "I think he might be interested in your *Isadora*. Can you get to London?"

"I'd get to the moon if I had to!" Sam looked as if his Christmases had come all at once.

Jerry tapped Sam on the shoulder and whispered something in his ear. Judging by the sudden scowl on Sam's face, it wasn't something he'd wanted to hear.

"Actually, Cador is on his way back from the Bahamas," I said. "Dennis told him about the wreck in the sound, but I know he'll be interested in anything that concerns the *Isadora*."

Sam's eyes widened in surprise. "He didn't mention this to me."

"You're in touch with Cador?" Now I was surprised.

"Well. Yes and no. I mean, we haven't spoken for a long time," said Sam. "But cool. This is great news."

"Great news?" Jerry raised an eyebrow.

"Yes, Jerry, it is." Sam threw his arm around his cousin's shoulders and mock punched him in the face. "Love you too, man."

Jerry pushed him off and turned back to the bar.

The whole exchange was very weird, but Randy didn't seem to notice.

"I'll try to get ahold of my client right now." Randy pulled his mobile out of his jacket pocket and left the dining room, adding that he would be back in ten minutes.

Sam drained his bottle of beer. As he lifted his chin, I noticed a reddish bruise on his jawline and pointed it out.

"How did you do that?" I said.

"Fell down those damn steps to the annex," said Sam.

"It looks nasty," I said. "I've got arnica somewhere if you'd like some."

Sam gestured for me to follow him. With one eye on Jerry's back, he lowered his voice and said, "Sorry about Jerry. Give him a drink and the monster comes out."

"I didn't notice," I lied.

Sam gave a sudden whoop of appreciation. "Blimey!" he exclaimed. "Will you look at what the cat dragged in!"

And there, framed in the doorway and making a grand entrance like two Hollywood vintage movie stars, stood Randy with Margot and Louise on either arm.

They looked stunning.

Louise wore a sea-green satin dress and Margot had found a slinky champagne sheath with thin spaghetti straps that I could have sworn I'd seen her sleep in, but even so, she wore it with confidence and flair. Masses of costume jewelry and pale cream feather boas—that I distinctly remembered moving to the Margery Allingham suite—completed their outfits. There was no sign of the bandage on Louise's injured hand, and I felt a surge of relief that she seemed to have recovered fully.

The next fifteen minutes were filled with animated conversation as Margot and Louise joined us at the bar and downed two cocktails each in swift succession.

"I think this 1930s theme is a good idea after all, Evie," Margot declared. "I can't believe that Dennis got that phonograph to work. I thought it was purely decorative."

"We need photos!" Louise suddenly exclaimed. "Where is Kim?"

"She's in the kitchen," I said.

"I'll use my own Instagram and tag the hotel." Louise scanned the room. "Where's the cat? We have to have the cat sitting on the bar."

There was no sign of Mister Tig.

"Never mind," Louise said. "Everyone stand by the bar— Jerry and Sam, go at the back, you're not in costume. Dennis, shake a cocktail or something."

As Louise barked orders—"stand here, stand there, do an Oprah smile"—which confused everyone until Louise showed us Oprah's signature cover girl look: shoulders raised, arms spread and a widemouthed smile. We had a lot of laughs with that one.

Louise posted a flurry of photographs. "Hashtag, hashtag, done, done, *done!*"

Finally, I was able to step out of the dining room to check my iPhone. I'd missed a call from Becky.

"I've rung everyone I can think of," she said. "No one has seen or heard from Ollie. I'm really worried. Are you positive he's not there? Did you look in his room?"

It was distinctly possible that he'd slipped back to Tregarrick and gone sulking to his room. The annex wasn't connected to the hotel, so none of us would have seen him.

"I'll go and look," I said. "But I'm afraid it'll have to be after dinner now." At that moment Margot emerged from the dining room and waved.

"There you are!" she exclaimed. "We're just about to eat!"

Promising to call Becky later, I disconnected the line.

"Please don't tell me that was Becky," she said.

I filled Margot in on our conversation. She rolled her eyes.

"Evie, one of the things I love about you is your concern for other people, but in this case, Ollie is a grown man and whatever is happening with Becky and Becky's father is frankly none of your business." She flashed a smile. "Trust me. I'm right on this."

"He does have our boat, you know," I reminded her.

"He'll show up!" Margot gave me a nudge. "Now come on, let's enjoy this evening."

I followed Margot back into the dining room to join the others at our table. Dennis's potent cocktails seemed to have set a lively mood and no one seemed to notice that I was preoccupied. I made a superhuman effort to be a good hostess and congratulated Kim on her magic. Somehow she had managed to rustle up a three-course meal from the freezer, beginning with carrot and coriander soup followed by lasagna—although she made a point of apologizing for the missing salad.

For pudding there was ice cream and a Cornish cheese board from the Cornish Food Box Company—Cornish blue, Miss Wenna Brie, Helford Camembert and of course, no cheese board would be complete without Cornish Yarg. The company had very generously sent us a sample to try out for next Saturday's open house.

When Randy started playing the white piano and Louise stood up and began to belt out songs from the 1930s in a truly terrible voice—"Stormy Weather," "As Time Goes By," "Cheek to Cheek"—I started to relax. I was worrying unnecessarily. I heard my iPhone ring in my purse, but this time I ignored it.

Sam challenged everyone to a limerick contest that Dennis

proved surprisingly good at and that left Margot crying with laughter. He continuously topped up our wineglasses and Randy continuously—though politely—refused. Even Louise tried to get him to drink, but he was adamant, and yet just as rowdy as Sam and Dennis. Their limericks became increasingly bawdy until Louise got unsteadily to her feet, picked up a spoon, tapped her wineglass and yelled, "Let's play cards!"

"Poker," said Sam.

"Strip poker!" Louise cried.

Kim laughed. "I'm in!"

"No," Margot squealed. "I don't know how to play poker."

"Yes, you do," Louise said. "You always beat the *pants* off everyone." There was a chorus of laughter. "Seriously. Never challenge Margot to a game of poker. She's such a good liar."

Margot pointed a finger at Louise. "That's because I learned from the best!"

The two friends grinned and in that moment it was easy to imagine them enjoying the nightlife of Los Angeles together.

Dennis stood up. "I'll get the cards."

"Try the Residents' Lounge," I said. "I'm not sure where I put them. We moved so much stuff out when Jerry started rewiring."

"And we play for money," Kim declared. "Fifty pence a hand."

"That's stupid," Louise said. "It's got to be five quid, otherwise it's not worth it."

"No, no," I said desperately. "Can't we play for buttons?"

"Buttons?" Louise scoffed. "How old are you? Twelve?"

"You'll have to count me out," said Randy. "I don't like to gamble."

Margot's eyes widened. "You don't smoke, you don't drink, you don't gamble . . . don't you have any vices at all?"

"I'll let you know tomorrow morning," Louise said, making her meaning plain. Randy's face remained impassive. "Of course he gambles," she went on. "Isn't dabbling in the stock market a gamble?"

"It's not the stock market. And I don't dabble." Although Randy was smiling, he seemed deadly serious. "People trust me with millions of dollars."

"Do you have to have a million to become one of your clients?" Kim demanded. I noticed her lipstick was smudged and her eyes glittered. "I've got a little nest egg."

"I'd like to see that little nest egg," said Jerry with a leer.

The two exchanged a look that went unnoticed by everyone except for me. Jerry's face was flushed and I was reminded of Sam's comment earlier about drink letting out the monster. He also seemed to be hitting on Kim and she seemed only too happy to reciprocate. I could have sworn that Jerry had mentioned he was married.

"And that's why you need to be smart now!" Louise slammed her empty wineglass down on the table. Dennis swiftly topped it up. "Invest! Protect your future!"

"I don't know the first thing about investing," said Jerry.

Sam sneered. "You are so full of it, Jerry."

There was clearly some kind of feud going on between the cousins.

"So why don't you tell us all at the table here exactly what it is you do, Randy?" Jerry sat back in his chair with a look of defiance. "I'm all ears."

"Jerry!" I exclaimed. "Randy is our guest."

"I make it a rule never to discuss politics, money or religion at the dinner table," said Randy. "But I tell you what, why don't you and I have a chat tomorrow?"

"I think now is as good a time as any," Jerry said.

"I agree," Kim declared.

"Okay," said Randy slowly. "But I'm afraid the ladies will find it boring."

"I won't," said Kim.

"Nor I," Margot agreed.

Louise grabbed the open bottle of wine from the table and topped up Kim's and Jerry's glasses. "Randy has the most exciting clients. Tell them, Randy. Don't be so modest!"

"We already know about the *San José*," said Sam. "Do you know the name of the investor, Louise?"

"Even if I did, I wouldn't tell you," Louise said. "Randy is all about confidentiality."

"Well, go on then," prompted Jerry rudely. "Start talking."

Randy gave a sigh. "Okay. But I want this noted that I am telling you all under duress."

Kim took out an imaginary pen and pretended to write on the palm of her hand. "Duly noted!"

"Well . . ." Randy began. "I'm a consultant for the Pinnacle Trust Group—"

"It's in Hong Kong," Louise said excitedly. "Tell them about the special fund."

When Randy hesitated, Louise jumped in again. "In that case,

I will," she said. "It's called Trust Fund M. and guarantees"—she held up both hands for air quotes—"'anything from twelve to twenty-one percent interest annually.'"

"That's impressive." Sam nudged Jerry. "Right?" But Jerry didn't react.

"Well, yes, it is," said Kim. "But to be honest, I'd be very skeptical about any company offering that kind of return."

Randy didn't seem to take offense. "My investors are in for the long haul. They expect to lose a little bit of money at the beginning."

Louise was now seriously drunk. "Tell them about the gas and oil wells in good old Texas."

"What kind of money is a little bit?" Kim demanded.

"A couple hundred thousand," said Randy.

"Dollars, that is," Louise declared.

"Ssh, babe." Randy's discomfort was growing by the minute, but Louise obliviously blundered on.

"Unfortunately, the syndicate is very small and the only way to get in is to wait for someone to die," said Louise.

"But you got in," Kim pointed out.

"I got in because I'm special." Louise laughed. "But Randy does all kinds of ventures."

"True," said Randy. "But those ventures are basically points-based syndicates."

Something about the word *syndicate* bothered me. I may not have had the hands-on experience that Margot had in movie production, but when Robert was alive, he had invested in various enterprises. I was fully aware of the basic concept.

"So you're saying that investors in a syndicate use their own money," I said.

"It depends on the venture," said Randy. "Obviously, my team calculates the risk. We're in it to make money for our investors—"

"And for yourself," said Kim bluntly. "I mean, let's get real here."

"Of course I am!" Randy reached for the Perrier to top up his glass. There was an uncomfortable silence.

"I think it's time for coffee," Margot declared. "Anyone?"

"I'll clear the table and make a *cafetière*." Kim got to her feet and began to stack the empty plates.

And then Jerry stood up and turned to Kim. "Here, let me help you with that. That way, I can supervise your appliances."

Then the music on the phonograph stopped.

"You can supervise my appliances anytime," Kim said in an audible whisper.

"Bad idea, Jerry," Sam said loudly. "Bad idea."

"You stay out of my business," Jerry retorted. "And I'll stay out of yours."

My iPhone rang. I ignored it, but it rang again. And again.

"Shouldn't you answer that?" said Louise. "It sounds like it could be important."

So I did.

Becky's voice was laced with anger. "Why are you covering for him?"

"Hold on a moment." I stood up, made my excuses to the table and headed for reception.

"Ollie's in his room," Becky declared.

"I haven't been to his room yet," I said wearily.

"He's there but he's not answering!" Becky exclaimed. "I used that app—'Find My'—you know, the one that locates your mobile. I know his password."

"Okay," I said again. "So what do you want me to do?"

There was silence on the other end of the line until I heard a few sniffles.

"I'm pregnant," Becky said suddenly.

I should have been surprised, but I wasn't. Becky's distress now made perfect sense. No wonder her father was angry. Becky was so young—not even twenty-one.

"Something is wrong. I know it," she said urgently. "Please, please. Just go and make sure he's all right."

I hesitated, but Becky's tears were just too much. "I'll call you back."

Chapter Ten

I didn't tell anyone where I was going. I just grabbed a waterproof hotel cape and left. Outside, the air was eerily still. There wasn't a breath of wind. It was as if Storm Iona were pausing to gather her strength before she would wreak havoc on our tiny island.

The annex was set behind a thick laurel hedge and accessed by a narrow flight of steps. I remembered Sam's warning about the steps being slippery, but they looked clear and clean from last night's rain.

Ollie's room was number five.

I rapped on the door and called out, "Ollie! It's Evie."

Nothing.

I knocked again, louder this time. "Ollie! I know you're in there. Please open the door."

But there was still no answer. I stepped back, conscious that there was no band of light shining under his door.

Suddenly, the cold, gloomy corridor of the annex seemed

menacing. I glanced into the small kitchen to see if he was in there, but it was empty.

Returning to Ollie's room again, I tried the handle. The door wasn't locked.

"Ollie?" I slowly pushed it open and stepped into the darkness. I flipped on the light. The room was empty, though the bathroom door was closed.

His space was predictably untidy, with the bed unmade. It smelled of stale beer and cigarettes. He wasn't supposed to smoke, but I knew he did—and not just cigarettes, either. I definitely detected the sweet, pungent smell of marijuana.

Clothing was piled on a hard-backed chair and on top of his chest of drawers was a muddle of spare change, balled-up scraps of paper and a comb. Ollie's iPhone was nowhere in sight. And then I saw something that made my stomach turn. Partially hidden by the paper was the boat key on its bright yellow foam fob marked Spare.

Ollie *had* come back.

I stared at the closed bathroom door again, conscious that my heart was beginning to beat a little faster. I knocked. "Ollie?" I said quietly. "Are you okay?"

But again, there was no answer. I tried the handle, feeling a draught on my feet coming from under the door.

I took a deep breath and entered the room.

The bathroom window was wide open. It was small—too small for Ollie to get through, even though it was the first thing that came to my mind. I closed it and just stood there, perplexed.

Where on earth was he?

And then I heard the sound of pitter-patter on the corrugated iron roof that quickly grew to a thunderous roar. Storm Iona had finally hit.

The noise grew louder until it sounded like the entire building was being struck by thousands of drumbeats. There was a clap of thunder and the lights flickered, went out and then came back on again.

I darted up the annex steps and tore along the narrow path to the kitchen entrance to the hotel. Within seconds, I was absolutely drenched.

There was another crack of lightning followed by an even louder boom of thunder as I burst into the safety of the building and bumped straight into Margot.

"There you are!" she exclaimed. "But you're soaked?"

Although the poncho had kept my body dry, my hair had fallen down and was plastered to my face. I quickly told Margot about Becky's call and finding the boat key in Ollie's room.

"That's weird," said Margot. "Becky must be mistaken. And you say it's the spare boat key?"

"Yes, that's the one I saw him take this afternoon," I said.

"But you also told me that Dennis said Ollie had both boat keys, remember?" Margot went on. "He must have just taken the other one."

"Aren't you just a bit concerned?" I said, irritated. "It's obvious he came back."

"Of course I am concerned, but more about Ollie's future here," said Margot. "He can't just please himself when he's on company business."

"Margot!" I exclaimed. "Something might have happened to him."

"Trust me, Ollie is the type who can look after himself—Oh, here is Louise." She waved to her friend, who was weaving her way over toward us.

Louise gasped. "Gosh, Evie, you do look wet!"

"My sister loves to dance in the rain," said Margot.

"Did Dennis find the brandy?" Louise asked. I could hear a slur in her voice.

Margot caught my eye. "I'm really tired," she said. "Aren't you?"

"Where's Randy?" I asked.

"Gone to write some emails," said Louise. "But we don't care! The night is still young! The party isn't over. You should join us, Evie!"

"I'd love to another time, but I need to go and dry my hair," I said. "Sorry."

"We'll see you tomorrow, then," Louise trilled.

Sensing my confusion, Margot added, "We're all meeting at ten-thirty tomorrow morning to walk to the wreck. We mustn't be late. You know what Dennis is like about punctuality."

On cue, Dennis appeared from the side hall with a bottle of brandy that Louise grabbed immediately. "You only have a short window of time on the seabed," he said. "It'll take forty minutes to make the climb down to Seal Cove. You don't want to take any chances."

Louise, Margot and I trooped upstairs, but I left the two of them on the landing and finally let myself into the sanctuary of our flat. I was desperate to take a shower, but wanted to get the call to Becky over and done with first.

"He must be there," Becky said in a low voice.

"Well, he's not."

"Dad's just gone to the kitchen," she said. "I can't talk for long. You checked the boat was there, right?"

"No," I said. "And I don't plan to tonight."

I heard a man's voice in the background that had to belong to Becky's father, who, in no uncertain terms, told her to get off her phone. She disconnected the line.

I was growing irritated with the Becky and Ollie drama but I still couldn't shake off the feeling that something was wrong. What was I supposed to do now? Go out in the rain and check that our boat was down at the floating pontoon?

I stood at my bedroom window and watched the storm in awe. The violence of nature never ceased to amaze me. Rain pounded against the glass; deafening thunderclaps reverberated across the sky. Bolts of lightning lit up the ocean. I thought of the schooner in the sound and the *Isadora* beyond Windward Point and wondered if they had perished in such terrible weather as this.

And then, all was quiet. The storm had passed. The gleaming supermoon, hidden now and then by unfurling dark clouds, finally emerged to take command of the night sky.

I was just about to turn out my bedside light when I heard a tap on my door.

It was Margot. "I saw your light was still on." She gestured to the end of my bed. "Can I?"

"Please do," I said. "Is everything okay?"

"Define *okay*." Margot flung herself full-length across the end of my bed, then rolled onto her side, resting her head on her elbow. It took me right back to all the postmortem conversations we used to have after our nights out in London.

"Well, put it this way," said Margot. "As you know, they haven't slept together yet, but she's determined that tonight is the night she wants to take things to the next level."

"Good luck to her," I said.

"I told Louise not to mix business and pleasure, especially if he's involved in financing our movie," Margot went on. "It's a huge mistake, but she's completely infatuated with him. She's had quite a bit to drink tonight and I don't want her making a fool of herself. I admit I was upset about how quickly she seemed to be able to move on from Chester, but to be honest, Randy seems like a nice guy . . . although—" She frowned. "I hate to say this, but there's something about him that—"

"Doesn't ring true?" I suggested.

"Exactly! I can't put my finger on it." Margot sat up and thought for a moment. "He reminds me of a . . . of a—"

"Politician?" I suggested again.

"Yes! It's like he's touting for votes. He knows all the right questions to ask and the right things to say."

"I know what you mean," I said. "Don't you think it's weird that he doesn't want to sleep in the same room as Louise?"

"Oh," said Margot. "I just thought he was being respectful."

"And as you said, he could just be after Louise's money."

Margot shook her head. "No, Louise says he's loaded." She pointed to the carafe of water and glass by my bed. "Do you mind? Otherwise I'm going to have a crashing headache to-morrow. I'm not used to so much alcohol. Louise was always a party girl and she hasn't changed."

I poured Margot a glass and passed it over. "We only have Louise's word that he's loaded."

"Hmm. You might have a point." She hesitated a moment before adding, "Actually, Louise wants half of the option money for *Lighthouse of Sorrow* up front."

"Margot, I don't like the sound of that," I said. "I thought you weren't going to have to spend your own money."

"It's complicated," said Margot.

"Well, how much is she talking about?" I asked.

"Fifty thousand dollars."

"Fifty thousand!" I exclaimed. "That's a lot! And where are you planning on getting that from?"

"The option was for a hundred," she protested, as if that made a difference.

"You didn't answer my question," I said. "The fifty thousand?"

"Rob a bank? Win the lottery?" She gave a heavy sigh. "I can't think about that now."

"Have you seen the agreement?" I persisted. "Presumably, there has to be one between the author and Louise . . . and you, for that matter."

"The details are still being worked out," said Margot. "You know, stuff like flying him first-class to the premiere, that kind of thing. The money will go into an escrow fund. It's all aboveboard—Wait. Did you hear that noise? Ssh! Listen."

We fell silent and yes, sure enough, I could hear what sounded like banging.

Margot frowned. "What *is* that?"

The noise was definitely coming from the floor below us. Then we heard a female voice shouting, "Let me in! Randy! Let me in."

"It's Louise!" I exclaimed.

"Oh my God, it sounds like she's trying to break into Randy's room!" Margot jumped off the bed. "This is exactly what I was worried about. She's going to make a total fool of herself. We have to stop her!"

We hurried down the back stairs and there, standing outside the George Goodchild suite, was Louise, dressed for the outdoors in her Burberry trench coat and knee-high boots with stiletto heels. The DO NOT DISTURB sign lay tossed on the carpet.

Louise's knocking became more insistent. "Randy!" she yelled. "Let me in! *Now!*"

I gasped. "What on earth is she wearing?"

"Louise!" Margot called out.

Her friend spun around and as she did so, her trench coat swung open to reveal a sheer black basque, miniscule panties and suspenders. She'd also been overzealous in her use of blush and red lipstick.

"Good grief," said Margot. "We need to get her back to her room. Quickly, Evie. Help me."

Personally, I thought we should just let Louise get on with it, but Margot was on a mission.

"He's not answering." Louise, eyes wild, rattled the door handle and hammered on it again. "I know you're in there! Sweetie. Babe. Honeypie. *Pleeeeeease* open the door."

"Let's go back to your room, Louise," I said, but when I

tried to prise her fingers from the door handle, she lashed out with her boot, catching me on the shin.

"Ouch, that hurt!" I squeaked.

"Why won't he open the door?" She hammered yet again.

Margot sprang forward and slapped Louise in the face.

I was shocked but not as shocked as Louise, who reeled backwards, clutching her cheek. "You hit me."

"Sorry, but you were hysterical." Margot turned to me all matter-of-fact. "Don't look so alarmed, Evie. Louise gets like this occasionally and this isn't the first time I've had to snap her out of it. Take an arm. Let's go."

To my surprise, Louise didn't protest. She leaned onto Margot and whispered, "Was I about to do something silly?"

"Yes, you were," Margot said firmly.

"You're such a good friend."

"Is everything all right up there?" Kim appeared at the top of the stairs, with Jerry close behind. "What was all that banging?"

"Thunder," I said. "Thanks for everything tonight, Kim. The meal was fabulous."

As we bore Louise away, we heard Kim and Jerry sniggering.

Once inside the Agatha Christie suite, Louise's knees buckled and she slithered down the wall, landing in a heap on the floor.

"Tired," she whispered. "So very, very tired." She promptly closed her eyes and began to snore.

Margot shook Louise's shoulders. "Louise, Louise," she said desperately. "Wake up."

But Louise's snoring grew louder.

"Now what?" I said to Margot. "We can't leave her like this."

Louise's legs were splayed out in front of her. Her trench coat was wide open.

"Is she wearing La Perla?" Margot looked closer. "Oh no! I've just had an awful thought. Wait there."

Margot headed to the bathroom, returning just moments later with an empty Ziploc bag. "This had six Ambien in it. She must have taken them all!"

"Mixed with the cocktails, the wine at dinner and the brandy—"

"*And* whatever else she was taking." Margot looked worried. "I didn't think she did party favors anymore."

My jaw dropped. "What? You mean . . . *drugs*?"

"Oh God," Margot wailed. "I hope she's not going to die."

"Don't be ridiculous," I said, although I wasn't altogether unconcerned, either. "But she might throw up. You'll have to stay with her tonight in case she does."

Margot regarded her friend, slumped against the wall like a discarded marionette.

"Help me get her into the recovery position," I said. "We'll wedge her in with pillows and cover her with a blanket."

After much debate, we decided to put a white toweling robe over Louise's undies and move her into the master bedroom. For someone so skinny, Louise was surprisingly heavy.

"I hope she doesn't wake up in the middle of the night," Margot grumbled.

"No . . . we hope she does," I corrected her. "Then we know she'll be okay. I'll stay with her while you get ready for bed."

As I waited for Margot to return, I went to draw the curtains but stopped in front of the window, awestruck.

The supermoon was huge. As it cast its dazzling light across the starry sky, Windward Point Lighthouse stood out in silhouette, a tiny speck against the wonder of the universe. It reminded me of the iconic bicycle shot in *E.T.*

And then a solitary light came into view in the dell below. It was moving fast and looked like a bicycle headlamp, but I knew it couldn't be that. The light seemed to float above the ground. It crossed the Galleon Garden and headed to the flights of steps that marked the tiered terraces all the way up to the top, to the coastal path, and from there, on to William's Wood. I watched the light crest the bluff and disappear from view.

Ollie? Could it be Ollie?

I watched for the light to reappear but it didn't.

Margot returned in her faded navy sweatpants and a hoodie. "Just as well I didn't throw these out," she said. "What's the matter? Why are you standing at the window?"

So I told her. Margot came to join me and stared into the night.

"I can't see any light," she said finally.

"It was definitely there," I said. "Do you think I should go and see what's going on?"

Margot's jaw dropped. "Are you out of your mind? It's one in the morning!"

A thought occurred to me. "It'll be low tide in two hours. What if it's Ollie and he's going out to the wreck?"

"Then let him!" Margot was getting exasperated. "Stop this! Evie. Please, can we talk about Ollie in the morning? I'm so tired. Help me arrange these damn pillows."

Margot grabbed one and pushed it into my arms.

Despite us having positioned Louise on her side on top of the vast bed, she continued to snore.

"I'll get the bucket from the cleaning supply cupboard," I said. "Just in case she throws up."

Moments later, I'd placed the receptacle strategically on Louise's side of the bed and left her and Margot, finally, to sleep.

Unfortunately, I was now wide-awake. Back in my bedroom, I was drawn to the window, unable to resist the temptation of looking for that light. I scanned the skyline, eyes fixed in the direction of the coastal path and William's Wood. Nothing. I was just about to turn away when my eye caught a tiny pinprick of light just to the west of the abandoned lighthouse, moving back toward the hotel.

I just had to know if it was Ollie. I had to know if the *Sandpiper* was down at the causeway. Margot had said I was out of my mind and maybe she was right.

I didn't hesitate. I pulled on my jeans and a thick sweater over my pajamas.

I'd never been afraid of what the darkness held, but even so, I grabbed the purse-size aerosol of Mace that Margot kept in the drawer by our front door. One of the habits she'd picked up in Los Angeles and that I'd ridiculed.

I took a flashlight, let myself out of our flat and tiptoed downstairs.

Chapter Eleven

The air outside seemed unusually still after the storm. I took my flashlight but didn't end up needing it. The supermoon was so bright, it illuminated my way.

I started to have serious second thoughts. What exactly was my plan? Pick a fight with Ollie in the middle of the night? Demand to know what he's been doing, just like a fussy mother hen? Even more embarrassing, what if it wasn't Ollie? Maybe it was Sam who had gone out to the wreck, or Randy, who'd said he suffered from insomnia?

But there was one thing that I could do. Check to see if the *Sandpiper* was moored at the floating pontoon.

As I descended the granite steps to the causeway, the sound of the sea grew louder. I spotted Ollie's battered dinghy tucked into a hollow in the small cluster of rocks above the waterline, but there was no sign of our boat.

Maybe the *Sandpiper* hadn't been tied up firmly and had broken loose in the storm, but it was unlikely. Dennis and

Ollie had built the floating pontoon in a sheltered natural rocky recess for that very reason.

Defeated, I turned back. Halfway up the steps I paused to catch my breath and noticed something odd. A batch of envelopes, held together by a rubber band, had been dropped among the aeoniums that grew out of the surrounding wall crevices.

My stomach gave a peculiar lurch.

It was junk mail, addressed to Margot and myself, care of our PO Box number that I'd specifically asked Ollie to pick up for me. The mail had been reduced to a clump of wet pulp from having been soaked in the rain. Of course, there was always the chance that it could have lain there for weeks unnoticed, but I didn't think so. I'd passed this spot many times and was sure I would have seen that clump before now.

I shoved the letters into my pocket and kept on going. As I took the top step, I caught my foot on the uneven flagstone and pitched forward, only just keeping my balance.

And then I saw them. There, on the ground, next to the first cast-iron urn, were four cherry tomatoes glinting in a moonbeam. Two more were in the flower border. I stared at them with a growing sense of unease. Ollie had also been instructed to pick up a list of salad items that included cherry tomatoes. With the sodden junk mail and now the tomatoes, it was too much of a coincidence. What's more, Becky had used the Find My app and located Ollie's phone in his room.

For whatever reason, Ollie must have come back to Tregarrick and gone back out again. He could easily have found the original boat key and left the spare in his room.

But where on earth was he now?

The tomatoes joined the sodden junk mail in my pocket. I headed back to the hotel.

. . .

It took forever to fall asleep, but I must have eventually because I was rudely awakened by Margot opening the curtains with a flourish and a cheery, "What time do you call this?"

A glance at my bedside clock showed that it was nearly a quarter past ten!

"If you want to walk to the wreck," she said, offering me a mug of black coffee, "you'd better get a move on. They're leaving in fifteen minutes."

I sat bolt upright and scrambled out of bed, blindly reaching for my clothes.

"Didn't you hear the phone ring in the kitchen?" said Margot. "Dennis was concerned when he hadn't seen you. It was just as well I came back to make more coffee for Louise."

I mumbled a thank-you. I felt groggy and struggled to gather my thoughts as the bizarre events of last night came flooding back. I took a gulp of coffee.

"Louise feels a little ropy and her ankle is bugging her and frankly, I'm exhausted, so that's why we're not walking out to the wreck," Margot finished saying. "Didn't you hear what I said?"

"Yes, yes, of course," I lied. "Do you know if Ollie got back safely?"

Margot rolled her eyes. "Oh my God! What is it with you? I have no idea. Just let it go."

"But aren't you worried at all?" I was going to add that I'd gone down to the floating pontoon and found the boat gone, but I decided against it. Ollie could well be downstairs right now and I was worrying over nothing.

"A little concerned, yes," said Margot. "But I am sure there is a perfectly logical explanation!" She pointed to the clock. "Get your skates on. We'll talk later—Oh, and don't forget to take your camera!" And with that, she left.

I glanced at my iPhone and saw I had a voice mail from Becky. I listened to it with growing disbelief. She said she must have made a mistake about thinking the blue dot from Ollie's Find My app was in his room, because when she checked it this morning, it had vanished. And yet that did not explain finding the junk mail in the rockery or the cherry tomatoes at the top of the steps from the causeway.

Margot said I just had to let it go. But I couldn't. Something wasn't right.

Grabbing my camera and slipping my iPhone into my pocket, I left.

I reached the landing just as Randy was replacing the DO NOT DISTURB sign on his door handle. He greeted me warmly. I thought he looked tired. There were big black circles under his eyes.

"How did you sleep last night?" I said.

"Very well," said Randy. "Just not enough of it. Running usually helps me to sleep, but this time it didn't."

My jaw dropped. "It was you!" I was overcome with relief and not just because I narrowly missed making a fool of myself had I bumped into him in the dark. "I saw a light and wondered what crazy person was out there in the middle of the night!"

Randy grinned. "I happen to love running in the dark. I run whenever I can, though it's a challenge with my insane work and travel schedule, and all the time differences."

"The supermoon was pretty amazing, wasn't it?" I said.

"Yeah." He agreed. "And seeing it illuminate the wreck in the sound was awesome."

So this meant that Randy hadn't known that Louise had been trying to break down his bedroom door. "Did you happen to see anyone else out there?"

"Nope," said Randy. "Just me and the moon."

I felt as if I were losing my mind, but I couldn't get rid of this awful premonition that something was wrong.

We headed down the back staircase, and I noticed a brown stain on the ceiling that hadn't been there before. The storm had done its damage.

Randy noticed it, too. "Looks like you might need a new roof at some point."

"I know," I said.

"If I were you, I'd take out a construction loan. You'd get a better rate of interest," he said. "Have you thought about adding an extension? Going up as opposed to out?"

"We can't do anything structural to the building." I explained that Margot and I were just chatelaines of the Tregarrick Rock hotel.

He seemed surprised. "You mean you don't own it?"

"No, we've leased the hotel from the Ferris Family Trust," I said. "We're on the hook for some of the repairs and general maintenance. I'm afraid the repairs have turned out far more expensive than we thought. The major ones have to be approved by Cador Ferris. He owns the estate."

"Ah yes." Randy nodded. "I remember. He's Sam's old school pal and he's in the Bahamas hunting for treasure, too." Randy thought for a moment. "And what about Sam?"

"What about him?" I said carefully.

"Do you know much about his dive boat business in Chuuk?" Randy asked.

His tone was casual, but I felt uncomfortable and he must have sensed it.

"Sorry," he said ruefully. "I can't help it. I've got to do background checks for my clients."

"Of course you have," I said. "But to be honest, he's only been here three weeks. You should talk to Jerry."

"I detected a bit of animosity there," said Randy. "Any idea what's going on between them?"

"Sorry. No," I said, and swiftly changed the subject. "It's a shame that Louise and Margot aren't walking out to the wreck."

"I'm not surprised," said Randy with a grin. "They were both really knocking it back last night. I hear there was brandy involved, too."

We reached the ground floor and, spying the office door, I had a sudden thought. "I just need to check on something in the office. I'll meet you in reception in a few minutes."

Randy left and I slipped inside just on the off chance that Ollie had returned and left my package in there. Of course he hadn't. Yet again, I had that sick feeling in my stomach. I thought of Mum, long dead now, who always said to trust my gut and that when it came to her two daughters, it was me, the youngest, who was intuitive while Margot was always too impatient. But in this situation, what was I supposed to do? Call the police and report a missing person?

I returned to reception, where Sam and Randy were engaged in animated conversation. Sam's mood from the night before had vanished and he seemed like a kid with a new toy. He was decked out in waterproofs and carried an oversize canvas rucksack.

"Forecast is predicting a bit of mizzle." Dennis appeared holding a black waterproof cape and a pair of Wellington boots. He set the boots down. The hotel always kept a supply for guests who were unprepared for the changeable weather. "Size twelve, as you requested."

"What's mizzle?" Randy switched his brown leather loafers for the boots. He wiggled his feet and nodded to Dennis. "Great fit. Thanks, mate."

"Mizzle is a misty drizzle," I explained to Randy. "It's sneaky wet rain."

"Isn't all rain wet?" Randy teased.

"Ah . . . but this is stealth rain," I said. "Wet air, really."

"And it's easy to get disorientated in mizzle," Dennis declared. "Vicar Bill told me that years ago someone walked the seabed and drowned. He'd lived on Bryher all his life, but the mizzle came in fast and the tide even faster."

"Yeah, I heard about that when I was a kid," said Sam.

Dennis picked the loafers up. "I'll leave these in the downstairs boot room."

"Has anyone seen, or heard, from Ollie this morning?" I asked.

Sam shook his head. "Nope. And believe me, I would have heard if he'd come back. My room is next to his and the walls are paper-thin."

"Is there a problem?" Randy asked.

"One of our employees didn't come home last night," I said. "And no one seems to know where he is."

"Isn't he staying with Becky?" said Dennis.

"No," I said.

"Ollie has a lot of friends, Evie," said Sam. "Maybe he just wanted to get away from his girlfriend for a bit of peace and quiet."

"Why would you say that?" I said sharply. "Is there something you know and we don't?"

Sam seemed startled by my tone. "Sorry. I didn't mean anything by it. I'm just saying that I've spent a lot of time with him over the past few weeks and it sounds like she's pretty high-maintenance. Don't you agree, Dennis?"

Dennis raised his hands. "I'm Switzerland. Don't involve me in this."

Sam checked his watch. "We need to go."

I had another idea and told Randy and Sam to go on ahead.

"We'll wait in the Galleon Garden," said Sam, "but don't be too long. Remember, we've only got a two-hour window and it'll take a good forty minutes to get down to the seabed and another fifteen to walk out to the wreck, and then we have to get back."

"I'm right behind you," I said, and took out my iPhone.

Dennis raised a questioning eyebrow.

"I'm going to call Pegasus Couriers," I said.

I knew Kevin, the manager, well. Margot and I had used his courier service a lot when we were in the throes of moving to Scilly.

"Ollie?" said Kevin, when he answered. "Sure, I remember. He came in yesterday around three, three-fifteen. He picked up the two packages."

Becky had said as much.

"A large box from Marvis Cameras in London for you and an extra-long mailing tube for a Sam Quick from Weno, F.S.M., wherever that is. Sam Quick was also the sender."

Thanking Kevin, I disconnected the line and relayed the conversation to Dennis. "Where is F.S.M.?"

"It's the Federated States of Micronesia," said Dennis. "That's where Sam lives."

Was this the water-blast pistol for his nephew? It seemed an odd thing for him to send to himself. Perhaps he wouldn't be so ambivalent about Ollie's elusiveness when he knew that his package was missing, too.

I looked at Dennis. He was always so hard to read. "Aren't you worried about Ollie?"

"I'll make a few calls," was all Dennis said. "We'll track him down."

I left him to it and hurried to catch up with the others.

It must have rained again in the night. Everything smelled fresh and clean. The flagstones were black and shiny, and the grassy bank that ran down to the dell sparkled in the morning sun.

Sam and Randy were waiting for me in the Galleon Garden, as promised. It was an outdoor museum of sorts and home to spectacular figureheads of all shapes and sizes. There were painted ladies, golden tigers and giant fish heads, to name just a few. Each figurehead stood in its own neatly clipped three-sided box hedge.

"And you say that the figureheads in this garden *all* come from ships that actually sank in these waters?" I heard Randy ask Sam.

"As I mentioned last night at dinner," said Sam, "Scilly was along the trading route from the Far East to the New World. At one time it was said that a thousand ships were able to seek shelter in the harbor at St. Mary's—Oh hey! Evie!" Sam waved a greeting. "Any news of Ollie?"

I shook my head and told him about my conversation with Kevin. "So Ollie must have picked up your package, too."

"That's strange," said Sam. "I've been tracking it, and it's not due to arrive until Monday."

"It must be important," I said. "You were listed as the sender as well."

"Yeah, I know," said Sam. "I bought it before coming here. You get the best Bazooka water-blast pistols out there and it wouldn't fit into my suitcase." He turned back to Randy. "Where was I?"

"You were talking about the Tearing Ledge," said Randy.

Sam went on to give a history lesson about a deadly rock formation that lurked under the water's surface. "Obviously, there was no radar or sonar technology in those days," he said. "I don't think I need to explain why it was called the Tearing Ledge."

Randy looked somber. "And having wooden hulls, those old ships wouldn't have stood a chance."

I looked at my watch, worried about the time. Sam had seemed so anxious to get going and now he was playing tour guide.

We walked on for a few moments until Sam stopped. "Ah . . . there she is. The Holy Grail." He pointed to the *Isadora* figurehead, which reminded me so much of Sleeping Beauty. She was painted with waist-length flaxen hair, fair skin and a touch of red on her bow-shaped lips. Her dress was sky blue and had a bodice trimmed in gold braid. *Isadora* had one hand raised as if shielding her eyes from the sun's glare. It was easy to imagine her on the prow of her ship, forging through the waves.

"When we were kids, Cador and I always dreamed of finding the *Isadora*," said Sam.

Randy stepped up and ran his hands over the smooth, burnished wood. "She's beautiful."

Sam beamed. "Isn't she? Of course, she looked nothing like that when she was found off Windward Point. The figurehead lived in a tank of salt water for months. There weren't so many rules and regulations back then."

As we left the Galleon Garden behind and headed for the steps up to the coast path, Randy bombarded Sam with questions about the *Isadora*—how many souls perished, what kind of cargo had she been carrying, and where Sam believed she had ultimately gone down.

We began the ascent. I soon fell behind and could no longer hear the conversation between Randy and Sam.

They were waiting for me at the top, where a small area of

wasteland commanded a spectacular view of the sound and the neighboring island of Bryher.

There, far out on the sand, stood what was left of the old schooner.

Randy and Sam were waiting at the top of what I assumed was the way down to Seal Cove. The path had been washed away and now resembled more of a gulley. It was strewn with rocks, boulders and scrub vegetation that zigzagged out of sight.

Down below, the carcass of the old schooner stood upright. Even from where we were standing, the wreck seemed far larger than I'd expected. There was something menacing about the stark wooden ribs that reached up to the sky. As someone who is afraid of the water, I couldn't help thinking how terrifying it must have been for those on board as the boat was torn apart on the Tearing Ledge.

"Well?" Sam demanded. "Are we all ready for this? Evie?"

"Yes, of course," I said.

"Let's go!" Randy exclaimed.

The sun disappeared behind a heavy bank of clouds, and Sam plunged through a tangle of gorse bushes. Randy followed, and I brought up the rear.

At first I was worried that Sam didn't know where he was going, but then, after fighting through waist-high prickles, we broke through and stepped onto a patch of mud-beaten earth.

Gesturing to the vista below, Sam said, "What you see exposed at low tide now would have represented high tide thousands of years ago. When we start to walk across the sound, you'll see the remains of human habitation—fish traps, hut circles and field systems that were used in the Bronze Age."

"And all these islands were just *one* land mass?" Randy said. "Bloody amazing!"

"Speaking of the Bronze Age," Sam went on. "Up behind us and to your extreme left is a burial chamber."

Randy and I turned to see a cairn of boulders nestled against the escarpment, twenty feet or so above us.

"It's been boarded up since I was a kid," said Sam. "The roof collapsed years ago, which is a pity because there are wall paintings inside."

I was impressed by Sam's knowledge of the island.

"Were you born on Tregarrick, Sam?" I asked.

"St. Martin's," said Sam. "But I spent a lot of time here with Cador."

Randy pointed to a distinctive crescent-shaped sandbar in the cove below that started at the base of Seal Rock and curved across the seabed. "What's that?"

"*That*, my friend, is our pathway," said Sam. "We walk on the sandbar because it's easier to follow. And keep your eyes open. The best time to beachcomb is always after a storm."

"So how do we actually get down to the seabed?" Randy asked.

Sam grinned. "Ah, that's the million-dollar question. There used to be an animal track at one time. Hopefully, it's still there."

Sam turned left and fought his way through some scrub and bushes, but he was right. There was a narrow track.

"Watch your step!" he yelled out. "Last night's rain has made this very slippery."

The track turned into the gulley we'd seen from above. Was this really the only way to get to Seal Cove?

Finally, Sam reached a wide slab of stone that protruded from the hillside.

"Seal Cove is directly beneath us," he said. "We're standing on an overhang."

I gingerly stepped to the edge and peered over. The rockslide had torn a channel through what had been the original path. Now there were more steep, uneven tracks, and flat grassy ledges that continued to zigzag all the way down to another slab of stone above the sand.

"It looks like a bit of a drop," I said.

"It's not too bad." Sam grinned again. "That's why we don't get people walking from Bryher to Tregarrick for afternoon tea."

I had a good view of the actual seabed now. It was a mass of rocks and boulders, too, interspersed with wide expanses of furrowed sand.

"Ready, Evie?" Sam asked.

I tucked my camera inside my coat for safety. Sam led the way, followed by Randy, with me bringing up the rear again. It was slow going. Sam was right—the path was slippery and treacherous. Many times I had to squat and half shuffle my way to the next flat surface. Here and there were banks of gorse and heather. Hopefully, climbing back up would be easier.

At last, we reached the ledge that I'd seen from the top. It was more of a shelf and it hugged the length of Seal Cove. Looking back up, I noticed a wide orange-brown band. It was a good twenty feet above us. With a jolt I realized what it was— the high-tide mark.

The thought of such a huge body of water rolling in made me nervous, and the "bit of a drop" to the sand had to be a vertical drop of at least ten feet. Pooled at the base was a mound of debris—bottles, ropes and plastic bags. It was filthy.

This whole thing was turning into a major mountaineering expedition. Margot and Louise would have hated it.

"Are you okay, Evie?" Randy asked.

"Yes, as long as we can get back up," I said.

Sam, and then Randy, turned around to face the side of the cliff and scaled down. They made it look so easy—even Randy did in his bulky waterproof cape and Wellies. I turned to follow, but then lost my nerve.

"Just jump, Evie," Sam called out. "We'll catch you."

The two of them stood below with arms outstretched.

"Come on!" Randy teased. "Trust us!"

So I closed my eyes and jumped . . . and promptly landed right on top of Sam, who staggered backwards and crashed onto the sand.

Randy roared with laughter. "Definitely not a Cirque du Soleil performance there," he teased. "Are you both okay?"

"I'm fine." I grinned. "I think I squashed Sam, though."

Sam pretended to be hurt. He doubled over and joked that he'd been rugby tackled by a herd of elephants.

We set off at a brisk walk in good spirits. I was determined to enjoy the day. Other than some shallow puddles, the water had completely disappeared, leaving long sections of the seabed in furrowed patterns dotted with shells and tiny pebbles.

The wreck was even farther out than I'd expected. She lay stranded like a beached whale, and as we drew closer, I was stunned at just how tall those wooden ribs were.

Strewn about the seabed were thick layers of crispy brown seaweed that had fused with vast amounts of plastic, rope, wires, bottle tops, light bulbs and aerosol canisters that had drifted in on the Gulf Stream. Some of the markings I saw showed that they had traveled huge distances from Canada, Japan, Russia and Spain. A pile of massive ropes that could have been used to tether ships at anchor lay like giant pythons across the sand. The amount of pollution and waste was distressing.

I fell behind to photograph a group of oystercatchers scavenging for food, and other wading birds—sanderlings with their winter plumage of pale gray and white, and turnstones with their beautiful tortoiseshell feathers. I picked up a handful of gorgeous shells for Margot—cowries, wentletraps, dogwhelks, periwinkles and baby sea potatoes. With each photograph I took, I made sure to use the wreck as a backdrop. These photographs were going to be great, and I'd be developing them myself!

I panned over a clump of tangled fishing nets that were wedged into an enclave. They were trapped beneath a rocky outcrop.

But then my eye saw something familiar, caught in the netting, that made my heart stop.

Sticking out from under the pale blue and orange nets was an arm, heavily tattooed with skulls and mermaids. For a moment I struggled to accept what I knew to be true. It was Ollie, and he was dead.

I began to scream.

Chapter Twelve

Somehow the three of us managed to get Ollie's body up to the first ledge.

Sam covered Ollie with his waterproof coat, but the coat kept sliding off. More than once I came eye to eye with Ollie's bloated and bloodied face. It looked as if he had suffered a mass of cuts and bruises from being tossed by the waves and smashed against the rocks.

Sam, visibly shaken, insisted that he stay with Ollie while Randy and I went to raise the alarm.

It was easier getting back up than down, but still exhausting. Randy was climbing like a man possessed, and in the end I shouted for him to go on ahead without me.

My mind was reeling. Nothing made any sense. How on earth did Ollie end up in Seal Cove?

I reached the hotel's rear entrance just as Dennis exploded through the door, his face pale and anxious. "I've called the coast guard and the police," he said. "I'm going out to wait with

Sam. I'm afraid I can't find Kim anywhere. No one is manning the phones."

"It doesn't matter," I said. "Did you take—?"

"The walkie-talkie, yes," said Dennis. "I left the other one on the counter in reception."

I found Randy there, too. He'd taken off his waterproofs and changed from his Wellies into his loafers. He was standing in a daze.

"I'll get your room key," I said. I realized I was trembling. All I could think about was Ollie's mangled features indelibly printed in my mind. I would never forget them.

Randy and I took the back staircase in silence. As we reached the landing, I was surprised to see Jerry emerge from the George Goodchild suite, closely followed by Kim—both having clearly ignored the DO NOT DISTURB sign that Randy had hung on his door.

A tide of red raced up Kim's neck and flooded her face. "The bathroom was low on loo paper." She gestured to Jerry. "And he had to check—"

"Something," said Jerry. "After the storm."

"Evie?" Kim regarded me with alarm. "What's the matter? You look terrible."

"Ollie's dead," I said bluntly. "He drowned."

Kim gave a cry of distress. "But . . . how? Where?"

"Seal Cove. I can't . . ." I noticed that Randy seemed fit to drop. "Excuse us. Randy needs to get into his room."

"Does Margot know?" Kim must have guessed by my expression that the answer was no. "I'll go and tell her."

I ushered Randy into his suite and mumbled apologies for

Jerry and Kim being in his room, but he didn't appear to be listening.

"Just give me a second." He leaned against the doorjamb and, for a moment, I thought he was going to pass out. And then it occurred to me. Seeing Ollie like that must have brought back awful, harrowing memories. He had to be thinking of Carrie.

I gently touched his shoulder. "I think you should sit down."

"Funny," he said quietly as I led him over to the leather sofa. "You think you're okay and then suddenly, it all comes flooding back." He forced a smile. "I just need a bit of time to process."

I couldn't help but notice how tidy Randy kept his room. In fact, the only indication that he was staying there at all was the closed laptop on the burr walnut desk over by the window. There were no books on his nightstand and no personal items on the dresser. Even his cabin-size holdall bag had been tucked out of sight.

"I'll ask Kim to bring you up some tea," I said.

"Tea in a crisis," Randy said wryly. "How very British. But no, thank you. I need to be alone. Can you tell Louise I will come and find her later?"

"Of course," I said.

"Evie . . ." he said slowly. "I'm sorry you had to find your friend. I . . . I know how you must be feeling."

"Thank you," I said. "I know you do. And I'm sorry for the memories this must be bringing up for you."

As I left Randy's room, I met Margot on the landing. "Oh God! Evie! Kim just told me!"

She looked immaculate with her leather trousers, a black

turtleneck sweater and a green scarf that made her Linda Blair emerald-green contacts even more startling.

For a moment I couldn't speak, and then it all came tumbling out. "Oh Margot. It was so awful. So terrible. I . . ."

"Come on, I'll make you a Margot special." She took my hand and I let her lead me upstairs to our flat.

I was filled with guilt. I'd been irritated by Becky's constant phone calls and messages, even though I'd felt something was off, too—enough for me to venture out in the middle of the night. But I'd never thought in a million years that Ollie would end up dead.

Neither of us spoke as Margot put the kettle on and waited for it to boil. She added a nip of brandy to our coffees, a heaped teaspoon of brown sugar and a dollop of Cornish clotted cream.

"Becky was right," I said finally, and told Margot everything.

Margot's jaw dropped. "Jeez. She's pregnant? That is so sad." She sat back in the chair and frowned. "There's something weird about all this."

"I know." I told Margot about my trip to the causeway in the middle of the night, the sodden junk mail I'd seen in the rockery and finding the cherry tomatoes at the top of the steps.

"Okay, yes, he could have found the original boat key," said Margot, "and the junk mail could have been lying in the rockery for a couple of weeks. The blue dot that Becky saw on Ollie's phone? A very possible mistake, but"—her eyes widened—"finding . . . tomatoes? I mean—that's just bizarre!"

"I told Becky he came back," I said. "And it's obvious. He went back out again while we were at dinner and got into trouble. He must have been caught in the storm after all."

We sipped our coffees. The brandy warmed my stomach and I began to feel a tiny bit better.

"Do you think we should still go ahead with the open house?" Margot asked.

"I don't know," I said. "We've spent so much money on preparations, and with all the advertising . . ."

"I don't know, either," said Margot.

"Poor Ollie," I whispered.

We fell into a miserable silence.

"You mentioned those packages from Pegasus Couriers," said Margot suddenly. "So if he did come back, where are they?"

I nodded. "I know. That's the thing. Ollie would have left mine in the office, but it wasn't there." I thought for a moment. "Maybe, since Sam wasn't waiting to help him at the causeway, Ollie couldn't carry everything and left the heavier stuff in the boat, intending to go back after dropping off—"

"The stuff he bought at the co-op for Kim?" Margot suggested. "But you only found the tomatoes. What happened to the other items on the list?"

We fell quiet again until she jumped up and motioned for me to as well. "Come with me."

"Where are we going?"

"Back to the annex. Fresh pair of eyes and all that," she said, adding with a grin, "and trust me, these green ones give me X-ray vision."

We trooped downstairs, where Kim was in reception talking on the phone. I heard her say, "I'm afraid you need to speak to the police. It's not for me to comment." She replaced the receiver. Spotting us, she added, "How can the newspapers have got wind of this already?"

"Bad news travels fast." Margot shot me a look and went on. "A strange question for you, Kim—you didn't have any lone tomatoes in your kitchen, did you?"

Kim frowned. "Excuse me? Believe me, if I had, I would have used them. Why?"

"No reason," I said. "We're just going to the annex. We'll be back in a minute."

"Wait!" Kim beckoned for us to come closer. Leaning over the counter, she scanned reception and whispered, "Where's Randy?"

"I assume he's still in his room," I said. "Why?"

Kim took a deep breath. She looked at Margot and then back at me. "I know he's a friend of yours, but—"

"But what?" Margot said sharply.

"There's something really off about that Australian."

"Why would you say that?" I was intrigued. Margot and I had both thought the same.

"Nothing," Kim said quickly. "Forget it. I shouldn't have brought it up."

"If you've got something to say, then you should say it now," Margot demanded.

Kim turned pink. "All I'm saying is that for someone who is traveling halfway around the world, he packs very light."

"Meaning?" I prompted.

"I just think it's odd," Kim went on. "I mean, Randy works all hours and yet he's just got his laptop and two changes of clothing. He rented that outfit he wore last night from Giggles, you know."

"Giggles?" I said.

"It's a fancy dress-hire place on St. Mary's," said Kim.

"Wait a minute," Margot said slowly. "How do you know all this?"

"Because I saw the tag in his tuxedo," said Kim.

Margot gasped. "Are you telling me that you looked through one of our guest's *things*?"

Kim's flush deepened, but then she straightened her shoulders with defiance. "Yes, and I'll tell you why."

"You'd better have a good reason," said Margot.

"Randy came down to the dining room for breakfast this morning and we got to talking. I told him I had a substantial nest egg and wouldn't mind some advice on investing it. What he said made me suspicious. And I know you're making that movie, and then there's Sam wanting to buy into a syndicate—"

"What do you mean, 'made you suspicious'?" I prompted.

"Randy mentioned it at dinner, remember?" Kim declared. "He said he could guarantee his investors between twelve and twenty-one percent interest per annum, which is unheard of. He said that if I gave him fifty thousand pounds, he could guarantee fifteen percent, but that if I gave him a minimum of a hundred, I would get a lot more ROI. I asked for details of exactly what I'd be investing my money in and Randy reeled off stocks that I'd never heard of and that aren't registered with the S.E.C. I checked. I asked for the names of his clients, but he said he was bound by client confidentiality."

"Of course he would be," said Margot. "Although, Louise is a client. Perhaps you should talk to her."

Kim's face fell. "I don't feel comfortable doing that."

"But you felt comfortable going through Randy's things," said Margot quietly.

Kim looked mortified. "I'm sorry," she said. "I don't want to make any trouble."

"Look, we're all upset," I said. "I know you mean well, but let's just focus on finding out what happened to Ollie. Okay?"

The phone rang again and Kim turned away to answer it.

I took Margot's arm and steered her out of reception, down the short hallway and out through the rear entrance.

As we skirted the building and approached the potting shed, Margot continued to grumble about Kim going through Randy's things. "And didn't you say that Randy had even put the DO NOT DISTURB sign on the door handle?"

But I was no longer listening. The potting shed door was ajar and while the padlock had been snapped shut, the hasp had not been fitted over the staple.

My hand tightened on Margot's arm.

"Ouch. What?" she said.

"The padlock," I said. "I distinctly remember closing this door and securing it with the padlock through the hasp, only, I never snap the padlock shut."

"You're positive?"

"Yes, I'm positive," I said. "Ollie and I moved the plants in there to protect them from the storm."

"So someone has been in there," said Margot. "Gosh, Evie.

You're freaking me out with that rabbit-in-the-headlights expression."

I ignored her and opened the potting shed door wider to look inside.

The light was behind me, so it took a few moments for my eyes to adjust to the gloominess. The wheelbarrow stood in the middle, filled with the plastic containers of plants.

I brought out my iPhone and touched the flashlight feature to pan the inside. All seemed the same as yesterday, with the gardening tools hanging from their hooks on the walls and the wooden slatted shelves laden with a muddle of terracotta pots.

"Well?" Margot peered over my shoulder. "What are you looking for, exactly?"

"I don't know," I admitted, but I continued to shine the beam into all the corners. I could feel Margot's breath behind my right ear.

"There!" she exclaimed. "On the floor. Under the bottom shelf."

I turned the beam as directed to see an upturned plastic tray of six tiny geraniums.

"Oh, poor plants," I exclaimed, and maneuvered my way past the wheelbarrow to retrieve them. I put them on the shelf and turned to inspect the others, uttering another cry of dismay. The plastic trays were haphazardly placed on top of each other. "My little plants are all crushed!" I turned to Margot. "Someone has definitely been in here!"

"What? Sitting in the wheelbarrow?" she teased.

"Can't you be serious for a moment?" I said. "I just don't see how one of the plants fell out."

Margot shrugged. "I don't have an answer for you. I'm sorry. Are we going to go to the annex or not?"

I nodded, closed the potting shed door and followed her.

"God, it's depressing here," said Margot as we took the steps down to the annex. She flipped on the light switch in the corridor. "Which room number?"

"Five." I suddenly didn't want to go in there and Margot must have sensed it. She took my hand. "Come on, sis," she said, and gingerly pushed open Ollie's door.

Ollie's room was just as I had remembered from last night. There was no sign of my package in the room, in the bathroom or in Ollie's wardrobe.

"God, it stinks of cigarettes in here," Margot muttered. "Can you smell . . . weed?"

"Yes," I said.

"I don't want to speak ill of the dead—"

"Then don't," I said quickly.

Margot started going through Ollie's chest of drawers.

"My package is hardly going to fit in a drawer!" I said. "It's a big box!"

"I'm not looking for that," said Margot. "You mentioned that Becky thought she'd seen Ollie's mobile in here. Maybe she was right and he stuck it in a drawer for some reason—"

"Or the battery went flat or he turned it off," I said, and sprang to join her in her search. Then I stopped dead.

"What?" Margot said.

"The spare boat key," I said. "It was on top of the chest of drawers. It was right there!" I pointed to the change and balled-up scraps of paper. "It's gone."

Margot looked blank. "It would be. He used it."

I shook my head. "But that makes no sense. It would mean that Ollie must have been somewhere on the island when I came looking for him last night after dinner. I thought he had used the original boat key that he'd mentioned he'd left in the glove box on the *Sandpiper*, but I was wrong. He must have come back to his room to pick up the spare."

"Maybe he was avoiding you?" Margot suggested.

I agreed that was possible. "Sam said he didn't see him, either."

"We were all at dinner," Margot pointed out. "Maybe Ollie didn't want to see anyone? Especially if he was going back out again."

"And we know he wasn't going to see Becky," I said. "So where was he going?"

"Maybe he was seeing someone else," Margot suggested.

I dismissed her suggestion immediately. "He was besotted with Becky."

"It does happen, you know," Margot persisted. "And he'd definitely want to keep that secret."

I thought of Sam's comment about Becky being high-maintenance.

But then I shook my head. "No. Because that means that Ollie must have gone out when the storm hit. He would never have done that."

I dropped to my knees to check if the boat key hadn't fallen onto the floor under the bed, but there was nothing there. As I scrambled to my feet, I heard a cry of surprise.

Margot thrust a scrap of paper at me. "Look!"

She had smoothed out one of the balls of paper. It was an itemized receipt from the co-op. I looked at the items charged: romaine lettuce, cucumber, avocado, Belgian endive, radishes and cherry tomatoes.

"Tomato-gate," said Margot. "This is confirmation that he definitely came back from St. Mary's."

"So where did the rest of the groceries go?"

"The kitchen?" Margot suggested.

Moments later, we were in there. The red-flecked Formica table and chairs, along with the battered two-seater sofa, made the room depressing. A corner unit housed the microwave and the kettle and a small fire extinguisher. On the wall was a television. Kim had told me that she and Jerry watched football in here together. Although clean, it was dreary.

"God, it's grim in here," Margot said, echoing my thoughts. "We'll definitely need to redecorate." She opened the fridge door. "Nothing apart from a six-pack of beer, a bottle of white wine and a bit of cheese—"

"And an untouched mug of coffee," I said, pointing to Ollie's pirate mug next to the kettle on the countertop. "Maybe he got a phone call and—"

"Left in a hurry," Margot said with a nod. "Damn. Let's face it. We've hit a dead end."

"Let's at least check the other rooms in the annex," I said.

"Whatever for?" Margot said.

"For the packages? The groceries? Ollie's phone?" I was becoming frustrated with the mystery of it all. "I don't know!"

"You're the boss," said Margot, and joined in the search, but we drew a blank in the other four rooms before stopping outside Sam's door.

"Well?" Margot demanded. "Aren't you going inside?"

"I don't think we should," I said. "And besides, I'm sure he'd have locked it."

Margot pushed me aside and tried the handle. The door wasn't locked at all. She pushed it open a crack.

"No, don't." I felt jittery and looked over my shoulder. "What if he comes back?"

"Won't he still be at Seal Cove with Dennis, waiting for the police?" Margot said.

"Maybe," I said, "but I really don't want to risk it."

"Go up to the top of the annex steps," Margot commanded. "And if you see him coming, just whistle."

I darted up the steps, scanning the path for any sign of Sam. It couldn't have been more than two minutes later when Margot joined me.

"Nothing," Margot said to my unspoken question. "No romaine lettuce on the chest of drawers. He's untidy, though. Clothing and towels all over the floor."

My iPhone pinged. It was an incoming text.

"It's Kim," I said to Margot. "The police are here."

Chapter Thirteen

"Hello, girls," said Patty. "Long time no see."

Detective Sergeant Patricia Williamson of the Devon and Cornwall Constabulary stood in reception, bearing a warm smile. Gesturing to a blue plastic crate full of groceries on the countertop marked with the Tesco logo, she said, "I timed my arrival well." She made a vague nod behind her. "And my trusty musketeers are bringing the rest of the delivery up from the causeway."

"That's very kind," I said. "Thank you."

Two police constables—freckle-faced Owen King and dark-haired Kip Granger—walked in carrying another crate each, followed by Sam and Dennis with two more.

"Is that the lot?" Patty asked.

"Yes. Five crates." Kim brandished her clipboard and pen, ready to check off the items. "Do you boys mind taking them into the kitchen, please?"

The "boys" picked up the crates and bore them away.

"Ah, Miss Winters," said Patty. "How are you settling into island life?"

Kim seemed surprised. "I'm sorry, but have we met?"

"Owen was working the harbor shift when you landed on our sacred soil." Patty offered her hand. "D.S. Patricia Williamson." She pointed to Kim's clipboard. "You seem very organized, but I would have expected nothing less given your extensive background in event planning." Patty flashed another smile. "Bit of a change from London for you, but it looks like the sisters have great plans for Tregarrick Rock. I don't think you'll get bored."

"I like to keep busy," said Kim.

"And congratulations on the excellent job you have done publicizing the open house," Patty went on.

"Oh. Thank you." Kim smiled. "Yes, I know what I'm doing."

"Flyers up all over the place, local sponsorships. Oh, and I love the arts and crafts exhibition. Very nice. Keeps the locals happy."

"That was Evie's idea," Margot put in.

"And Instagram!" Patty enthused. "I follow you religiously—or should I say, I follow Mister Tig. Judging by his latest posts, it looks like you already have guests here."

"They're friends of Margot's," I said. "We're not officially open yet."

Patty nodded. "Nothing like a trial run. And where are these guests of yours now?"

"Louise is resting," Margot said as Kim excused herself. "And I assume that Randy is still in his room—Evie?"

"Yes, he was pretty shaken up," I said. "He was with us at . . . when . . . at Seal Cove."

"I'm looking forward to meeting"—Patty glanced down at her notebook and tapped it with her pen—"Mr. Campbell and Mrs. Vanderhoven. Kip was on harbor duty this week, so I've missed out on the welcome party *again*." She gestured to the back office. "New computers, a new printer—is that a scanner as well?"

Patty didn't wait for an answer to her question. "Mind if I look around?"

Or that one, either.

She inspected the gaping holes in the walls and seemed to find the dangling wall lights fascinating, before walking over to the picture window and staring out at the terrace.

Of course, we expected Patty to make an appearance at some point in the afternoon, but as lunchtime came and went, Margot and I both hoped she had returned to St. Mary's with the coastguard or the medical launch or—to quote Margot—"on her broomstick." I still wasn't prepared for how nervous she made me feel.

It wasn't that we disliked Patty. In fact, had she been anyone other than a policewoman, she could have been a fun friend to have. I guessed Patty was around the same age as Sam. Margot thought she should have been a model, with her sweetheart face, pixie haircut and large Bambi brown eyes, but behind the perfect smile was a woman of steel. Patty had a knack for appearing friendly until you realized you had been beguiled and fallen into her trap.

There was reportedly "no crime on Scilly"—one of Patty's favorite turns of phrase—a fact she put down to vetting all incoming visitors as they arrived by sea, or by air on St. Mary's. Given that there were only four police officers who serviced all 142 islands—97 percent of which were uninhabited—I was convinced that Patty had to pay for a network of local spies. She certainly seemed to know everyone's secrets—including ours.

Patty took off her outdoor navy peacoat and folded it over her arm to reveal a tailored pin-striped suit and crisp white shirt. It looked like she would be staying.

"Can I hang that up for you?" I offered.

"No. I know where the cloak cupboard is," she said, heading out of the room. She knew her way around the hotel, too.

Patty reappeared. "We already ate lunch, but we're hoping to scrounge a cup of tea."

"Kim mentioned she'd made a Victoria sponge earlier," I said.

"And ask a few questions, naturally," said Patty. "It's all very tragic. Very tragic indeed."

"How is Becky taking the news?" I said.

"In a terrible state," said Patty. "And not helped by her father, unfortunately."

"What about her mother?" Margot asked.

"Irene?" said Patty. "Gone with the wind years ago. Fell in love with a sailor. Seems to run in the genes. And of course, Becky's an only child." Patty flipped to another page in her notebook. "I have my theories about poor Oliver Martin, which I'd really love to run past you."

"We do, too," I said.

Patty seemed surprised. "Well. Excellent. In that case, shall we adjourn to the Residents' Lounge? My feet are killing me in these new boots."

"We're finishing up the refurbishment," I said as we passed through the archway. Jerry was sweeping the floor. "Sorry for the mess."

Still, it was vastly improved since yesterday, when there had been chunks of drywall, mounds of dust and bits of wood, paper and general detritus scattered all over the floor. Old wiring had spilled out of the gaping holes, sockets dangled from the skirting board and wall lights swung from their fixtures. But Jerry had got a lot done today, and now all that was left to do was the plastering and painting.

"Gerald Arthur Quick," Patty exclaimed. "Well, goodness. I am surprised."

Jerry stopped sweeping and scowled. He didn't look exactly happy to see Patty.

"Ma'am?" Kip appeared in the doorway. "Refreshments are on their way. Oh, Jerry. Glad to see you're still at it."

Jerry scowled again but didn't comment.

"Ma'am?" Kip said. "I believe you owe me a fiver."

Patty stuck her hand in her jacket pocket and withdrew a five-pound note. "Just goes to show I'm not always right."

Margot caught my eye and raised a quizzical brow.

Patty noticed our silent exchange. "Let me fill you girls in. I bet Kip that Jerry wouldn't last five minutes working for the family firm. I was so certain that he would miss the thrills and spills of the stock market."

Jerry rolled his eyes. "That was five years ago, Patty."

"I realize that," Patty went on. "But go on, admit it. Don't you miss watching that little ticker tape crawl across the bottom of your computer screen?"

"No," said Jerry firmly. "I don't miss it at all." And with that, he picked up his broom and stomped out of the lounge.

This was odd. I distinctly remembered Jerry claiming at last night's dinner that he knew nothing about the stock market. In fact, Kim had had to explain it to him.

Jerry had never mentioned his previous job to us—but then, we hadn't asked him. We'd taken Vicar Bill's recommendation at face value and when Jerry said his cousin would be helping him, we'd accepted that, too. With every passing day I was beginning to see just how inexperienced—and trusting—Margot and I were at this hotel business.

Patty took in the room. "Hmm. Now, where should we sit?"

The existing furniture—leatherette armchairs, occasional tables, a dark red Chesterfield sofa, a long teak coffee table and two wingback chairs—had been moved into the center of the room and covered with dust sheets.

Margot walked to the Chesterfield and whipped off the cover. "We can sit here."

Patty perched on the arm of the Chesterfield as Margot and I sat side by side.

"I'll jump straight in," said Patty. "Would you know if Ollie had any money problems?"

"Money problems?" I was surprised. "Why are you asking?"

Patty's brown eyes stared steadily into mine. "Why do you think?"

My feeling that Ollie's death wasn't straightforward deepened. "Well. Yes. He asked for an advance on his paycheck," I said. "He told me that Becky's twenty-first birthday was coming up and he wanted to buy her a bracelet that she'd admired."

"Our Becky does have expensive tastes," said Patty. "Has he ever asked for money before?"

"He asked me on two other occasions," Margot put in.

"So he was strapped for cash." Patty flipped back a page.

I found I had to spring to Ollie's defense. "He doesn't get paid a lot—"

"But he gets free food and accommodation," Margot pointed out.

"And with Becky being pregnant," Patty mused. "I assume you knew about that?"

"We only just found out," I said.

"Do you think Ollie was a trustworthy person?" Patty said.

"Yes, of course," I said, and looked to Margot, but Margot just shrugged.

"I sense some hesitation there." Patty cocked her head. "Do you think otherwise?"

"Margot doesn't trust anyone," I said.

"And Evie trusts everyone," Margot shot back, but she cracked a smile. She hesitated. "I did catch Ollie coming out of the Agatha Christie suite about three weeks ago."

"He was probably looking for Jerry," I said, and went on to explain to Patty that the modem was kept in the turret room, which was accessed through the Agatha Christie suite. "With the hotel being rewired," I went on, "whenever the power is turned off, Jerry has to reset the modem."

"No," Margot said firmly. "This was long after supper. Ollie's room is in the annex and he had no reason to be in there."

"You didn't mention this to me, Margot," I said.

Margot shrugged again. "I asked him what he was doing and he said that Kim had told him to fetch the silver ice bucket because she was cleaning all the silver."

"And did he fetch the ice bucket?" Patty said.

"Ollie said he couldn't find it in there," said Margot. "I just thought he seemed a bit furtive."

My heart sank. I wish Margot had voiced her suspicions to me before.

"Vicar Bill called me last night to say that a piece of jewelry was missing from his sister's jewelry box," Patty went on. "According to the valuation, it was—I quote—'a step-cut sapphire and rose-cut diamond set cross in platinum and gold.' Try saying that when you've had a few beers."

Margot looked confused. I quickly filled her in about the parquetry jewelry box that Kim and I had found in the Agatha Christie suite.

"But I am curious," Patty went on. "Lily Travis has been dead for months. Why did you wait so long to return her stuff to her brother?"

"Vicar Bill was supposed to remove all Lily's possessions from the Agatha Christie suite weeks ago," I said. "But I suppose he hadn't got around to it, and what with everything going on here—"

"Ah yes. The fire," said Patty. "I hope you were insured."

"We didn't claim on our insurance," Margot said. "Dennis was able to put the fire out before it took hold."

"Are you implying that Ollie stole this necklace?" I was dismayed.

"Evie always sees the best in people," said Margot. "I'm just a little bit more cynical."

"And seeing the best in people is a lovely quality to have," Patty said, "but these are theories. Just theories."

"Perhaps Ollie owed someone some money?" Margot said suddenly. "Maybe an unpaid debt."

"Before we jump to conclusions," said Patty, "I want to know what's happening to our tea and cake."

Margot needed no excuse to leave. "I'll go and find out."

Patty turned to a new page in her notebook, pen poised. "Why don't we get a timeline of Ollie's movements yesterday?"

I nodded.

"It seems that you knew Ollie better than your sister," said Patty. "Did you notice that he was worried about anything yesterday?"

"Just talking to Becky's father," I said. "At the time, I didn't know that she was pregnant."

"Becky told me that her father had offered Ollie money to leave her alone," Patty said. "When was the last time you saw Ollie?"

"After lunch yesterday afternoon. About two-thirty," I said. "He was running an errand for me to St. Mary's. He took the *Sandpiper*—that's the hotel cabin cruiser. I assume there is no sign of our boat?"

"The coastguard is out looking," said Patty. "So Ollie wasn't going to St. Mary's just to see Becky?"

"No," I said. "He was checking our PO Box, picking up a

package for me at Pegasus Couriers and stopping by the co-op for some things for supper. I spoke to Kevin at Pegasus Couriers and Ollie picked up two packages around three-fifteen."

"What was Ollie picking up for you?"

"Camera equipment for my darkroom," I said. "And a water pistol for Sam's godson."

"Ah yes, Sam." Patty wrote something down. "I heard he was back."

"Sam was waiting for Ollie down at the floating pontoon to help him carry the stuff," I said. "But Ollie never showed."

Patty carried on scribbling.

"Our PO Box is next door to Pegasus," I went on. "So Ollie would have made a quick stop there before going on to see Becky."

Patty duly wrote that down, too. "Now, Becky tells me that he got to Godolphin Court at about three-thirty and that he left in a hurry around four-fifteen."

"He would have gone to the co-op after that," I said.

"The harbormaster confirmed that Ollie left around five forty-five. Hmm." She frowned.

"I can't believe he was in the co-op for over an hour," I said. "The receipt is still in Ollie's room. But the items he bought there are missing."

I went on to tell Patty about the cold coffee in the annex kitchen, the random tomatoes at the top of the steps leading down to the causeway and the sodden junk mail. "The spare boat key was in his room last night when I checked after dinner, but it was gone this morning."

When I mentioned that Becky had tracked Ollie's phone to

the annex, Patty nodded. "She told me that she had managed to hack into his phone. Naughty girl. And yes, we found it."

I gasped. "You found Ollie's mobile? Where?"

"In his pocket. It's water damaged and the battery is flat, but we'll see what we can get from it," said Patty. "So—without wanting to assume too much, we agree that Ollie came back to the island, returned to his room and went out again much later."

"But that doesn't explain the missing packages or what happened to the items he bought at the co-op," I pointed out. "Ollie knew that Kim needed the stuff for supper. Wouldn't he have taken them straight to the kitchen?"

"Your guess is as good as mine," said Patty.

"Margot and I think that Ollie got a phone call," I said. "It's the only logical explanation I can think of. It would have been high tide when he tried to dock at the floating pontoon and maybe, because of the storm, he changed his mind and thought the deep water quay—that's William's Quay—on the northeast side of the island would be safer—"

"That's what I think, too," said Sam. Neither of us had heard his footsteps. "The Atlantic and the Celtic Sea meet at the northern end. Everyone knows that the sound is plagued with riptides and dodgy currents." His face twisted in anguish. "Poor bastard."

"Yes, poor bastard indeed," said Patty quietly. "Come and join us. I'd like to talk to you."

Chapter Fourteen

"I didn't have a chance to give you my condolences earlier," said Patty. "I'm so sorry to hear about your mum. I always had a soft spot for Marie."

"Thanks," Sam said. "She'd been in a nursing home for a long time. It was expected."

"How many years had you been away from Scilly now?" Patty went on. "Twenty, isn't it?"

"Seventeen," said Sam.

"Must be weird coming back," Patty said. "I take it you won't be staying for long, though. The call of the ocean and all that."

"I'll be getting back after this job is done," said Sam.

"And your godson's birthday," I reminded him. "Let's hope his present turns up."

A flicker of surprise crossed Sam's face, but he gave a wry smile. "Yeah. Me too. Cost me a fortune in shipping."

"What was it?" said Patty.

"A Bazooka water-blast pistol," said Sam. "Top-of-the-line."

Patty nodded. "My son would die for one of those!" She smiled again. "Evie tells me that you were staying in the annex next to Ollie's room."

"Yeah," said Sam. "And no, I didn't hear him come back last night."

"That's right." Patty consulted her notebook. "Time-wise it would have been when you were at dinner. And you waited down at the causeway until it got dark, I believe?"

Sam nodded. "I assumed he wasn't coming. Don't get me wrong, he was a good kid, but reliability wasn't his forte."

"I disagree," I said. "Yes, Ollie was forgetful, but I found him reliable."

"No offense, Evie," said Sam. "But you only saw one side of Ollie."

Patty looked steadily at Sam. "Were you guys friends?"

"We talked, sure," said Sam. "I've only known him since I came here, but I liked him. We talked about wrecks and stuff." Sam lowered his eyes and shifted his feet.

"Go on, out with it," said Patty.

"Look"—he took a deep breath—"Becky wasn't the only one. Ollie was a bit of a dark horse when it came to women."

I felt a stab of disappointment. Margot had wondered about the same thing. "Why would you say that?"

"I told you," said Sam. "The walls in the annex are thin, and I overheard a couple of conversations that were, shall we say, X-rated."

"But they could have been with Becky," I protested.

"Unless she changed her name to Stephanie," said Sam.

Patty scribbled in her pad. "Thank you. Helpful. Hopefully, we'll find evidence of that in Ollie's phone."

"Maybe he stopped to pay her a visit on his way home," said Sam. "She lives on Bryher."

"The island on the other side of Seal Cove," I said.

"Exactly," said Sam. "And he would have needed to cross the sound on the way back, which is where I'm convinced he got into trouble."

I frowned. "I don't buy it," I said. "Ollie knew that Kim needed the groceries for supper."

Sam shrugged. "I'm just saying."

"I'll definitely want to talk to you again about this Stephanie." Patty looked over to the archway, where I saw Randy and Louise hovering in the entrance. "Ah, your trial-run guests, I believe." Patty beckoned them in. "Welcome to our little party."

I wondered how long they had been standing there and how much they had heard. Randy seemed to have recovered from this morning's ordeal, but Louise definitely looked a little ragged around the edges. She was nursing her voluminous Birkin bag.

Kim and Dennis—along with Margot—were right behind them, carrying two trays—one with a freshly baked Victoria sponge and a stack of plates and paper napkins, and the other a pot of tea, a *cafetière* of coffee, a jug of milk and a bowl of sugars and artificial sweeteners.

"Why don't we make the room more comfortable?" said Patty. "Gents . . . actually, in the spirit of equality, ladies, gents, all and sundry, everyone just pitch in and rearrange the furniture so we can sit down and get cozy. Dennis, can I have a quick word with you in reception? Kip, Owen—you come, too."

The four of them left the Residents' Lounge while the rest of us set out the chairs and moved the Chesterfield so we were all able to sit in a circle.

Everyone found a seat.

Patty and Dennis returned without Kip and Owen. Patty headed to the fireplace, which was covered in a large sheet of durable plastic that had been taped over the 1970s built-in teak wall unit and fake fire. She stood with her back to it. "My favorite spot. The detective always has to stand in front of the fireplace."

There was an atmosphere of uncertainty. Patty just had that way about her. Kim passed around tea, coffee and slices of cake. Patty ate one slice in about three seconds flat.

"Sorry," she mumbled through a mouthful of crumbs. "That was delicious. So this is everyone? Oh wait! Where is the cat?"

As if on cue, Mister Tig sauntered in with his tail held high and made a beeline for Louise, who seemed thrilled to welcome him onto her lap.

"Jerry's not here," I said.

"I'll go and find him," Sam said.

"No, you stay here, Sam," said Patty. "Dennis can do the honors—oh, that reminds me. Has anyone thought to inform Cador about Ollie's demise? I hear he's out in the Bahamas."

"He is on his way back," said Dennis. "He knows about the wreck in the sound but not about Ollie. He should be here tomorrow evening."

"Any idea of his E.T.A., Dennis?" Patty asked.

"I'm not sure if he will fly back through Nassau directly to Heathrow or change in Miami," said Dennis. "Either way, he's got three connecting flights and a train or if—"

"Just the E.T.A., luv," said Patty.

"Between sixteen and seventeen hundred hours tomorrow."

"Did Cador know Ollie?" Patty asked.

"I would think so," said Dennis. "Doesn't everyone know everyone on Scilly?"

Patty turned back to Sam. "So will this be the first time you will see Cador since . . . the incident?"

Sam laughed. "Patty, that all happened a long time ago."

"It wasn't funny at the time," Patty said. "Bit of backstory here for you Hollywood film people . . . I'll see if I can give you the logline."

Kim frowned. "The what?"

"It's a two-sentence summary of a movie," said Margot. "They're quite hard to do, actually."

Patty thought for a moment. "Two inseparable childhood friends hunt for long-lost treasure, but when they fall in love with the same woman, their friendship takes on a dangerous—"

"Very clever," said Sam. "And as I said, it happened years ago."

Patty ignored him. "Again, for you Hollywood people, let me fill in the gaps. Sam stole Cador's girlfriend, Natalie—who just happens to be Jerry's youngest sister—after the World Pilot Gig Championship in 1991."

"How incestuous!" Louise said.

"Isn't it just?" Patty said. "The thing is, there isn't much choice around here when you grow up on an island. We all went to the same school. All hung out at the same bar. If you're a Scillonian, chances are you're related somewhere along the line, biologically or otherwise."

This definitely went a long way to explain how Patty seemed to know so much about everyone.

"I grew up on the Isle of Wight," said Louise. "Same kind of thing, but I managed to escape."

Patty turned to Sam. "How is Natalie, by the way?"

"Happily married to someone else and living in Ireland, but thanks for asking," said Sam.

"Now, why didn't I know that? I must be slipping." Patty took a gulp of tea. "Rumor has it that Cador is hunting for rich investors for his marine salvage business. What do you think, Mr. Campbell? Aren't you a hedge fund manager or high-flying financier? Would you invest in a bit of treasure hunting?"

If Randy was surprised that Patty seemed to know what he did, he didn't show it.

"If you're asking if I would personally invest, it would depend on the risk," he said easily. "Confirmation of a wreck, authenticating artifacts—yeah, tempting. But I have plenty of clients who do invest in equity fundraising who would want to get involved."

"I bet you know all the big shots like—let me think"—Patty frowned and then brightened—"Mark Zuckerberg?"

Randy looked startled. "Er. No."

"How about Richard Branson? I bet he'd be up for a bit of treasure hunting," said Patty. "Safer than his quest to orbit the earth."

For the first time, I saw a flicker of annoyance cross Randy's perfect features before he said, "Yes, I am a hedge fund manager. No, I do not personally know Mark Zuckerberg or Richard

Branson, and as for being a highflyer, I would say that's true only if you count the number of air miles I rack up every year."

"By the way, how is the training coming along for the Ötillö Swimrun?" said Patty, switching gears. "I see you've registered. Brave man."

"Um. Good. Yes, thank you." Randy now seemed very uncomfortable. "How did you know that?"

Patty pointed to Mister Tig, still sitting on Louise's lap. "The cat told me. Just kidding. As I mentioned to the 'sheilas' earlier—love the Australia slang for girls—I follow Mister Tig on Instagram and he seems to have taken a great interest in you. Great job, by the way, Kim."

"Thanks," said Kim.

We fell into an uncomfortable silence.

Patty surveyed the room. "While we wait for Dennis to find Jerry, let's do a warm-up exercise before I really get stuck in with the questions." Patty poured herself a second cup of tea. "Let's go around the room and say three things about ourselves, one of which will be a lie."

Louise gave a nervous laugh. "Seriously?"

"I'll start. My name is Patty. I've been married three times, I play the trumpet, and when I visited Berlin, I brought back a tiny piece of the Berlin Wall."

"The trumpet is the lie," said Sam.

"You don't remember?" Patty scoffed. "I played the trumpet in the school band and you played the triangle."

"And the tambourine, let's not forget that," said Sam. "Cador played the maracas."

"In that case, the Berlin Wall is the lie," Margot declared.

"Nope," said Patty. "I was a foreign exchange student in Germany. By the way, I thoroughly recommend visiting the Stasi Museum if you ever get to Berlin. How else do you think I learned my interview techniques?" Seeing everyone's worried expressions, she added with a grin, "That wasn't the lie. The lie . . . I've not been married three times. I've been married four, so I can see how easy it is to get in a muddle with one's love life. Like poor Ollie, or"—she pointed to Louise—"you."

"Me?" A look of panic came over Louise's face. "I've not been married four times."

"That's my lie, not yours," said Patty. "Now it's your turn in the hot seat."

"Really, this is ridiculous," said Louise. "But okay." She closed her eyes. "I have a black belt in judo. I've kissed Brad Pitt, and I've been to the Playboy Mansion."

"Impressive." Patty nodded. "I'll go for Brad."

"Wrong," Louise said smugly. "I do not have a black belt in judo."

"Randy?" Patty said. "You're up next."

Randy leaned forward. "Sure. My name is Randy Campbell. Let me see—I always take a bath at five forty-five local time wherever I happen to be, I have won three Ironman triathlons and I can bench-press two hundred pounds."

"Gosh, I'm glad I know what time to bring you in a towel," Louise teased.

"Now, isn't that romantic?" said Patty. "And what a gorgeous couple you make. Let's hold the two-facts-and-one-lie game for a minute, because I just love to hear where-did-you-meet stories. It gives me hope. So . . . where *did* you both meet?"

"Los Angeles," said Louise.

"Next thing we know we'll have Oprah flying in by helicopter," Patty joked.

"She will when they put in a helipad," said Louise. "Oprah and I are Facebook friends."

"We're hoping to attract high-profile clientele," Margot chimed in.

Dennis returned with Jerry and both sat down.

Patty gave a nod of acknowledgment before adding, "So—Louise, you're a—?"

"Publicist," said Louise. "At least I was. I'm pivoting at the moment from publicist to producer. You could say I'm a hyphenate."

"A hyphenate." Patty nodded. "Right."

"You get writer-directors and writer-producers. I'm a publicist-producer." Louise shot Margot a smile. "Margot and I are producing a movie together."

I stole a look at my sister, who had a polite smile plastered on her face.

"It's based on a book called *Lighthouse of Sorrow*," said Louise. "It won a lot of prizes in the seventies. Did you read it?"

"Doesn't ring a bell, but back then I was still learning to read." Patty smirked.

"Margot's a brilliant producer," said Louise. "And this movie definitely is Academy Award material. It's a cross between *Love Story*, *Cast Away* and *Das Boot*—that's German for 'the boat.' We're just finalizing the funding."

"And presumably you are bankrolling this Academy Award–winning production, Mr. Campbell?" Patty asked.

Randy gave a gracious nod. "Part of it. Yes."

"Ah, so you're mixing business with pleasure. Lots of moonlit walks." Patty gave a knowing smile. "Incredible supermoon last night, too. I assume you all went outside to gaze at it. I know that I did."

"I didn't see it," said Louise. "I was already in bed."

"I wonder if Ollie saw it as he fought for his life," said Patty quietly.

Suddenly, the atmosphere had changed. There was a deadly silence.

My eyes met Randy's and in them, I saw the horror of finding Ollie's mutilated body that I knew must be reflected in my own. Margot reached for my hand and squeezed it.

"Yes, not only tragic since he was going to be a father," Patty went on, "but . . . there is no other way to say this . . . we have reason to believe that Oliver Martin was murdered."

Chapter Fifteen

I heard a cry of disbelief and realized it was coming from me. Margot grabbed my hand tightly. She was deathly pale.

"What?" Patty said with mock surprise. "Do you think I just came here for the cake?"

I couldn't speak. My deepest fears had been realized.

Sam finally spoke. "But . . . I thought it was an—"

"An accident?" Patty said. "Really?"

"Why do you think it wasn't an accident?" Margot demanded.

"Seriously?" Patty cocked her head in that annoying way she had. "You really think I'm going to lay all my cards on the table right now? But since you forced my hand, Ollie was strangled."

She paused for this horrific fact to sink in. Once again Ollie's mangled face flashed through my mind. Margot squeezed my hand even tighter.

"He'd been in the water for quite a while in rough sea conditions, so it's hardly surprising that his body was so badly damaged. I'm waiting on confirmation from Derek, but I'm confident it was a homicide." She picked up a knife and cut herself another slice of cake.

"Who is Derek?" Margot asked.

"Derek is the pathologist," said Sam. "Who just happens to be one of Patty's ex-husbands."

"Excuse me," said Randy. "No offense, and I know you are just doing your job, but I can't see what any of this has to do with Louise and myself. We've just arrived and we're leaving on Monday."

"No one is going anywhere," said Patty.

Margot opened her mouth to protest, but Patty held up a hand. "Besides, I am sure you can help with our enquiries."

"I don't see how," said Louise. "Randy and I have never even met this poor guy."

"Is that so?" said Patty, looking directly at Randy, who stared steadily back.

"But this could take days," Margot grumbled. "You can't keep our guests here hostage."

"I've got to get back to L.A.," Louise exclaimed.

"I'm confident that we'll have confirmation first thing tomorrow—maybe even tonight if Derek pulls his finger out." She smiled. "Happily, it was an amicable divorce." Patty turned to Louise. "Are you friends with all of your ex-husbands?"

Louise turned pale. "I'm not sure what you are trying to say."

The question was so out of left field that I was taken aback.

Margot sprang to her friend's defense. "Louise has just lost her husband, actually."

Unfortunately, Louise picked that moment to grab hold of

Randy's hand and clutch it tightly. Mister Tig opened one eye but didn't stir.

"Nothing like a shoulder to cry on," said Patty dryly. "Remind me, when did your husband pass away?"

"With all due respect," said Randy. "It's none of your business." He was smiling, but his blue eyes were cold.

"Maybe. Maybe not." Patty smirked. "And this is where the A, B, C rules of policing come in handy. Let me enlighten you.

"*A* is for *assume* nothing. I'm not going to assume you have never met Ollie before, Randy." She ticked off her fingers. "*B* is for *believe* nothing. So I will not necessarily believe anything any of you tell me here . . . especially when it comes to these two sisters, who have led me up the garden path on more than one occasion. Lastly, *C* is for *challenge* everything. So expect to be . . . well . . . *challenged.*" Patty popped a bite of cake into her mouth and turned to a fresh page in her notebook. We waited for her to finish chewing.

I saw Louise shoot Randy a quizzical look, but he just stared ahead. Patty's A.B.C.'s made me wonder. Randy had been outside after the storm last night. He'd also been running the coast path above Seal Cove. He claimed to be in training, but since we'd known him all of five minutes, he could easily be lying.

"Right. This is the bit I always like." Patty flashed a smile. "Where were you all yesterday between the hours of five forty-five, when the harbormaster saw Ollie's boat leave St. Mary's, and say, seven this morning?"

"Seven? This morning?" I was surprised. Margot and I exchanged puzzled looks.

"But we know that Ollie came back to Tregarrick after five forty-five," I declared. "It must have been much later than that."

"Five forty-five and seven this morning is what we're working with," said Patty firmly, and turned to Louise. "Let's start with the lovebirds."

Louise looked to Randy for reassurance. He gave her a nod.

"I arrived in the afternoon around three, took a bath and almost got electrocuted." Louise grinned but then grew serious again when no one else reacted. "Randy arrived about five. We spent what was left of the afternoon together before going to dinner in the dining room."

"Do those times align with your recollection, Dennis?" Patty said, adding, "For those who don't know, Dennis is an excellent timekeeper."

"Not quite," said Dennis. "Mrs. Vanderhoven checked in at fifteen oh five and Mr. Campbell at sixteen fifty-seven."

"We had a little party," said Margot. "I think we all got to bed around midnight."

"Ah. The witching hour," Patty said.

"It was later than that," I said to Margot. "Remember? You came into my bedroom for a chat."

"It was later for me, too," said Randy. "After dinner, I went out running."

"In the dark?" Patty blinked.

Louise gasped. "You . . . were out the whole time? Oh. My. God!" A relieved smile spread across her face. "Wait . . . so you're saying that you didn't hear anyone knocking on your door?"

Randy frowned. "What? No. Why?"

"No reason," said Louise quickly.

"Excuse me. Can we continue?" Patty said. "Was this run before or after the storm?"

"It was after the storm," said Randy.

"Goodness. You do take your marathon training seriously," Patty exclaimed. "And what a beautiful night it was with the supermoon to light your way."

"I saw nothing at all," said Randy. "I ran the entire coast path, taking the steps down to the causeway. I didn't see any boat moored there other than a dinghy that had been tucked high up on a ledge. Ask Evie. She saw me."

I acknowledged that I had seen him. "It was about one in the morning. I found it hard to sleep and was admiring the moon," I said. "At first I thought it could have been Ollie out there. That he'd come back and was going out to look at the wreck."

Patty regarded me with interest. "Now, that's a very good point, Evie. I hadn't considered that. What would the tide be doing around that time?"

"It would be going out," Dennis cut in. "But still far too high to walk on the seabed."

"Far too high," Sam agreed. "Ollie told me he'd never been down to Seal Cove. He would never have found the path on his own. Besides, he was excited about going there with me."

Patty nodded and continued scribbling. "So, Evie, when did you realize that it was Randy out there running and not Ollie?"

"Randy told me it was him this morning," I said.

"I see," said Patty slowly. "So you didn't actually identify Randy as the runner out on the coast path."

I hesitated. "Um. No. I suppose not."

"So you *assumed* that Randy was telling the truth?" Patty said.

"Well, I saw a light," I said. "And why would he lie?"

"Why indeed," Patty mused. "Perhaps Louise can confirm that Randy was out running?"

"Louise was asleep," Margot said.

"I took some sleeping pills and just passed out," Louise said. "The next thing I knew, it was the morning."

"So where was Mr. Campbell when you woke up?" Patty demanded.

"I would have assumed he was in his own room," Louise ventured.

"Excuse me?" Patty's eyes narrowed. "You aren't sleeping in the same room as Mr. Campbell?"

"Of course they aren't," Margot exclaimed. "As I said earlier, Louise's just been widowed."

"Right. Okay." Patty kept her focus on Randy. "So basically, you have no alibi for the wee hours and there is no alibi for Louise, either."

Margot raised her hand. "I was with Louise," she said. "She was very ill. She must have eaten something that disagreed with her."

"She can't have," Kim protested. "Otherwise we'd all be ill. It was only lasagna!"

"That's right. Only lasagna." Patty looked at me and I caught the barely perceptible warning nod to not mention the missing salad. "And where were you, Kim?"

"Kim was with me," said Jerry. "Dennis and I were helping her wash up. And Sam had already gone to bed."

"Golly, this sounds like musical chairs." Patty turned to Sam. "So no alibi for you."

"Or me," I echoed.

Patty turned to a fresh page in her notebook. "Other than Sam, did anyone else know about Ollie's secret friend Stephanie?"

"Secret friend?" Margot shot me a look as if to say *I told you so*. "You mean another girlfriend?"

"Dennis?" I said. "Did you know anything about this? You spent more time with Ollie than anyone. You must have talked a lot when you were building the floating pontoon."

"Ah yes." Patty nodded. "Male bonding."

"A little," Dennis admitted. "He mentioned an ex-girlfriend, but he referred to her as his ex. I didn't know her name."

"An ex," I said firmly, and looked directly at Sam. "Perhaps you heard wrong."

Sam shrugged. "I know what I heard."

Suddenly, Patty stepped forward to put her empty cake plate back on the coffee table. "Delicious, thank you, Kim. Excuse me for a quick moment. No one leave this room. I'll be right back."

We fell into an uneasy silence. Louise and Randy got out their phones and started scrolling.

Margot leaned over and said in a low voice, "Cui bono? Who benefits? Nobody in this room, that's for sure."

I looked around the Residents' Lounge at Dennis, Sam, Jerry, Kim, Louise—still stroking the cat—and Randy. I couldn't think of a single motive, either.

"And you have to admit we don't know much about Ollie's past," Margot went on.

"I hope you're right."

"What about Becky's father?" Margot said. "You told me that he couldn't stand Ollie. That he offered money to Ollie to keep away from his daughter and Ollie refused. What if . . . what if he went one step further and ordered a hit!"

Despite the seriousness of the suggestion, I actually laughed. "Don't be daft. This isn't Hollywood."

"Margot's got a point." Louise put her phone away, clearly eavesdropping. She didn't bother to keep her voice low. "I mean, you only have to read the newspapers. They're full of stuff like that. I think you can get a gun for hire for about two grand. Pretty cheap if you ask me."

I shook my head in disbelief and once again, the image of Ollie's face filled my vision. "But he wasn't shot, was he?" I whispered. "He was strangled, and that's very personal."

"Can we stop talking about this?" said Sam suddenly. "This isn't Hollywood, you know. He was a good kid."

"I don't like the way she asks the questions," Louise declared. "It's like we're all guilty. Don't you agree, sweetie?"

Randy didn't answer. He was too busy texting.

"Her technique is a bit unorthodox," I said. "But you have to know that the police complete background checks on everyone who comes to work on the islands. It's just what they do."

Margot nodded. "And trust me, Patty knows how to dig up the dirt. Maybe that's why Ollie was murdered. Maybe he discovered a secret. I mean, everyone has secrets, don't they?"

"I don't," Louise said firmly.

"Nor do I," Kim declared.

"I just wish she'd get on with it." Louise yawned. "Are we waiting here to find out what happened to Ollie or just being grilled for her amusement?"

"You're here for my amusement," said Patty as she returned bearing a small Gucci duffle bag.

"Oh. My. God!" Louise squealed and jumped to her feet. "You found my luggage!"

"Vicar Bill made a special trip to the ticket office to pick it up just for you," said Patty. "Poor man brought it all the way up the steps in person."

Louise was ecstatic. "Thank you, thank you!" She went to take it, but Patty swung the bag out of her reach.

"As Lee Corso would say, 'Not so fast, my friend.'" Patty flashed a smile. "You've got some very incriminating merchandise in here. I think you'd better sit back down."

Chapter Sixteen

Louise turned ashen. "It's private. Just personal possessions, truly."

Margot leaned into her friend and whispered, "What does she mean by 'incriminating'?"

"I need to use that coffee table," said Patty. "Can you take the trays back to the kitchen, Miss Winters?"

Kim did as she was told and started to clear away the plates, cups and saucers.

"And you can tell Vicar Bill that he's welcome to join us once he's recovered from his arduous climb," said Patty. "But we don't want the parrot."

"It's a macaw," Margot muttered.

Kim left with the tray of dishes.

Everyone seemed riveted by the presence of the Gucci duffle bag that Patty set on the coffee table like a magician's top hat.

"This is an invasion of privacy," Louise mumbled. "I can't see what my bag can possibly have to do with this guy's death."

"Ollie," I said. "His name was Ollie."

"Sorry," Louise said quickly. "But you know what I mean."

Moments later, Kim returned with Vicar Bill, a grizzled seafaring man dressed in his usual threadbare jacket and dog collar. Mister Tig jumped off Louise's lap and made a beeline for him. Vicar Bill took one of the wingback chairs and invited the cat to settle on his lap.

"Ready, everyone?" Patty said. "Louise Vanderhoven, I'm going to ask you a question and I want you to be very careful about how you answer."

"Okay," said Louise in a small voice. She hugged her Birkin bag closer.

Randy put down his phone, suddenly interested in the proceedings.

Patty took a deep breath. "Are you a drug dealer?"

Sam gasped. "Bloody hell!"

"Of course not!" Louise exclaimed. "How dare you accuse me of such a thing!"

Patty unzipped the duffle bag and began removing an assortment of plastic bottles and packets of pills. "You've got quite the pharmacy in here, haven't you?"

Louise looked mortified. "It's my medication," she said. "I suffer from insomnia and anxiety!"

I could see disdain written all over Randy's face. He edged a few inches away from her on the Chesterfield.

"Let me see." Patty picked up a bottle and inspected the label. "Ambien for insomnia. Check. Paxil for anxiety—although, personally, I prefer St. John's Wort. It's not so addictive. You should try it." She picked up several foils. "Diet pills, more diet pills—really? You can't weigh more than a hundred pounds . . . Oh . . . Adderall for focusing—I could do with some of that. Vicodin for—?"

"My ankle," Louise snapped. "I rolled it."

"Is that a genuine Birkin bag?" Patty asked, suddenly changing tack.

"Yes," said Louise.

"Give it to me," Patty demanded. "Now!"

"No." Louise hugged the bag childishly to her chest. Randy wrestled it away and thrust it at Patty.

Everyone looked tense as Patty sifted through Louise's bag. She withdrew an aerosol can of Mace.

"I never go anywhere without it," Louise said sulkily. "And no, I didn't take it into the cabin on the plane. I packed it in the hold."

"And . . . ooh . . . what do we have here?" Patty held out a small white sachet.

"Don't touch that!" Louise shrieked, but Patty had already upended it onto the coffee table. Four tiny blue pills tumbled out.

Everyone leaned in for a closer look. You could have heard the proverbial pin drop.

"Well, I never," Patty said, wide-eyed. "MDMA—that's ecstasy, for the layperson."

There was another collective gasp. Margot put her head in her hands in despair, and Randy edged even farther away from Louise on the sofa.

"I rarely use them," Louise pleaded. "I bought them online—"

"We have zero tolerance for any form of drugs being brought into Scilly," Patty said coldly. "I'm afraid I'm going to have to arrest you and report you to the immigration authorities in the United States, where I suspect you will lose your green card. I know you don't have U.S. citizenship, because I checked."

Louise seemed close to tears, and when she reached for Randy's hand, he pointedly ignored her. Her extraordinary behavior outside Randy's room was beginning to make sense. The White Lady cocktails weren't the only cocktails Louise must have taken last night.

"Which brings me to you, Mr. Campbell," Patty said. "I think I just might have to have a little look in your suitcase in your room."

"Randy hasn't done anything." Louise was getting hysterical. "This is all a terrible misunderstanding."

Patty dismissed her protests with a cutting sweep of her hand. "Mr. Campbell, you live in Hong Kong—"

"This has absolutely nothing to do with me," Randy snapped. "I hardly know this woman and I do not support drug use of any kind. If you want to look into my suitcase, then go ahead. I have nothing to hide."

"I swear, Randy. I swear," Louise went on desperately. "If anyone is supplying drugs"—she pointed at Margot—"it's *her*!"

Margot's jaw dropped. "I did no such thing!"

"*You* gave me those pills last night!"

"For your *insomnia*," Margot exclaimed. "And by the way, thanks for throwing me under the bus, Louise."

I sprang to my sister's defense. "Margot was just trying to help."

"Personally, I think insomnia is psychosomatic," said Patty. "I have no secrets, so I sleep like a baby every night, which is more than I can say for the people in this room—apart from Dennis, because he is perfect."

Dennis smiled.

Randy stood up to leave. "I'm not sure what is going on here, but this most certainly does not involve me."

"Sit back down, sir," said Patty. "I don't care about your personal lives, but if you are both involved in a drug-smuggling operation, then I can assure you, I take no prisoners. Ollie has always been on our radar."

"What has Louise's personal pharmacy got to do with Ollie?" I demanded.

"I will tell you," said Patty. "Another reason that Ollie was not popular with Becky's father was because he was partial to a bit of wacky baccy."

Of course, I knew this to be true, but it hardly seemed evidence of serious criminal activity.

Patty turned to Randy. "Perhaps Mr. Campbell here was supplying him with something a little stronger? Perhaps that's why you met our Becky at Godolphin Court hotel?"

"Hotel?" Louise exclaimed. "What hotel?"

"You can come on in now, luv," Patty called out.

I recognized Becky straightaway. Dressed in leggings and a baggy sweater, she wore her strawberry-blond hair pulled back into a ponytail. Her face was pale and haggard.

"This is Ollie's girlfriend, Becky Godolphin," said Patty.

There was a stunned silence.

I had half expected Becky to come, but the tide was in. I couldn't understand how she had got here—or Vicar Bill, for that matter.

"You look confused, Evie," said Patty. "Don't be. We police have extraordinary powers and out of the kindness of our hearts, we laid on a boat. Why don't you take a seat, Becky, luv."

I moved over and gestured for Becky to sit next to me. To my astonishment, she gave Randy a small smile of recognition.

"I'm so sorry for your loss, Becky," said Randy.

"Wait, do you *know* each other?" Louise demanded.

I was just about to ask the same question.

"Becky's father owns Godolphin Court hotel," said Patty. "And Becky works in reception from time to time."

"The what? Where? But . . . I don't understand," Louise said.

"Didn't Randy tell you that he was staying on St. Mary's before he came here?" Patty asked.

"Blimey!" Margot muttered.

If Randy was surprised that Patty had known that, too, he didn't show it. I'd assumed he'd traveled straight from Hong Kong. Not only that, Margot and I had even suggested that he and Louise should stay at Godolphin Court when he first arrived. He had made no indication of having stayed there already. But then I remembered the way that Patty had responded when Louise had insisted they'd never met Ollie before. Patty had known all along.

It was obvious. Randy was hiding something.

"Come on, Randy," said Patty. "Let's get your Tripadvisor review."

"Five stars," said Randy easily. "Very pleasant."

"Wait a minute," Louise said. "*When* did you stay at the whatever it's called?"

"Godolphin Court. Let me see." Patty consulted her notebook, although I suspected she didn't need to. "Wednesday."

"But today's Saturday," Louise exclaimed. "I don't understand why you didn't say."

"And Randy spent one entire day in the library," Patty went on.

"The *library*?" Louise echoed. "Whatever for?"

"I just like libraries," Randy said simply. "Nothing wrong with that."

"But how did *you* know he was in the library?" Louise said to Patty. She was clearly upset, and any attempt to play down her true feelings for Randy had flown out the window.

"I know because my friend Charlotte works there," said Patty. "Apparently you asked her for some reference books on shipwrecks? Pretty girl with long dark hair. Red-framed glasses."

"Ah yes, that's right. She was very helpful." Randy seemed completely unfazed by this revelation. "I'm flattered that she would make a point of mentioning I was in there."

"You're unforgettable," said Patty.

"I flew in earlier than I'd planned, that's all," Randy said smoothly. "There's no mystery. I just took a couple of days to unwind, take in a bit of history, see the sights—"

"Pop into Giggles for your fancy dress costume," Patty said. "Sorry. I mean period attire."

"That's right," said Randy.

"Why didn't you tell me you were coming in earlier?" Louise seemed to be struggling with this piece of news. "I could have met you there."

"Why indeed?" Patty cocked her head. "So you were expecting Randy to come directly to Tregarrick Rock, Louise?"

"We live in different countries," said Randy. "I'm in Hong Kong at the moment—"

Patty snapped her fingers. "But your accent is . . . Australian? South African maybe?"

"That's right," he said. "I've moved around a fair bit."

"And Louise lives in Los Angeles. Hmm," Patty mused. "Personally, I've never found that long-distance relationships work." She turned back to Becky. "And you remember seeing Randy talking to Ollie yesterday afternoon."

It was another classic Patty move. Change the subject. Keep people off guard and then go in for the kill.

Becky nodded. "Yes. It was in the hotel lobby. I was speaking to a guest on the phone. Ollie was waiting for me to finish my call and Mr. Campbell wanted to get his room key."

"So you and Ollie had a little chat," Patty declared.

"You talked to Ollie." I was amazed.

"I didn't know who he was at the time. Why would I?" said Randy. "We hardly exchanged more than two words."

"And what two words did you exchange?" Patty said mildly.

Randy rolled his eyes in exasperation. "I can't remember. There were a couple of boxes on the floor and I made a comment that they looked awkward to carry. To be honest, I thought he was a delivery guy." Randy shrugged. "Oh, and yeah. We talked about the other islands and which ones to visit and I mentioned I was going to Tregarrick Rock."

"You mentioned Tregarrick Rock," Patty repeated. "Didn't Ollie offer to bring you over in the *Sandpiper*?"

"I didn't have a chance to ask him," said Randy.

"Yes," Becky said. "Because Dad turned up."

Patty tapped her top teeth with her pen and regarded Randy with suspicion. "Interesting. Did Ollie meet you in your room?"

"Oh, for Pete's sake!" Randy roared with laughter. "I am a hundred percent against any form of drugs. Surely you're not suggesting I did some kind of drug drop."

"Stranger things have happened," said Patty. "It's not the first time that Ollie has got caught up in something he shouldn't have."

"What do you mean?" whispered Becky.

But Patty didn't answer. She was watching Randy, and so was Louise.

"Caught up in what?" I said.

Patty didn't answer that question, either.

The idea of Louise and Randy being involved in drug trafficking was too ridiculous for words, but I knew how Patty operated. I'd seen her do it before. She'd throw out outlandish claims until, eventually, those poor souls being questioned became so confused that they finally cracked. But this afternoon, Randy held his own and just sat there, a polite expression on his face.

Finally, Patty backed down. "Sorry, folks," she said. "We're just trying to get an idea of Ollie's movements and talk to everyone who he has come into contact with. Hopefully, forensics will be able to get his call log off his mobile, but for now, it's old-fashioned police work, don't you agree, Evie?"

I nodded.

"So let's go through this again." Patty flipped back through her notebook. "Before Ollie leaves for St. Mary's, he asks Evie for another pay advance."

"He asked me, too," Kim chimed in. "I gave him twenty pounds."

"What about you, Dennis?" Patty said.

"Fifty the first time, but when he asked me a second time, I said no."

"Are you saying that Ollie has asked to borrow money from you before?" Patty said.

Dennis nodded. "That's right, and I gave it to him. I didn't expect to get it back, either."

Patty turned to Sam and Jerry. "What about you two?"

Jerry gave a snort of disgust. "Yeah. I gave him ten quid."

"Sam?"

"Yeah, ten," said Sam.

Patty didn't answer, just jotted on her pad again, but I looked at Sam as he sat in one of the wingback chairs. His knee was juddering a mile a minute and his fingers were working on the old fabric armrest. He seemed anxious.

"So as Evie and I have already concluded, Ollie was strapped for cash," said Patty. "He goes to the mainland to supposedly pick up the packages from Pegasus Couriers for Evie and Sam."

"He wasn't expecting to pick up Sam's package," I pointed out.

"I tracked it and it was supposed to arrive on Monday," Sam put in.

Patty inclined her head in acknowledgment.

"Why should that matter?" Margot said.

"Because the devil is in the details," Patty declared. "Ollie bumps into Randy at Godolphin Court, where Ollie has gone to see Becky," Patty went on. "There is a disagreement between your dad and Ollie. Right, Becky?"

Becky nodded. A lone tear trickled down her cheek.

"No need for us to go over that again, luv," said Patty gently. "Just tell us what happened after."

Becky swallowed hard and fought to compose herself. "Ollie picked up the packages and left. He was upset. He promised to call me later."

Patty turned back to Randy. "And where were you during this exchange?"

"I don't know anything about that," said Randy. "As I told you, I spoke two words to the bloke, got my key and went up to my room to pack."

As I watched Randy closely, I was struck by how odd it was that he had stayed at Godolphin Court and not told Louise about it. I could see why Patty would be suspicious of his story. I was, too. Maybe there was a connection to Ollie after all.

"And then we have the necklace that was stolen from Lily's jewelry box," said Patty, suddenly.

"Wait a minute," said Kim. "Are you talking about the parquetry box that Evie and I found in the Agatha Christie suite yesterday?"

"I am indeed." Patty nodded. "I suppose we could always ask the cat, eh, Vicar?"

I'd forgotten all about Vicar Bill sitting partially hidden in the wingback chair by the picture windows.

Louise's expression was comical. "The cat?"

"Mister Tig sees everything," said Patty. "And our Vicar here speaks kitty."

"The Agatha Christie suite has not been touched since Lily died," Margot put in.

Louise was horrified. "Someone *died* in my bed?"

"Oh yes. Suffocated," Kim said with relish. "With a cushion. Isn't that right, Jerry?"

"Can we not go off-piste?" Patty said. "The vicar checked the contents of his sister's jewelry box and a valuable sapphire and rose-cut diamond cross is missing."

Becky gasped. "Is . . . is this—?" She put her hand down her sweater and pulled out a necklace. "Is this what you are looking for?"

There were cries of shock.

"That belonged to my sister," Vicar Bill exclaimed.

"Oh. My. God!" Louise whispered.

"Told you so," Margot declared. "I knew Ollie was up to something that night."

I was upset, but that was nothing compared to Becky, who was finding it hard to stem the tears that coursed down her cheeks. I put my arm around her shoulders and gave her a hug.

"Do you want to tell us how you got it, Becky?" Patty said gently.

"Ollie gave it to me for Valentine's Day," she whispered.

"Guv," came a voice from the archway. It was Owen with Kip. "We've done the annex. Shall we start upstairs?"

"No need now. We've found the necklace," said Patty. "Well, that saves us the trouble of searching the rest of the hotel."

"Excuse me?" said Margot. "You can't just do that without a warrant."

"True, but now we don't need one." Patty smirked. "I had a hunch that Ollie might have had something to do with it and I was right."

"Guv," said Owen again. "Can we have a word?"

Patty joined her two police officers in the archway. They moved out of earshot.

I hugged Becky again. She was a mess. Margot caught my eye and mouthed, *What the hell?*

Patty returned with Kip. "Becky," she began. "Do you think you are up to going to the annex with Kip? We might have missed something in Ollie's room."

"The receipt for the co-op is on Ollie's chest of drawers," I reminded her.

Patty nodded.

Becky didn't need any encouragement. She couldn't wait to get away. She got up and left.

"Owen has found something rather interesting in your room, Sam," said Patty.

Sam sat up. "But it was locked."

"My apologies," said Patty. "He mistook your room in the annex for Ollie's. Dennis had given us the master keys."

Owen came into the center of the room holding two objects—one long and thin, and the other rectangular and bulky. Both were wrapped in our hotel towels. Sam stiffened.

"Nice use of our towels," Margot muttered.

"Are you going to tell us what these are, Sam?" asked Patty.

A flicker of annoyance crossed Sam's features, but then he just shrugged. "I suppose now is as good a time as any." With a pointed glance at Randy, he said, "You wanted proof of treasure for your hotshot investor. Now you will have it."

Chapter Seventeen

Having set Louise's Birkin bag—together with the contents—on the floor at her feet, Patty turned her attention to Sam's mysterious objects on the coffee table.

"Are they fragile?" she asked him.

Sam seemed very pleased with himself. "Nope."

Patty picked up the smaller one first and unwrapped it. She produced a heavily tarnished two-pronged fork and a metal spoon.

"What are they?" Margot asked.

"It's a set of seventeenth-century cutlery. I found them in the sand." Sam pointed to the larger object. "Along with that."

"That" turned out to be a sword. It, too, was tarnished and thick with crud.

I wasn't the only person in the room who was intrigued. We all were. Randy was perched on the edge of the Chesterfield, his body tense with anticipation.

"I told you that the best time to go beachcombing was after

a storm." Sam smirked and glanced pointedly at Randy again. "I found them when I stayed behind with Ollie's body. It seemed hardly the right time to boast about finding a couple of artifacts."

I just didn't know what to say. Ollie had been lying dead, and Sam decided to go beachcombing?

"And then what?" said Patty. "You just popped them into your shopping bag?"

"I always take a rucksack with me," said Sam. "Not just for ropes and emergency supplies but in case I find something. Which I did."

"Anyone else see this rucksack?" Patty asked.

I raised my hand. Of course I had. We'd had to use the ropes to haul Ollie's body off the beach, but at the time I wasn't paying attention to anything other than Ollie. And yet something struck me as odd. The rucksack hadn't looked big enough to hold a sword as well as Sam's equipment, but then I remembered that Sam had said that he found the artifacts after Randy and I had left for help. Sam could have carried the sword but surely, if he had, wouldn't Dennis have noticed?

"Are they from the *Virago*?" I asked.

Sam grinned. "Once I've cleaned them up, I will have a better idea of which vessel they came from."

"I'd like to take a closer look at that sword." Randy gestured to Patty to pass it over.

Before Patty had a chance to do so, Sam had jumped up and handed Randy the cutlery instead. "And it's not a sword by the way. It's a cutlass, and it won't tell you much until I've treated it. I think you'll find the cutlery far more interesting."

Louise didn't seem that impressed. "If that's cutlery, wouldn't there be a case or something?"

"Unlike metal, glass and ceramics," said Sam, "leather or silk would never have survived the salt water. Under all that crud, you'll find they're made of silver filigree and parcel-gilt."

Randy turned them over. "It's hard to see anything."

"If they're not from the *Virago*," I said, "which vessel would they be from?"

Sam took a deep breath, clearly enjoying having a captive audience. "I'm ninety-nine percent certain that they came from the *Isadora*."

"The *Isadora*!" I exclaimed. "But—"

"Don't be so bloody stupid," hissed Jerry. "You don't know what the hell you're talking about."

"Oh, don't I?" Sam was beaming from ear to ear.

I was taken aback by Jerry's reaction and, catching Margot's eye, saw that she was, too. "But didn't she sink beyond Windward Point?" I said. "That's the other side of the island. Cador said—"

"I've always maintained that Cador was wrong," said Sam. "The *Isadora* sailed up the sound, not around the point."

Dennis cleared his throat. "No offense, Sam, but the whole of Scilly knows that the *Isadora* figurehead was found north of Windward Point."

"And you know as well as I do that a wreck with known coordinates can drift ten miles or even farther—and that's just with ships that we know went down during World War II," said Sam. "And this was in the days of expert navigators and meticulously kept records." He paused for a moment. "What about the ships that went down five hundred years ago?"

"It's true," Louise chimed in. "I found out all about drifts when I was doing research for our movie, Margot."

"Just humor me," said Sam. "Take a good look at the handle on the fork. Hell! Everyone take a look!"

Randy did, then he passed it on around the room. We all examined the utensil, but to be honest, it was hard to see anything. The pieces were just too heavily tarnished.

"Can't you see those marks?" said Sam. "They're actually initials. This belonged to someone who was traveling on the *Isadora* and I can prove it."

"Ship records don't go back as far as the seventeenth century," said Dennis. "Passenger manifests didn't begin until the 1800s—sorry. I always get asked these kinds of questions from our hotel guests."

"That's right," said Sam eagerly. "But I bet you haven't heard of a publication called *Emigrants in Bondage* by Coldham? I went to a lot of trouble to get it. The book is almost impossible to find."

"Oh, for goodness' sake. Go on, spit it out before we all die of suspense," Patty cried.

"I quote, 'Between 1614 and 1775, more than fifty thousand English men, women and children were sentenced to be deported to the American colonies for crimes ranging from the theft of a handkerchief, to bigamy or highway robbery—'"

"Bigamy?" Louise exclaimed. "Seriously? Why would anyone be deported for bigamy? I mean . . . what if someone wanted to get divorced but the spouse had just gone and vanished? If you ask me, that's grossly unfair."

Sam seemed confused. "What? Um. Anyway, where was I?"

Patty regarded Louise with curiosity. "It's still a crime today, as we all know. Parliament passed the Bigamy Act in 1603."

"Well, that's ridiculous," Louise exclaimed. "I mean, if you live in Tibet, you can have as many husbands as you like."

"As I was saying," continued Sam, "we've got access to the names of those who were transported to the colonies, the charges against them, the dates and places of sentencing, the ports of arrival and"—he paused dramatically *again*—"the names of their ships."

"Go on," said Randy.

"Don't you see . . . the *Isadora* was not just transporting gold and precious stones," Sam enthused. "She was carrying fifty convicted criminals, too."

"So . . . you're saying that the cutlery belonged to a convicted criminal?" I said. "Surely a convicted criminal would never have owned something so fine."

"I'm pretty sure these initials are J.T.P. and stand for Jessica Tully-Paulette," said Sam. "She was a lady of great social standing but, unfortunately, tried and convicted for bigamy."

"And what about the Mormons? They have loads of wives." Louise was clearly not going to let this go.

"It's a bit of a stretch if you ask me," grumbled Jerry.

"For God's sake," Sam said, exasperated. "It all checks out. Her name was on the *Isadora*'s emigrant embargo list. These definitely belonged to her."

"So, if I understand correctly," Randy said, "what Sam is trying to say is that the *Isadora* does not lie north of the lighthouse. If she's not there, then where is she?"

"No, I'm not saying that," said Sam. "I'm just saying that she passed through the sound. But finding these gives us a place to start looking for the debris trail. This is exactly why we need a R.E.M.U.S."

"A what?" Margot said.

"It's an acronym," said Sam. "The letters stand for Remote Environmental Monitoring Units—*R-E-M-U-S*. They're A.U.V.'s, or autonomous underwater vehicles, that look like torpedoes, but instead of carrying explosives, they carry remote-sensing tools like side-scans, multi-beams and sub-bottom profilers. These machines can get down into difficult places—under coral reefs or in underwater canyons."

"I'd like to take a look at the cutlass," Randy said suddenly.

"Oh, that," said Sam dismissively. "It's just a cutlass."

"'*Just* a cutlass'!" Patty exclaimed, and before Sam could protest, she handed Randy the cutlass.

Randy peered closely at the crud-coated metal. "I can make out some letters, but I can't quite see what they are." He handed it to me. "Can you?"

"They're not letters." I ran my fingernail over the surface. "More like lines, or maybe symbols of some kind."

"Forget about the cutlass, man," said Sam. "It's the cutlery that's the prize."

"Evie's got all kinds of magnifying stuff and chemicals in her darkroom," Margot suggested. "You could take a closer look in there. Didn't you do some kind of art restoration course, Evie?"

"Paintings, yes, but never this kind of thing," I said. "You're right, though. I know the basics."

"I'd just like a closer look," Randy insisted. "No offense, Sam, but I've got to watch out for my client."

Sam shrugged. "Sure. But I don't think it'll teach you anything other than what I am telling you now."

"Yeah. I get that." Randy nodded. "But if you expect him to cough up a load of dough for your R.E.M.U.S., he will expect a business proposal along with concrete evidence that there's something down there."

"Sure thing, but I'll be honest—no offense, Randy. If you want that, then before we go any further, I want a written agreement," said Sam. "It would be easy to push me out of this. I've seen it happen before."

"I'm a notary," said Kim. "We can make it official right now."

"Cool," Randy said. "But let me talk to my client first. I appreciate your enthusiasm, but he can be a canny bugger. And obviously, he'll want good faith money, too."

"How much good faith money?" Jerry demanded.

Sam ignored Jerry's question and looked to Randy, his expression earnest. "This is exactly the kind of thing your client would jump at." He stopped and paused dramatically. "We're going to find the *Isadora*."

"Cador's going to be stoked about this," said Dennis.

"Yep, he sure will," Sam agreed.

"Looks like your boyhood dreams are about to come true," said Patty. "And just think, if you hadn't found Ollie, you'd never have found those artifacts in the sound, either. Good old Ollie. Frankly, I find this conversation about hunting for treasure callous and insensitive. Shame on you, Sam."

There was an ugly silence. Sam's face flamed red. He looked down at his lap. Patty's tone took me aback, but she was right. I'd been feeling exactly the same way.

I looked at the small gathering in the Residents' Lounge. It was unlikely that Dennis or Kim had had anything to do with Ollie's death and so that left Louise, Randy, Jerry and Sam. Randy's presence at Godolphin Court was too much of a coincidence to dismiss lightly. And Margot and I had both felt there was something off about him.

There were two other possible suspects, Becky and her father. But Becky had an obvious alibi on St. Mary's, and it was too far-fetched that her father had organized a Hollywood-style hit on her boyfriend.

Patty's gaze rested on Sam and then Randy, and in that moment I knew that her suspicions mirrored my own.

Was it possible that one of them had murdered Ollie Martin?

Chapter Eighteen

After dropping that cliff-hanger, Patty checked her watch. "Where can I set up my interrogation chamber? In here would be ideal."

"There's a corner in the reception area," said Margot. "Jerry and Sam need to get this room finished."

"Suits me," Patty said. "Louise, why don't we start with you? I'm fascinated by your personal pharmacy."

We all stood up. Patty retrieved the Birkin bag and led the way out, with Louise following meekly as if being taken to the gallows.

Sam rewrapped the cutlery and cutlass in the hotel towels.

"Wait—Evie." Randy stepped in front of me. "When would be a good time for Sam and me to make use of the equipment in your darkroom?"

"How about tomorrow morning?" I was desperate to get back to the flat. I was incredibly upset over Ollie's death and emotionally drained from Patty's revelations.

"Yeah, and you have work to do, Sam," Jerry said, joining us. "Remember our agreement."

"Yes, Jerry," said Sam. "I remember our agreement. You won't let me forget it, either."

The moment we were inside our flat, Margot and I looked at each other in utter amazement.

"Tea first, I think." Margot headed for the kettle and switched it on. I set out the teapot and mugs. Neither of us spoke until we had cups of tea in front of us.

"So who do you think did it?" she demanded, but didn't wait for me to answer. "I have my theories. I mean . . . Ollie stole Lily's necklace. He's bad news. I wouldn't be surprised if there were a lot of people who weren't happy with him. And what about this mysterious Stephanie who Sam mentioned?"

"She's an ex," I reminded her. "What do you make of Sam?"

"He's just a treasure-hunting geek." Her face grew serious and her eyes searched mine. "Why?"

"What about the stuff he miraculously found on the beach?" I said. "I mean . . . he was treasure hunting with Ollie lying there dead? Who does that?"

"Treasure-hunting geeks," said Margot. "And in fairness, Sam did say that beachcombing is best after a storm. He must have seen the stuff lying there on the sand, so he would hardly leave it behind."

"That's true," I admitted. "What about Randy? I saw him out running, Margot. You have to admit that's odd."

Margot opened her mouth to speak, then closed it.

"I know Louise is your friend," I said. "But Randy isn't . . ."

"Again, what would be his motive?"

"This isn't a Hollywood movie," I said. "Sometimes things are messy and don't fit into logical boxes."

"Amen to that," said Margot.

We fell silent for a moment, wrapped in our thoughts.

"What do you think about Ollie and Randy meeting at that hotel?" I said. "Do you think they knew each other before?"

"Of course they didn't know each other," said Margot with scorn. "How could they? That's just Patty being Patty and trying to do her usual smoke-and-mirrors thing."

There was a knock at the door.

"It's Louise," came a voice. "Can I come in?"

"I'll leave you to your friend," I said, but Margot shook her head. "No, stay here." She called out, "It's open!"

Louise entered. She looked subdued and anxious, although I did notice that she had reapplied her lipstick.

"Do you have any wine?" Louise exclaimed. "That police-woman is brutal."

Five minutes later, the three of us were sitting at the table nursing glasses of Holy Vale pinot and had moved on to eating Kim's homemade cheese straws.

"Randy and Sam are eating dinner tonight and talking money," said Louise. "Kim's supposed to be drawing up an agreement."

"You can eat with us," said Margot. "Lamb hotpot. It's Evie's recipe and it's delicious. Now. Take a deep breath and tell us everything."

"Well, Patty wasn't joking when she said she learned her interview techniques from the Stasi." Louise took a large gulp of wine. "She kept asking me all these questions about Randy. Half of them I couldn't answer. And then she changes tack and suddenly, I find myself telling her . . ." Louise hesitated. "Actually, there's something I need to tell you."

Margot reached for the wine bottle and topped up our glasses. "I have a feeling we're going to need this," she muttered.

Louise took a deep breath. "You remember that Sam was talking about the woman who was deported to the Americas for bigamy?"

"Er. Yes," said Margot. "The one who lost the cutlery." My sister gave an unattractive snort. "Cutlery. *Cutlery*. It sounds so . . . boring. Why couldn't this woman have lost a tiara?"

But Louise didn't laugh. "Well . . . the marriage to my first husband was . . . should we say . . . not exactly legal."

"You married him for a green card," Margot declared. "I guessed as much."

"Jamie wanted to work in Europe," Louise went on. "So it was a mutually beneficial arrangement. He was gay and sweet and lovely and then . . . he just vanished off the face of the earth."

"But don't the immigration people make you jump through hoops to prove that it wasn't a marriage of convenience?" Margot said.

"Oh yes," Louise agreed. "We created fake everything—a fake wedding with photographs, fake bank accounts. I mean . . . we were already friends because we worked together, so it was very easy. But when I met my second husband—Marcus—I couldn't find Jamie anywhere. So . . . we just went ahead and got married."

"You committed bigamy," Margot said flatly.

"In a way, it's rather funny," said Louise. "Jessica Tully-Paulette, or whatever her name was, got a free passage to Virginia and I had to pay a fortune for mine. Do you know how difficult it is to get a green card?"

"Yes, I do," said Margot. "But that's not the point."

"The good news is that Patty isn't pressing charges," said Louise.

Margot's eyes widened. "For *bigamy*?"

"That . . . or my medication," Louise said.

"But the medication is for personal use?" said Margot. "She's not still thinking you're some kind of drug dealer, is she?"

"Louise also had ecstasy," I pointed out. "That's a Class A drug."

"Oh. Right," Margot said.

Louise stared miserably into her wineglass. "Patty said that if I helped her, she would let it all go on one condition—"

"Which is—?" Margot prompted.

Louise took another deep breath. "She wants me to look through Randy's things. His suitcase, to be precise."

Margot gasped. "But . . . that's illegal. Isn't it?"

"Look through Randy's things for what?" I said.

"I.D. Proof of who he works with," said Louise. "Anything business-related."

"Did you ask her why?" I said.

"Of course I did," Louise retorted. "But she said it was on a need-to-know basis. That woman is crazy."

"She can't possibly ask that of you," Margot exclaimed.

"Well, she did," said Louise. "I don't really have a choice, do I?"

It looked like Louise was trapped although I had to admit

that I was definitely curious as to what Randy was up to. "You'll have to do what she says."

"Evie's right," Margot agreed.

"Wait." Louise gawked. "You mean, you think . . . Patty thinks Randy must have something to do with Ollie's death?"

"Why else would she ask you to spy on him?" Margot declared.

"But . . . but he wouldn't hurt a fly!" Louise protested. "I know him."

"Do you?" Margot said darkly. "You've known him all of five minutes!"

I held up my hand. "Wait a minute. Louise—did Patty actually accuse you of bigamy? Did she tell you she had proof?"

Louise went very still. "Not exactly. I mean . . . she asked me questions. I suppose—"

"Oh Louise!" Margot wailed. "That's what Patty does! Oh. My. God. She makes out that she has the dirt on someone and before you know what's happened, you tell her everything that she needs to know!"

Louise was incredulous. "I'm an idiot! Wow. And I fell for it."

"So just to be clear," said Margot, "Patty is threatening to expose your illegal first marriage to Immigration and Customs Enforcement unless you look through Randy's stuff."

Louise nodded. "I hope immigration will at least let me collect my cats before I'm deported."

Louise grabbed a cheese straw and nibbled the end but set it down again. "Oh Margot. I'm so sorry. I think I've ruined everything."

"Don't be silly," said Margot before adding, "Ruined what, anyway?"

Louise seemed close to tears. "Randy is very proud of his reputation," she said. "He's got all these fancy clients who will drop him like hotcakes if they get a whiff of any kind of scandal. And of course, he wasn't happy about the ecs . . . um . . . my medication." She took another gulp of wine.

"Does this mean he might drop out of the movie?" Margot feigned disappointment, but I saw a glimmer of hope in her eye.

"Not exactly. He's all fired up about that stupid syndicate idea with Sam," said Louise. "Now he's saying that backing our movie is too risky unless we form a syndicate, too."

"I really don't want to do that, Louise," said Margot.

"You can't drop out now! I bought the option!" Louise cried. "Please don't drop out. And what about Brian? Don't you want to get your revenge?!"

"Look, let's all talk about this tomorrow," I said quickly. "It's been a horrific day. Why don't you and Margot go and relax with another bottle of wine and I'll put dinner together?"

"We can relax right here in the kitchen," said Margot, clearly not wanting to be alone with her friend.

"I'm making a salad," I said. "Dressing on or off?"

"On the side," they choruséd.

I headed for the counter, but as I got the ingredients out from the salad drawer in the fridge, I thought about the cherry tomatoes again. This was where I'd hit the inevitable dead end. I tried to go through the timeline again but found it hard to focus with Margot and Louise chattering in the background about Hollywood movies. But more than once, Margot's eyes met mine and I could see that she was just putting on a brave face.

Somehow I got through dinner and when Louise upended an empty bottle of wine, I was glad to offer to go to the wine cellar and get another.

I bumped into Kim and Jerry in reception carrying trays of used plates and glasses. Dennis brought up the rear, holding two empty wine bottles. Kim had cooked again and they'd eaten in the dining room.

"Are you sure you don't need me to stack the dishwasher?" Dennis asked Kim.

"Jerry's offered to help me," said Kim. "But thanks."

"In that case I'll turn in for the night," said Dennis.

"Where are Randy and Sam?" I asked.

"Still talking," said Dennis. "Sam's started on the brandy." I detected a hint of rare disapproval. Just two days ago Sam and Jerry had been relegated to eating their meals in the annex. Sam certainly hadn't wasted any time making himself at home. I wasn't sure if I liked it.

"Any update on Cador?"

"No," said Dennis. "So that's good news. It means he's in transit."

"I'll go and grab the brandy bottle," I said.

I went into the dining room and discovered two very excitable grown men acting like teenagers. On the table was a hand-drawn map of Tregarrick Rock, with a large asterisk marking where the *Isadora* went down north of Windward Point. A series of dots passed through the sound. Presumably, this was the debris trail that Sam had been talking about.

"Here's the lovely Evie." Sam's eyes glittered and he was clearly drunk. "Have a brandy with us."

"You mean with you," I said, gesturing to Randy's bottle of Perrier. A printed document lay next to Sam's place, along with the cutlery.

Sam saw me looking and grinned. "We've reached a stalemate."

Randy shrugged. "It's just business, man." He gestured to the document. "Sam won't sign until I've revealed the name of my client."

"And Randy won't sign until he's looked at the cutlass with your fancy equipment," said Sam. "And I told him it's soaking in the bath and needs another few hours."

"Oh?" I said. "What are you using?"

"Just my magic mixture." Sam wiggled his eyebrows. "A secret recipe."

Randy got to his feet. "I'm going to turn in. Got to check a few emails."

"Me too." Sam picked up the nearly empty brandy bottle and gave it a critical eye. "Just enough for one for the road."

As we left the dining room, Randy suggested we three meet the following morning at ten in my darkroom in order to take a closer look at Sam's artifacts.

"Great!" Sam exclaimed. "You won't be disappointed."

We bumped into Jerry in reception. He did not look happy. "Oh, Randy," Jerry said suddenly. "Can you spare ten minutes? Got a quick question for you."

"Sure thing," said Randy. "You know my room number. Just knock on my door. I'll be up for a little bit longer." And with that he bid good night and left.

"Why do you need to talk to Randy?" Sam demanded.

"None of your business," said Jerry.

Sensing an argument brewing, I headed to the basement, pausing at the top of the steps to flip on the light. On my way back up, armed with two more bottles of Holy Vale pinot, I stopped. Sam and Jerry seemed to be having a heated discussion.

They were trying to keep their voices low, but I couldn't help but hear Sam say, "You'll get your damn money back," and Jerry answer, "You're a bloody fool." Their voices grew fainter and I assumed they'd moved somewhere else.

It seemed that Jerry was dead against Sam's financial endeavor. I couldn't help being struck by the parallel with me and Margot. I hadn't been too happy about her decision to go into business with Louise and Randy, because I was looking out for her. It sounded like Jerry was doing the same for Sam.

When I got back to the flat, Louise had left and Margot, having already loaded the dishwasher, was wiping down the surfaces with a cloth.

"Where's Louise?" I asked.

"She peaked," Margot said. "About five minutes after you left, she suddenly got tired. I'm relieved. I couldn't handle another night like last night."

"Nor me," I said. "I'm exhausted."

But I found it hard to get to sleep. Twice I got up and stood at my window. Dark clouds screened the moon, but there was no Randy out running tonight.

I went back to bed for the third time, intending to read my book—*A Man Lay Dead* by Ngaio Marsh—but I'd barely got through three pages when there was a loud click and my bedside lamp went out. At first I thought the bulb had gone, but when the overhead light didn't turn on, either, I knew we'd had yet another power cut.

I resorted to counting sheep and must have finally drifted off to sleep because I was awoken by a flashlight thrust into my face and a voice screaming, "Come quickly! Come now! Oh my God!"

I sat bolt upright. My heart was racing and I couldn't see who was standing over my bed. "Put the flashlight down!" I shouted. "Who—?"

"Oh Evie, Evie." I was shocked. It was Kim and she was hysterical.

"What on earth is going on?" Margot burst into my bedroom.

"It's Jerry! He's in the basement," Kim cried. "He's dead. Jerry's dead."

Chapter Nineteen

Dennis materialized in a T-shirt and tracksuit bottoms. He was also carrying a flashlight. "The basement, you say?"

Kim nodded. As the four of us, flashlights in hand, made our way down the back stairs to the first-floor landing, Randy and Louise—dressed in matching white toweling robes—emerged from the George Goodchild suite. They had flashlights, too—something that Kim had recommended we put in every nightstand throughout the hotel.

I was surprised to see they were together.

"We heard screaming." Louise was clutching Randy's hand tightly. "What's going on?"

"There's been an accident," Margot said. "Please go back to bed."

"Jerry's been electrocuted!" Kim was distraught. "He's dead!"

"I'll come with you." Randy turned to Louise and kissed her on the forehead. "Margot, will you stay with Louise?"

"Stay with me," Louise begged. "Please."

Kim and I followed Randy and Dennis down the stairs in silence. As we passed through reception, shafts of moonlight caught the dial of the longcase clock. It was three twenty-five in the morning.

"I'll call for the air ambulance," I said, but knew I was wasting my breath. Jerry was dead. No one would be coming out to Tregarrick Rock tonight. We'd have to wait until the morning.

I stood with Kim at the top of the steps that led down to the basement.

"Stay here," said Dennis. "Randy and I will handle this."

"I can't go down there, Evie," Kim whispered. "I just can't."

"I'll stay with you," I said, but glanced downstairs, where, in the beams of the collective flashlights, I saw the blackened form of Jerry Quick. He was lying on the basement floor wearing what was left of his blue-striped pajamas. A horrible smell of burning flesh wafted up toward us.

I led Kim back to reception. She started to shiver. Dressed in a slinky silk robe and with bare feet, I wondered what on earth she'd been doing roaming the hotel at this ungodly hour and how she came to find Jerry in the first place.

I guided her to one of the two-seater sofas, just as Margot reappeared. "Louise has gone back to Randy's room to wait for him there." She sat beside Kim and took her hand. "Are you okay?"

"I feel cold," she said.

"It's shock." Margot looked to me. "Let's go up to the flat."

Suddenly, I realized with a jolt: "Someone needs to go and tell Sam." With the annex being a little way from the hotel and built low against the hillside, it was unlikely that he'd have heard anything.

"Can you do it?" said Margot. "You're so much better at that kind of thing than I am."

It was pitch dark as I made my way around the building to the annex and navigated the steps. I flipped on the light in the corridor—the annex was on a different electrical circuit than the main building—and tapped on Sam's bedroom door.

"Sam!" I called out. "It's Evie."

"Who?" came the groggy reply.

"Evie," I said louder. "Please. It's . . . it's important."

"Wait a minute." A band of light appeared under his door, and seconds later Sam opened it. "Evie?"

He was dressed in his boxer shorts. His confusion rapidly turned to alarm. "What's the matter?" he said. "What's happened?"

I struggled to get the words out. "It's . . . Jerry."

"What do you mean?" Sam said sharply. "What's happened to Jerry?"

"He . . . he must have touched . . . power . . . electric . . . Sam, I'm so sorry," I whispered. "Jerry's dead."

Sam uttered a cry of horror. "Holy mother of God. No!" He shoved me aside and took off in a blind panic, not stopping to throw on any clothing or shoes.

I just stood there, feeling wretched. I took in the chaos of the bachelor bedroom, glancing briefly at a large glossy poster of a sunken Japanese submarine tacked up on his wall—*Dive Truk Lagoon*.

I closed the door and hurried back to the flat.

Margot and Kim were sitting side by side on the sofa under a pale blue chenille throw, nursing brandy balloons.

I poured myself one and wriggled under, too.

No one spoke for a while until Kim started to fidget. "I'm going to tell you, because it will all come out tomorrow anyway."

"Go ahead," said Margot, shooting me a quizzical look.

Kim took a deep breath. "I slept with Jerry on Friday night—"

"Oh Kim!" I exclaimed.

Margot pursed her lips with disapproval. "You do know that Jerry is married—"

"I didn't know it at the time," said Kim. "It only happened the once. I'd had too much to drink and I swear, the moment he told me he was married—in the kitchen tonight, in fact—I broke it off. You have to believe me."

"So why were you walking around the hotel in the middle of the night?" I asked.

"I couldn't sleep. I just lay there feeling horrible. I was upset and angry," said Kim. "I got up to make myself a cup of tea and realized the power was out. I don't know when it went out or how long it had been out for, but I knew that Jerry would go down and fix it. Jerry always, *always* switches the power back on whatever the time, day or night." Kim wiped away a tear.

"So you went to do it yourself," I said.

"I was worried about bumping into him," Kim went on. "So I just waited and waited and when it still hadn't come on, yes, I went to the basement and . . ." She closed her eyes and squeezed them tightly as if to blot out the memory.

"You found him." I gave her hand a reassuring squeeze. "It must have been awful."

"Yes, it was, but—" Kim's eyes snapped open and what I saw in them was fear. "It could have been me lying there. I mean, obviously something was wrong with the electrics."

"But it wasn't you," I said quickly. "You're okay. You're safe."

Kim took a deep breath. "I'm . . . I'm scared."

"Of who? Patty?" I exclaimed. "True, she's insane, but—"

"No, not Patty." Kim hesitated. "I'm scared of . . . Randy."

"Randy?" Margot and I chorused. "Whatever for?"

"When Jerry and I were clearing up the kitchen after dinner, he told me that he'd arranged to meet Randy for a quick nightcap and that he'd come and find me later."

"But I thought you said that you and Jerry had an argument," I reminded her.

"That was before the argument," said Kim. "He got all jealous about me spending time with Sam and Randy and that's when it slipped out that he was married." She gave a snort of disgust. "Bastard. So I . . . I told him to go to hell." She looked up, her face twisted in anguish.

"You weren't to know," said Margot crisply. "And frankly, if he was cheating on his wife, he deserved—"

"Not helpful, Margot!" I cut in. "Kim, was Jerry's conversation anything to do with the syndicate Randy is forming with Sam?"

Kim nodded. "The agreement stipulated that everyone had to put in fifty thousand pounds to start with. Sam owes Jerry a lot of money. Sam promised to pay him back after his mother died—there was money in her will—but then Sam decided he wanted to put all of it into this new venture. Jerry was upset."

"Understandably so," I said.

"The money they're investing is going into an escrow account," Kim went on. "Apparently it's a condition of Randy's fancy Californian client. But of course, he won't say who this client is."

I remembered hearing the words *escrow account* and *Cayman Islands* on the walk to Seal Cove the day before. Now it seemed a lifetime away. So much had happened.

"An escrow account." Margot nodded. "That's perfectly normal."

Kim took another mouthful of brandy. "The thing is . . . do you remember when you discovered Ollie's body and found Jerry and me in Randy's room?"

I nodded.

"Jerry told me that he didn't trust Randy," said Kim. "But he wouldn't tell me why."

Jerry hadn't been the only one.

"Jerry knew that Randy had gone out with you and Sam that morning to Seal Cove," Kim continued. "He knew that Randy wouldn't be back for hours." She bit her lip. "I know I shouldn't have, but he wanted the key to get into Randy's room and he asked me to go with him."

I had always suspected there was more to that run-in than Kim having to replace a few loo rolls.

"And that's not all," said Kim.

Margot and I waited patiently while Kim took another

mouthful of brandy. "Jerry . . . he . . . he tried to access Randy's laptop, but it was password protected."

"He did *what*?" I was appalled. "What on earth for?"

"Of course it would be password protected," Margot exclaimed. "It's got financial information on there." She shook her head with dismay. "We'll have to tell Patty all of this. You do know that, don't you, Kim?"

Kim said nothing. She just sat there looking mournful.

"We don't have to tell Patty everything, do we?" I said to Margot. "Jerry's death was obviously an accident and whatever he was doing in Randy's room doesn't alter the outcome." I looked to Kim for reassurance but found none. "Does it?"

Kim went very quiet until she said, "I don't think it *was* an accident."

"What?" Margot and I chorused again.

"We've had tons of power cuts, but this was a major voltage fail in the middle of the night," said Kim. "I mean, even when we had that storm on Friday night, the power didn't go out, did it?"

"Like Evie said, it was just an accident," Margot declared. "Jerry can't have reconnected something properly."

"No." Kim shook her head vehemently. "Jerry knew what he was doing. He was very good at his job."

I was incredulous. "Are you saying it was deliberate?" I looked at Kim's earnest, tear-streaked face. "You think Randy wanted Jerry dead? But . . . how could he possibly have done it?"

"I don't know!" Kim wailed. "Maybe he thought Jerry would make Sam change his mind about the money, so he wanted him out of the way."

"That's ridiculous!" Margot exclaimed. "Jeez, Kim. Maybe you've been watching too many Hollywood movies."

Kim's accusations were freaking me out. I could see that there was a connection—even if we didn't know exactly what it was yet—between Ollie and Randy, but Jerry and Randy? That made no sense at all.

But then I remembered how savvy Randy was about electrics. I was in the basement when he and Jerry had been discussing the pros and cons of various amps.

Maybe Kim had a point.

I turned to Margot. "I hate to say this, but up until Randy and Louise arrived on the island everything here has been fine."

"Randy, possibly. But Louise?" Margot shook her head. "Never. What you see is what you get with Louise. She's hopeless at hiding things and if anything, far more trusting than even you. Look at how she totally bought into Patty's threat to report her!"

"Speaking of Patty," I said, "I can guarantee she'll be back here first thing tomorrow."

"God, yes," said Margot. "We'd better brace ourselves."

Chapter Twenty

We were back in the Residents' Lounge sitting in the same places as yesterday, only Jerry's was taken by a thin, disheveled man with large owlish eyes behind heavy black-framed spectacles. I'd seen him briefly when he had arrived with Patty, but he'd been hurried down to the basement before the introductions were made.

It had been a wretched morning as we tried to keep ourselves busy while the police did their part, and Jerry was finally taken away and put on the medical launch bound for St. Mary's, where his body would join Ollie's in the morgue.

Louise pleaded a headache. Randy said he had work to do, and Sam—who had seemed far more upset than I'd expected him to be—kept to his room until we were summoned to the lounge at noon.

Once we'd all sat down, Patty moved to her favorite spot by the fireplace and called for silence. She was wearing the same suit as yesterday but sported a maroon shirt that brought out the color of her brown eyes.

"This is Derek Lombardi," said Patty. "Yes. My ex-husband. He's anxious to sample your excellent baking, Kim." Patty pointed to the coffee table, where Kim had set out the brownies she'd baked that morning.

Derek stood up and grabbed two, along with a paper serviette. Patty ate a brownie, too. No one else seemed hungry.

Patty surveyed the room. "Well, here we all are again and, crikey—as they say down under—*two* deaths in one weekend. I don't know about any of you, but I don't believe in coincidences."

No one answered. I stole a glance at Louise and Randy, sitting hand in hand on the Chesterfield sofa.

Patty turned to her ex-husband. "Derek? Why don't you do the honors? I suggest a quick recap of Ollie Martin first. What do you think? Dead before or after he hit the water?"

"Allow me to explain," said Derek. "Typical signs of drowning are foam in the airways and overinflated lungs. It is also true that spurious postmortem injuries may be created by boats, by underwater objects or by the hands of the deceased dragging on the bottom. Perhaps being caught on coral or struck against the rocks."

"Get on with it Derek, luv," said Patty.

"The deceased died by asphyxiation," said Derek. "Ergo, he was dead upon entering the water. Death was not by drowning." He paused to take a sip of tea. "Ollie also suffered a blow to his face that was so severe, it knocked out a front tooth."

Patty consulted her notes. "All okay with that? Any questions?"

I raised a hand.

"Evie?" said Patty. "You have something to say?"

"What time do you think this happened?" I asked.

"We've come across some anomalies, so I'd rather not be pinned down," said Derek.

"Go on," said Patty. "Give it a try."

"Well before midnight," he said. "The young man's body had been in the water for at least twelve hours when he was discovered, but as I say, there are some anomalies and we are doing further tests."

"Did you manage to talk to that Stephanie person on Bryher?" I asked.

"We did," said Patty. "According to her, there is no romance there. Apparently they were an item last summer but managed to stay friends. But then she would say that, wouldn't she?"

"So you're *assuming*," I said, "that Ollie did not go to Bryher? There is a window of time still unaccounted for after he left the co-op and picked up the *Sandpiper*. Maybe he met Stephanie somewhere on St. Mary's?"

"We are double-checking her story," said Patty. "Derek? Moving on to Jerry."

Derek cleared his throat again. "Jerry was electrocuted when the power was turned back on and he touched the light switch in the basement. It looks like it wasn't earthed."

"The light switch?" I exclaimed. "But—how?"

"That's not possible," said Sam. "I put the ground rod in myself yesterday." He was visibly distraught. "You saw me outside, Evie. Remember?"

I agreed that I had. Sam looked so upset. It was awful.

"All I am telling you is that the ground rod had not been connected properly," said Derek.

Sam was beside himself. "You're saying it's my fault?"

"We're not saying it's anyone's fault," said Patty gently. "The power outage was caused by the dishwasher, washing machine and tumble dryer. They had timers that were all set to come on at the same time, namely at two a.m. The system overloaded and the power went out."

Sam pointed an accusatory finger at Kim. "Then it was *your* fault!"

Kim bit her lip and looked down at her lap.

"Which brings me to my next question." Patty checked her notebook. "As I said, the power went out at two a.m. and yet Kim raised the alarm shortly after three-fifteen, according to Evie, who checked the clock in reception at three twenty-five."

Kim just sat there looking miserable.

"What made you go looking for Jerry in the middle of the night?" Patty demanded.

Kim straightened her shoulders. "I wasn't looking for Jerry. I was going downstairs to make a cup of tea. I couldn't sleep. The power was off. I went down to the basement to check the fuse box and found . . ." Her last words were just an incoherent mumble.

"Are you sure that's what happened?" Patty demanded. "I know for a fact, because he's married to my friend, that Jerry is a hard dog to keep on the porch, and let's face it, with your track record . . ."

A tide of red raced up Kim's neck and flooded her face. "I knew you'd dig that up," said Kim bitterly. "I was fired for having a ten-year affair with my boss. Okay?"

There was the most excruciatingly awkward silence. No wonder Kim had been upset when Jerry had come clean.

"That's not quite the whole story, though, is it?" said Patty. "You threatened to expose his creative accounting to the shareholders unless—"

"He left his wife," Kim said.

"You got a nice severance package," said Patty. "So not all bad. But this time, you must have been angry that, yet again, a married man had let you down."

Kim's jaw dropped. "I didn't know Jerry was married until I found out last night. We only began to spend time together when we discovered we both supported Chelsea. It was nice to have someone to cheer on the team instead of watching the games on TV on my own."

"Personally, I think Chelsea sucks," said Patty. "I'm a Manchester United fan myself. But, as the old idiom goes, never judge a book by its cover. And let's face it. Jerry wasn't just an electrician."

At this comment, the room fell silent.

"Did you know that Jerry was day-trading illegally, Kim?" Patty asked.

"Day-trading?" Kim was aghast. "No, but why would I?"

"Jerry was banned for life for insider trading, isn't that right, Sam?" Patty said.

"I have no idea," said Sam. "I knew he'd left the city under a cloud, but I didn't know why."

"But why did he pretend he didn't know anything about the stock market?" Kim sounded bewildered.

"The burner phone," I remembered. "I found it in the turret

along with a scrap of paper with letters on it. I thought it was Jerry's, but he denied it and said that it belonged to Sam."

"We'll want to see that burner," said Patty.

"You mentioned letters, Evie?" Randy broke in. "Those could be stock ticker symbols."

"Yes, Randy," said Patty. "What do you think about all this? You're the expert."

He shrugged. "Your guess is as good as mine. But if you say he was trading illegally, then clearly he wouldn't have wanted me to know about it—"

"Because that's what you do," said Patty. "Not illegally, however."

Randy nodded. "I also keep strange hours because of the different markets, so it makes sense that Jerry would be doing the same. He'd definitely have to rely on the Internet if he was working around the clock. Day-trading is volatile and involves massive risk. It's not my thing."

"And for those who don't know," Patty said, "what markets would be open in the middle of the night, G.M.T., that is?"

"Australia, New Zealand, Hong Kong, Shenzhen and Shanghai," said Randy.

"And obviously, you'd stay awake to watch those same markets," Patty said.

"That's right," said Randy.

I knew that Hong Kong was eight hours ahead of the U.K. because, in my other life, I dealt with a gallery in Victoria. One o'clock in the morning in the U.K. would therefore be nine in Hong Kong, when the market would open.

"Let's go back to last night again, Randy," said Patty. "When the power went out . . . weren't you tempted to go and see why it hadn't been switched back on again? Especially if you were in the middle of some lucrative international deal?"

Randy gave an easy smile. "First of all, I'd finalized my lucrative international deal last night after dinner. And secondly—do I really have to explain?" Randy took Louise's hand and gave it an affectionate squeeze.

"I see," said Patty. "So you only knew about Jerry's unfortunate accident when—"

"We heard Kim screaming upstairs," said Louise. "Randy's room is under Margot and Evie's flat."

"Okay, so . . . we have Margot and Evie in the flat, Randy with Louise, Sam all alone and Kim roaming the halls, looking for Jerry. Who am I missing?"

Dennis raised his hand.

"Ah yes, Dennis, I assume you were alone as well." Patty looked over to Derek. "What do you think?"

"I'm leaning toward a tragic accident," said Derek. "Whoever touched the light switch outside the darkroom in the basement would have got electrocuted. It could have happened to anyone."

Patty checked her watch. "We need to go, Derek, otherwise we won't make it."

"That's it?" Margot was stunned. "You've asked all these questions and now you're just leaving?"

"Yep. We are," Patty declared. "Our son, Danny, has a soccer game this afternoon and we promised we'd be there."

Derek got to his feet and thanked Kim for the brownies.

"Enjoy the rest of your Sunday," said Patty. "If I were you,

I'd start painting this room. Oh, and it goes without saying that Ollie's room and the basement are out of bounds. I put a bit of crime scene tape up just to remind you. We'll get the forensic team over as soon as possible. I still have a couple of questions about Ollie's timeline. So expect a phone call from me later today."

And with that, she and Derek left.

"So we're free to go?" said Louise with amazement.

"Yes," I said. "But as you must have gathered, no one can get off the island until tomorrow anyway. Patty knows that. She's not finished with any of us yet."

Randy ran his fingers through his hair. "Haven't we told her everything?" He seemed agitated. "I'm not sure what happened there."

"Why do I get the feeling we're in a sinking boat and Patty the shark is closing in?" Louise grumbled.

"Because you're right," said Margot. "She is."

"Derek said that it could have happened to anyone," I said suddenly. "In fact . . . oh." I couldn't finish my sentence.

I'd been planning on meeting Randy in the darkroom this very morning. I would have touched that light switch. It could easily have happened to me.

Chapter Twenty-One

After a desultory lunch of French baguettes stuffed with mozzarella, Kim's homemade pesto and sliced beef tomatoes, I left the others in the Residents' Lounge with their paintbrushes and headed outside to do some gardening. The slate-gray sky matched my mood. There would be more rain before the afternoon was out.

As I passed the spot where Sam had put in the new ground rod, I stopped to take a look. The soil had been pushed back into the hole and patted down in place. Nothing looked out of the ordinary. Jerry's death must have been a freak accident.

I headed for the potting shed, removed the padlock and retrieved the wheelbarrow full of plants.

I knew someone had come into the shed on Friday night. Could it have been Ollie? Had he come to get something in here? One of the gardening tools perhaps? But why?

It seemed hard to believe that just two days ago Ollie had

been standing here with me, drinking coffee out of his silly pirate mug and talking about the love of his life. I thought of the stolen sapphire-and-diamond cross that Ollie had given to Becky for Valentine's Day. What else had Ollie been stealing?

Now that I knew Becky was pregnant, I understood a little more about their relationship. Cyril Godolphin must have hit the roof when he found out, and I can't say I blamed him.

Oh Ollie. What had you got yourself into?

As I worked alone, accompanied by the sound of birds, I was joined by Mister Tig. He sat down on one of my freshly planted begonias and began to wash himself, but at the sound of approaching voices, he darted off.

Randy and Louise, dressed in Wellies and waterproofs, waved a greeting. Randy was carrying a small canvas rucksack.

Louise had a smudge of eggshell-blue paint on her nose.

"Is the painting finished?" I asked.

"Most of it," said Louise. "I can't tell you how boring painting is. We're off to Seal Cove. Randy wants to show me the wreck."

"You won't see anything now," I said. "The tide turned at lunchtime today."

"I know," said Randy. "But the view will be worth it."

"Will you be all right walking?" I said.

"Randy strapped my ankle," said Louise.

"She took an Advil," said Randy. "Just the one. From now on, I'm in charge of her personal pharmacy."

Louise gave Randy a look of complete adoration. So much for Randy's zero tolerance on drugs.

"Randy forced me to leave my bag behind," Louise grumbled. "I feel quite naked without my mobile."

"I want her to be in the moment and not taking photos for Instagram," said Randy. "And I told her that there is no phone service anyway." Randy gestured to his rucksack. "I had to bribe her with chocolate."

I waved them off, promising to meet up for cocktails at six-thirty.

It can't have been more than twenty minutes later when I became aware of being watched. At first I thought I was imagining it, but then, looking up, I caught a flash of dark red behind the laurel hedge.

"Hello?" I called out. "Is that you, Margot?"

There was no answer.

"Becky?" I called out again. "Becky? Is that you?"

There was still no answer, but whoever it was had not moved away.

I got to my feet and, armed with my trowel, approached the hedge.

"Look, I know someone is there," I said. "I can see you."

A blond woman around my age with shoulder-length hair stepped out from the shadows. She was dressed in a red parka, jeans and hiking boots.

The woman looked exhausted. Dark rings bloomed under haunted pale green eyes. She just stood there looking at me. It was very unnerving.

I regarded her with suspicion. My first thought was that she could be connected to Ollie. Was this the infamous ex-girlfriend, Stephanie? How had she got across the causeway? I noticed that the bottoms of her jeans were wet, which meant that if she *had* walked over, she'd been lurking on the grounds for quite some time.

"Can I help you?" I asked.

"Where is he?" she whispered.

I was struck by a horrible foreboding. "Who are you looking for?"

"My brother," she said. "My name is Carrie."

For a moment I thought I was imagining things and could only stare.

"Your brother? Your brother, Randy?" I said. "But you're supposed to be . . ." The pain and anger in her eyes told me all I needed to know. It was what I had always suspected deep down: Randy Campbell was a fraud.

I had no idea why Carrie was here, but I knew I had to get her out of sight before Randy and Louise returned.

She didn't protest as I hurried her up the back staircase and into the safety of our flat. Margot's confusion turned to disbelief and then to indignation as Carrie explained that Randy's real name was Noah.

"He told us you had drowned," I said.

A shadow of disgust crossed Carrie's face. "Of course he did."

"I'm still not sure how you came to find him here," Margot said.

"Instagram," said Carrie.

Margot and I looked on in astonishment as Carrie scrolled through a number of images of Randy—Randy standing in front of the Tregarrick Rock hotel entrance, Randy and

Mister Tig, Randy in the dining room, Randy out on the terrace. In each one, Kim had done an excellent job with her hashtags—#triathlete, #ironman, #TregarrickRock, #Scilly, #OtilloSwimrun.

"I've been looking for my brother for a long time," said Carrie. "I started searching social media using triathlon or Ironman tags and then, by chance, I heard about the Ötillö Swimrun. I knew it would be the kind of thing that Noah would want to do. And I got lucky. I knew that he wouldn't use his real name, but I'd recognize his face anywhere."

"Wait a minute," I said suddenly. "You live in Australia, don't you? Randy only arrived on Friday. How could you have—?"

"Yes!" Margot agreed. "It's impossible for you to have found this out and got here so quickly."

"I've been in London," said Carrie simply. "And if you don't believe me, I can show you hotel receipts and give you the name of the taxi company that was very happy to drive the two hundred and eighty-five miles from London to Penzance. From there, I flew by helicopter to St. Mary's, and from there, took a water taxi to Tregarrick before crossing the causeway on foot. Satisfied?"

I regarded the bedraggled young woman sitting in our kitchen. She'd certainly gone to a lot of trouble to get here.

"Look. No offense," I said. "All we've got is your word for it and the photograph that Randy keeps in his pocket of you."

"Exactly!" Margot chimed in. "How do we know that you're not an ex-girlfriend or an ex-wife or something?"

Carrie gave a bitter laugh. "Wow. He's really charmed you,

hasn't he?" She went back to her iPhone. "Perhaps this will convince you."

We sat beside her and looked at her iPhoto library. There were dozens of photographs of Randy and Carrie together, many of them as kids. Side by side, their likeness was unmistakable.

"My brother is the biggest con man who ever lived," Carrie said bluntly. "He even conned me—his own sister—and my husband and all our friends. Everyone trusted him with their savings."

"Trust Fund M.," I said.

"You've heard of it." Carrie sneered. "Ridiculously high returns on investments. He had the right paperwork, fancy letterhead, fake backup to prove it was bona fide, only it wasn't at all. Noah would use our money to fund his luxury lifestyle, and throw the odd bone to those poor unsuspecting bastards who believed they were making money."

"He gave a check to Louise," I said. "Remember, Margot?"

"I can guarantee that he used the money she had already given him to make it seem like she was making money," Carrie declared.

"You mean, he was operating a Ponzi scheme," I said.

Carrie nodded. "But now Noah's moved on from that. His latest thing is forming syndicates for crazy expeditions—with money up front, of course. Then, when they fail, he reminds them of the risks that he'd outlined at the beginning."

"That's despicable," Margot whispered.

"Oh, my brother likes to make a big show of having money," said Carrie. "But at the same time he pretends to be modest.

He always gets other people to do his dirty work and take the fall."

A sickening feeling began to pool in the pit of my stomach. I thought back to that first dinner on Friday night and how Randy had insisted that he didn't want to talk about money. It was Louise who had insisted he should. She had been his cheerleader. Louise had also introduced Randy to all her friends, and it was she who had bought the option on *Lighthouse of Sorrow* for my sister.

"Louise told him I had a huge divorce settlement," said Margot. "He thought I was loaded."

"And Sam had his inheritance," I said.

"And Kim's settlement money," Margot added.

"My brother is a master manipulator," Carrie continued. "He's a good listener. He befriends you and he knows exactly the right thing to say to gain your trust. He spends a lot of time researching his marks—it's part of his strategy. He likes to impress everyone with his knowledge."

I thought back to Randy's offer to help me find a construction loan for the roof, and how I had explained about my financial situation and that Margot and I were just chatelaines of Tregarrick Rock. When Randy had realized that I didn't have any money, he'd just let me be.

"My brother is an opportunist," said Carrie. "He also never wastes time on something, or someone who he knows won't pan out. He cuts his losses and moves on to the next."

Margot reached for my hand and squeezed it. "We've had a lucky escape."

"Noah is clever, but then he learned from the best. Our dad,"

Carrie went on. "Ask for your money back and he smiles and says, yes, of course. But he only gives a little bit back, claiming that there was an opportunity that came his way and was just too big to miss. Naturally, you believe him. Why wouldn't you? And then, when things get too hot to handle, he simply vanishes into thin air."

Margot reached for the phone. "We need to call the police right now."

"No!" Carrie shouted. "Sorry. I mean, we can't. Not yet. If he so much as sees a blue light or suspects *anything*, he'll be gone."

"We're on an island—he has nowhere to go," I said.

"Trust me, he'll find a way out," said Carrie. "He always does. He goes into every one of his little projects with an escape plan. *Always*. Why else do you think he's never been caught in the last eight years?"

"*Eight years?*" I whispered.

"I don't care. I'm calling the police," Margot said again.

Carrie was adamant. "Noah *mustn't* know I'm here. We need a plan. We need to catch him and keep him here, and then call the police."

"What did you have in mind?" I said nervously.

"What kind of manpower do you have?" Carrie asked.

"Sam, Dennis, Kim, Louise, Evie and myself," said Margot. "Six."

"Seven, including me." Carrie nodded again. "We can manage with seven, as long as we have the element of surprise."

I was becoming increasingly anxious. "Your plan is for us to *overpower* him? He's incredibly strong."

I remembered Patty's silly truth-and-lie game when Randy

claimed he could bench-press two hundred pounds. Even if that turned out to be a lie, it wasn't worth the risk.

"But what if it goes wrong?" I said. "What if someone gets hurt? The police may not even be able to get here tonight at all."

"Dennis is a former marine," Margot said suddenly. "And Sam's a diver. They're strong enough. What do we need? Ropes? We can lock him in Evie's darkroom in the basement."

"Good idea. He wouldn't be able to get out of there," I said. "The walls are solid rock." I'd also had a lock installed to make sure that I wasn't interrupted when developing my photographs. "Oh wait. Damn. We can't. Patty said that the basement is out of bounds. Remember?"

"I'm not afraid of Patty," said Margot. "And besides, do you have a better idea?"

I didn't.

I thought back to Jerry again. He'd suspected Randy all along and Randy knew it. Randy had told us that he'd worked in construction before. He'd certainly known about amps and fuses, because I'd heard him talk to Jerry about the electrical circuits.

What if Randy had tampered with the ground rod in some way? There was a handy shovel conveniently in the unlocked potting shed and with the freshly dug soil, it would have been very easy to do. It would also confirm my belief that someone had been in there.

And then there was Louise. Suddenly, after keeping his distance physically, Randy seemed to have had a change of heart, and now I could see why. Louise had given him the perfect alibi for last night. But then I was struck by the most horrible thought. If Randy had got rid of Jerry in cold blood, would he get rid of Louise?

"Has Randy ever deliberately hurt anyone?" I said slowly.

"Define the word *hurt*," Carrie said. "If you mean destroyed lives, yes. He's destroyed a lot of lives. But physically?" She shook her head. "No."

"That might change if he's cornered," Margot pointed out.

The phone rang, making us all jump. It was Dennis.

"I just wanted to let you know that Randy and Louise are not back from their walk yet. Do you want me to go out and look for them? It's mizzling and they could easily get lost."

I told Dennis I would call him back in five minutes.

When I repeated Dennis's concern, Carrie's face fell. "Then it's too late. He's already gone."

"He can't have gone!" Margot exclaimed. "I told you. He can't get off the island without a boat."

"There's Ollie's dinghy," I said. "But he won't get far in that. It's got a slow puncture."

"I'm telling you," Carrie said, "he's already gone. And you forget, he's a very strong swimmer."

"Hear me out," said Margot. "Even if he can get to St. Mary's, he's still stuck. The first flight out from St. Mary's to Penzance isn't until midmorning tomorrow. The *Scillonian* sails late afternoon, so it's unlikely he made it today. However good a swimmer Randy is, he can hardly swim twenty-eight miles to Penzance. And what about his passport? Money?"

"He took a rucksack with him," I said. "Maybe it was in there? We need to check his room."

I took the set of master keys off the hook.

"What if he comes back?" Margot exclaimed.

I thought of Kim's excuse. "Maybe he's run out of loo paper."

Chapter Twenty-Two

Armed with three loo rolls, I let myself into the George Good-child suite.

I breathed a small sigh of relief—Carrie was wrong. Randy hadn't left. His laptop computer was still on his desk. I opened his wardrobe and sure enough, his clothes were there, as well as the 1930s suit from Giggles.

Randy would be returning. I dashed back to our flat.

"So he'll come back for his laptop," said Margot. "That's when we'll get him. We'll be waiting."

"I know this is a crazy question to ask you, Carrie," I said. "But . . . Randy mentioned that every day he takes a bath before dinner at five forty-five—"

"Of course!" Margot exclaimed. "Patty's stupid two-truths-and-one-lie game!"

"He hates baths." Carrie regarded us in amazement. "Don't you understand? He's gone. He can always buy another laptop.

He can save everything to the cloud. He's probably already wiped that hard drive clean."

"So what do you suggest we do?" I said.

"And if he isn't coming back," Margot said, "what about Louise?"

"We *have* to call the police," I said.

Carrie reluctantly agreed. We rang Patty, and Carrie told her everything. When she put down the phone, she looked shattered. She told us that Patty would be coming over by boat and that we were to sit tight and wait.

"There's no way I'm doing that," Margot said hotly. "We have to find Louise."

"I agree, but we must be careful," I said. "Despite Carrie believing that Randy has already gone, what if he hasn't?"

"Maybe he's planning to do a runner tonight?" Margot suggested.

"We need to tell the others what is going on," I said. "We can't do this alone."

We summoned Dennis, Sam and Kim up to the flat where, once again, Carrie told her story.

They were just as appalled as we were. Sam, in particular, was shocked about just how close he'd come to giving Randy his inheritance. He shared his belief that Randy had killed Ollie and Jerry, too, but Carrie was adamant this was not true.

"Say whatever you like about my brother," she said. "He is not a killer."

"So why make a run for it?" I demanded.

Carrie looked at me with scorn. "Because that's what he

does. He disappears and then turns up somewhere with a brand-new identity."

"We should all split up," Sam declared. "I'll head out to Seal Cove—"

"We can't do anything to let him suspect we know what's going on," I said. "They could be on their way back."

"Not if he's swimming," said Carrie.

"But he might not be swimming," I pointed out.

"Wait . . . so, Carrie, you think that Randy might have swum to where . . . St. Mary's?" Sam was aghast. "Has he any idea how strong the current is in the straits?"

"Oh God," Margot exclaimed. "What if he took Louise as a hostage or something?"

"How far is it to St. Mary's?" asked Carrie.

"About three miles," said Dennis.

"The Ironman swim section is three miles," said Carrie grimly. "He could swim there no problem."

"But then what?" Margot said. "He arrives in St. Mary's completely soaked to the skin? We already know he didn't take anything with him."

"Do we?" said Carrie. "He could easily have preplanned the whole thing."

"We're wasting precious time," Margot said. "We have to find Louise."

"I'll stay with Carrie to make sure she keeps out of sight," Kim said. "Just in case Randy shows up."

"Good idea," I agreed. "Dennis should remain in reception, too. Act as if everything is normal."

Sam wanted to come with us, but Dennis felt that it would be better for him to stay close by in case Randy did return.

"I don't like this," said Sam. "You girls need a man with you."

"It's better this way." Although I was reluctant to admit that Sam could be right. "Margot and I can bluff our way out of it if we meet them both coming back. But seeing you with us might arouse suspicion."

"No, it wouldn't," Sam protested. "I'd be looking after you."

"We don't need looking after," Margot retorted.

Dennis handed me a walkie-talkie and two flashlights.

"Where should we start?" Margot said.

"I know that Randy wanted to show her Seal Rock . . . and . . ." But then I had such an awful thought that I couldn't finish my sentence.

Margot turned pale. "What? Why do you have that weird look on your face?"

I thought of the treacherous path that zigzagged down to the ledge and the long drop onto the sand. "Because it is the perfect place for someone to have an accidental fall."

Margot set her jaw. "Then that's where we go first."

The light was fading rapidly by the time we reached the wasteland on the top of the bluff. Neither of us had said a word. I could hear the sound of the breakers crashing against the rocks below. In the dim light there was very little to see now. What remained of the wreck had disappeared above the rising water.

We took the same way that Sam had shown me yesterday. Margot and I only got as far as the overhanging ledge.

There was no sign of Louise.

The more I thought about it, the more I was certain that Carrie was right, however far-fetched it might seem. Randy had gone. Earlier in the afternoon he could have easily swum across to Bryher. From there he could have stolen a boat and then—freedom.

Margot gripped my hand so hard, it hurt. "Seal Rock's covered," she whispered. "If Louise . . ." Tears glistened in her eyes. "Oh Evie." She stared bleakly out over the sound. "What if he really did push her off?"

"Carrie said he wasn't violent." I remembered how difficult it had been to navigate the animal tracks yesterday, and with Louise's bad ankle, perhaps she had fallen. "I think she's here somewhere. I just have a feeling. But she might be hurt."

We both started screaming out Louise's name.

And then the wind dropped.

We both heard something. A sound. A scream.

"Shh! Listen!" Margot hissed.

It was faint but it was there. It seemed to be coming from above us, up by the Bronze Age burial chamber. We called out Louise's name again and this time we heard hysterical cries for help.

Louise was still alive.

We clambered up to a small mud-hardened plateau that fronted the burial chamber. A portal stone stood on either side of the entrance, which had been blocked by a large sheet of custom-made timber, spray-painted with the words *Danger: Keep Out*. The makeshift door was secured horizontally by a rusting iron bar that was lodged into iron rings, screwed into the stone on either side.

Louise was trapped.

The iron bar was easy to remove, but the timber was heavy and awkward. Hearing Louise's convulsive sobs seemed to give us superhuman strength.

"We're here!" shouted Margot. "It's okay! We're here!"

Finally, Louise tumbled out onto the grass. Her face was smudged with dirt and her blond hair was matted with blood from a nasty cut on her forehead, but she would be okay.

"Thank God, oh thank God," she cried. "I thought I was going to suffocate in there! I didn't have my phone! I could have died! I could have died!"

"But you didn't," said Margot briskly. "And here we are."

"What happened to your head?" I asked.

Louise reached up and touched her hair, shocked to find her fingertips coated with blood. "The roof was so low. I must have hit it," she said.

I stepped away to radio ahead to Dennis. I told him that we'd found Louise safe, but that Randy had fled.

Louise sank onto the grass. "All I could think about was Ralph Fiennes in *The English Patient*. You know . . . the bit where he goes for help and leaves Kristin Scott Thomas in the Cave of Swimmers and she dies."

Margot dropped down beside her and took her friend's hand. "We saw it four times, didn't we?"

Louise struggled to hold back her tears. "I could have died in there if Randy hadn't gone for help. Where is he?"

At this comment, Margot and I exchanged looks of astonishment. Surely Louise didn't really believe that her being trapped in the chamber was an accident?

"We don't know where he is," Margot said. "And it wasn't Randy who raised the alarm. Evie and I have been out looking for you."

"I don't understand." Louise's bewilderment was extraordinary to behold.

"Randy is no Ralph Fiennes," Margot said. "He's done a runner."

Louise's face went through a series of expressions until the horrible truth dawned on her. "You mean he *deliberately* left me in there to die? But why?"

I sat down on her other side and took her other hand. Together, Margot and I told her about Carrie and what we knew about Randy—or Noah, or whatever other names he went by—so far.

"So . . . he's a con man and a killer," Louise whispered. "And I'm a stupid old fool."

"He was a very clever con man," I said. "We were all taken in. He won't get away with it." But even as I said it, I was struck by the awful thought that he just might.

For a long moment Louise didn't speak. "Can we sit here for a minute? I . . . I don't think I can face the others quite yet."

"Why don't you tell us what happened?" I said gently.

"We had a lovely walk. He told me he saw a seal, but I didn't believe him," said Louise in a dull voice. "The tide was coming in, but Randy still thought we should go down as far as we could. Oh!" She clapped her hand over her mouth. "You don't think he planned to—?"

"Of course not," I said quickly, but I had wondered.

"But how did he persuade you to go inside the burial chamber?" Margot demanded.

"Randy said there were Bronze Age wall paintings in there—"

"Even though there is a sign that says *Danger: Keep Out*?" Margot seemed incredulous. "Gosh. You're even more gullible than my sister!"

"Thanks," I muttered.

"He told me that Sam had told him that it was a precaution for curious guests," said Louise. "It was perfectly safe."

"And then . . ." Margot prompted.

"Randy was quite the gentleman. He said, 'After you.'" She gave a dry laugh. "*After you!* Ha! It was so dark in there. He was right behind me, trying to get his flashlight to work on his mobile. He told me the wall paintings were a long way back—it's huge inside, by the way. The next thing I know is that he's not behind me anymore and I can't get out."

I was stunned. "You didn't hear anything at all?"

"Well. Yes. I heard a scrape and a heavy thump that I now realize had to be the timber being put into place." Louise shook her head, still struggling to accept the obvious. "I can't believe he would do that."

"Did he say anything to give you an idea of what he was thinking?" Margot asked.

"Like what? 'Enjoy yourself in there'? 'Take a nap'? 'Write a poem'?" Louise's bottom lip began to quiver.

Margot gave her a hug.

"How long do you think you were in the burial chamber for?" I asked.

She shrugged. "I don't know. It felt like forever."

But it had probably been enough time for Randy to get away.

Margot regarded her friend with frustration. "Didn't you ever think that Randy was too good to be true?"

Louise shook her head again. "I was too loved-up to care. I couldn't believe my luck. He was so gorgeous. So handsome."

"And someone who only wanted to sleep with you when he needed an alibi," Margot said brutally.

"An alibi?" Louise frowned then pulled a face. "Oh. Great. That makes me feel like even more of an idiot, although—" She thought for a moment. "There was something that I thought was a little strange in his room. I had a look around when he was making a call from the bathroom. It was in his holdall."

"What was?" Margot and I demanded.

"A hotel key," said Louise. "And some boring business periodicals, and a town map of St. Mary's and a receipt for Giggles. Let me see what else, the empty rucksack. Oh—and a list of sailing times from St. Mary's to all the other islands."

"Wait," I said sharply. "The key. Was it for Godolphin Court?"

"I don't know," said Louise.

"And . . . in his holdall, was there a passport? Or money?" I asked.

Louise shook her head yet again. "A little money in his wallet. But no passport."

"Oh my God. That's it!" I exclaimed. "I bet he's got all his stuff at Godolphin Court!" Seeing Margot's confusion, I added, "I knew there was something that had been bugging me. Remember when Patty asked Randy what he and Ollie had been talking about that afternoon at the hotel?"

"Something about visiting the islands," said Margot. "Why?"

"Randy told Ollie he was going to Tregarrick Rock," I said excitedly. "But Ollie didn't offer to take him across even though he would have been traveling back around the same time!"

"Okay. Yes. Possibly," said Margot. "That's assuming Ollie was coming straight back. We still don't know if he made plans to see the Stephanie girl."

I shook my head. "Becky said that Randy was in reception and had asked for his room key. Wouldn't he have had to check out earlier in the day? Like noon. Randy turns up on Tregarrick Rock with one very small bag and—"

"He kept his room at the hotel," Margot finished. "Oh God! You are right! That's where his stuff is, and maybe Ollie found out what Randy was up to and then Randy had to get rid of Ollie when . . . um . . . actually, I'm not sure when it could have happened."

"That's the problem," I said. "Opportunity. When would Randy have had the opportunity?"

"Randy was with me from when he arrived around five until he went to change—"

"So there was a window of opportunity right there!" I exclaimed.

Louise shook her head. "No. We were only apart for about thirty minutes and during that time we were exchanging text messages."

I recalled meeting Randy on the landing outside his room to go down for cocktails. He certainly hadn't looked like a man who had just committed murder.

"And then we were all at dinner together," Margot declared.

"After dinner," I said quietly. "It had to have been then." But then I remembered. "Derek said Ollie had been in the water for at least twelve hours, so it would have had to have happened much earlier."

"But Derek also said there were anomalies, remember?" Louise reminded us.

"We can drive ourselves insane with this," said Margot. "Right now we need to radio Dennis and get him to tell the police to go straight to Godolphin Court. I can guarantee he'll be there."

"And I want to be there when they catch him, too," Louise declared.

But when we got back to the hotel, we were in for a surprise. There was a commotion in reception, a buzz of excited voices and waterproofs being passed out to Kim and Carrie. And then I spied the tall man in his early forties. I'd forgotten just how tall and Nordic-looking Cador Ferris was, with his golden skin and white-blond hair.

Margot gave a cry of surprise. "Is that Cador?"

Hearing his name, Cador turned and saw us. Although he smiled, his expression was grave.

Moments later, Dennis was handing out more waterproofs to Margot and Louise, while Cador and I exchanged the briefest of greetings. He looked shattered. Dark rings bloomed beneath his piercing blue eyes. He was understandably rattled. We all were.

"I'm not coming with you," I said.

Cador nodded. "I know how much you hate boats. We'll talk more when all this is over." And with that he swept out of reception, with the four women chattering like a gaggle of geese.

I was suddenly incredibly tired. The events of the day and all their devastating revelations had finally caught up with me. I leaned on the counter and said to Dennis, "Fill me in."

"Cador heard about Ollie from one of the fishermen who ferried him over from St. Mary's to Tregarrick," said Dennis. "Cador immediately called me, I told him everything and he just stopped at his place to dump his gear and grab his boat. Then he came straight over the causeway. When you radioed in to say that Randy had fled, Cador was only too anxious to take the girls to St. Mary's."

I suddenly realized that I hadn't seen Sam. "Did Sam go with them?"

"Yes. When Sam knew Cador was coming, he went down to meet him," said Dennis. "You'll be glad to know that your hunch was right," he went on. "Randy did keep his room at Godolphin Court. Not only that, he ordered room service this evening."

"You're kidding." I was surprised. "That's a bit bold, isn't it?"

"That's what Becky told Patty," said Dennis. "Soup of the day."

"But . . . how did he get to St. Mary's without a boat?" I was astonished. "Did he actually *swim*?"

Dennis shrugged. "It wouldn't have been difficult to swim to Bryher and steal a boat from there."

Carrie was right. Randy had had everything planned, right down to the last detail.

I stood in reception, at a loss. I just didn't know what to do with myself. Though I was exhausted, at the same time I was mentally wired.

"I don't know how you stay calm, Dennis," I said. "I really don't."

Dennis just smiled. "Go and look in the Residents' Lounge and see what you think. Kim didn't get very far with the vacuuming."

The Residents' Lounge looked fresh and clean. The furniture was still in the middle of the room, but that was just as well since there was so much dust and dirt scattered over the bare floorboards. The room was 99 percent finished. It only needed a second coat of paint. If, after all this, we decided to go ahead with the open house, we'd be ready.

The Miele stood plugged in and ready to go. I put my mobile on the windowsill and turned on the machine. As I vacuumed, I couldn't help but feel that I'd missed something important.

I replayed the afternoon's events. Randy and Louise had left around two-thirty for their walk. Carrie turned up about twenty minutes later and it wasn't until around four or four-thirty that we realized Randy had flown the proverbial coop and locked Louise inside the burial chamber. He would have had plenty of time to get to St. Mary's.

But something was really bothering me. Verifying that Randy had a room reservation at Godolphin Court had just meant making a phone call. Yes, Randy had ordered room service, but had it been delivered and *signed* for by Randy, or was it just left outside on a tray?

There was something else. As Carrie had said, Randy had escaped capture for years. Why would he have left his hotel key in his suitcase? Randy was anything but careless. Had he wanted Louise to find it and—just as we all did—draw the conclusion that he was hiding out there?

I'd feel better if I could speak to Becky myself and ask her to check that Randy really was at Godolphin Court. I'd left my mobile on the windowsill with her number in it. I turned off the vacuum cleaner just as I heard the phone ring in reception. Dennis didn't pick up. Then the ringing stopped and began again. Dennis still didn't pick up. I went to reception. It was empty.

When the phone rang a third time, I answered it myself.

It was Patty and her voice was tense. "Thank heavens," she said. "Are you all right?"

I felt an unexpected jolt of alarm. "Yes? Why?"

"Randy isn't at Godolphin Court," she said tightly. "It was all a trick. His room is empty. There was nothing in there at all. No clothes. No passports. Evie." Patty's voice went very quiet. "He must still be at Tregarrick Rock."

I looked around the empty reception room and my throat constricted with fear.

"You've got the boys, though, yes?" Patty asked.

"I . . . I don't know where Dennis is," I said.

"But Sam. You have Sam, don't you?"

"I thought Sam was with you?" I said.

"No," said Patty. "It was just Cador and the four girls who turned up, guns blazing, so to speak."

Thank God. Sam was still on the island, too.

"Sam must be in the annex," I said to Patty.

"Don't go there," said Patty sharply. "Don't leave the hotel. Don't even try to find either of them. Where are you, exactly?"

"In reception," I whispered.

"Does your own office have a lock and key?"

I croaked a yes. I could hardly speak, I was so terrified.

"Go straight there and lock yourself in," said Patty. "We'll get the chopper over as soon as we can."

She rang off.

And then the power went out.

Chapter Twenty-Three

Instinctively, I darted under the hinged countertop and dropped to the floor, scooting into the corner of the back office.

Randy must have disconnected the power in the basement.

My first thought was to send a text for help, but I realized that I had left my mobile on the windowsill in the Residents' Lounge when I'd dashed back to reception to answer Patty's call on the landline.

Where was Dennis? Where was Sam? I felt sick with fear. Every nerve in my body was primed for flight, and yet I knew I had to stay perfectly still.

Then came the sound of footsteps. A beam of light slowly crept toward me along the floor. I shrank farther into the corner, closed my eyes and held my breath.

There was a loud ding on the service bell.

"Evie," said Randy. "I know you're there."

I didn't answer.

Randy must have found a storm lantern. He set it on the counter, where it cast an eerie yellow glow.

I knew he could see me. I could feel his eyes on me.

"I am not going to hurt you, I promise," he said. "I just need your help."

"Where is Dennis?" I managed to say.

"Taking a nap in your darkroom," said Randy. "He'll have a headache, but he'll be okay."

I struggled to stay calm, but I was shaking all over. "How do I know you're speaking the truth?"

"I'll show you if you like," said Randy. "That is, after you've helped me."

I didn't answer.

The silence between us lengthened until Randy said, "Evie? I know you're still there. I told you. Dennis will be fine. Don't make things difficult. It's just the two of us."

But it wasn't just the two of us. Sam was somewhere, too, and given that Randy hadn't mentioned Sam, perhaps he didn't know. I felt a tiny surge of hope.

"Yeah," said Randy. "I saw a group of people heading back to the causeway like the hounds of hell were on their tail."

Of course, it would have been dusk when the party headed for the causeway and hard to see who exactly was who in those identical waterproof capes.

He gave a chuckle. "Louise was right when she said the view from the turret was awesome."

"So that's where you were hiding." I tried to keep my voice steady. "Yes, Cador Ferris came to the rescue with his boat."

"Aw. My timing sucks," said Randy. "I would have liked to have met him."

I took a deep breath. "They all left except for Dennis." I waited for Randy to correct my lie, just to make sure he didn't know that Sam had not gone with the party, but he didn't.

"If you don't come out, I'll just have to come in and join you," Randy said. "We can be nice and cozy together."

"No. It's okay." I scrambled to my feet. Having the counter between us was at least some form of protection. I knew I could get out by the swing door behind me. The corridor would be dark, but I could make a run for my office—or even the annex, but I dismissed the annex idea straightaway. What if Sam wasn't there? I'd be cornered. But then again, if Sam wasn't in the annex, he'd soon realize that there had been a power cut and come and find out what was happening.

I made a decision. It was better to stay in the hotel.

There was a shelf under the countertop where Dennis kept the hotel register, pens, scissors and a silver letter opener. Keeping my hands low and out of Randy's line of vision, I tried to slide the letter opener into the pocket of my jeans. I missed. It fell to the floor with a clatter.

"Seriously, Evie?" Randy leaned in. "Hands on the counter where I can see them."

I did as I was told. My heart was pounding so loudly, I was certain that he could hear it. I was so scared, I felt numb.

"I wasn't doing anything," I lied. "I accidentally knocked something off the shelf. I don't understand what's happening."

"I saw you out on the terrace with Carrie," Randy said quietly.

My heart sank.

"And you don't want to listen to anything my sister says," he went on. "She's schizophrenic. Been in a mental health facility since she was a teenager."

"Why did you tell me she was dead?" I said. "That was a wicked thing to do."

"The Carrie I grew up with *is* dead," said Randy. "I'm sure you can relate to that. I bet your relationship with your sister is nothing like it used to be when you were kids. People change."

For a split second I faltered. It was true. Carrie had appeared unbalanced and hysterical and Margot and I had only heard her side of the story.

"Despite what Carrie may have said or what you may think about me, I'm not a killer," said Randy. "I haven't hurt anyone."

But I knew that this was patently untrue. "You just admitted to me that you hurt Dennis," I said. "And what about Louise, to say nothing of what you did to Ollie and Jerry."

"I have no idea what you're talking about with Ollie and Jerry," said Randy. "As for Louise, I knew you'd find her eventually. She was perfectly safe in there."

Randy's blue-eyed gaze held mine. I didn't look away, but my fists were clenched so hard, I could feel the nails cutting into my flesh.

"So it's just you and me," said Randy. "We're all alone."

I offered a prayer for Sam to reappear but said, "Yes. Just you and me."

Randy studied my face in the yellow light of the storm lantern. "What's going on in that little head of yours?" he said.

"I already know that the cops are on their way back from St. Mary's, but we've still got plenty of time."

"Your Godolphin Court diversion didn't work," I said.

Randy laughed. "Of course it worked. I just wanted everyone out of the way. Now I need a boat."

"But you know we don't have one," I said. "To be honest, I thought that swimming was more your thing."

"Yeah, well, I would have done that had the tide not been so high, and had there not been, what do you call it—mizzle? I didn't want to get lost in that. Anyway, I should have been more specific. I don't need a boat. I want that dinghy."

I hoped my face didn't betray my elation. How far would Randy get before the dinghy began to take on water? Certainly not to St. Mary's. He'd be lucky if he made it across the sound.

"Where is the outboard engine?" Randy demanded.

"It's in the dinghy," I said. "Ollie put it in there to weigh it down before the storm hit."

"Right, let's go," said Randy.

"Why did you kill Ollie?" I said. "At least tell me that."

Randy actually laughed. "Is that what you think, Evie?"

"That's what the *police* think," I lied. "And you will get caught. You have to know that. Isn't it better to turn yourself in?"

Randy still seemed stuck on Ollie. "The police really think I killed that kid?"

Keep him talking, Evie. Where the hell was Sam?

"Why did you meet Ollie at Godolphin Court?" I asked.

"It was a coincidence," said Randy.

"But you *did* speak to him," I insisted.

Randy gave a heavy sigh. "I told you. We talked about me

visiting the other islands. Nothing more. He detected my accent and knew I was a tourist. The minute Becky's dad walked into the lobby, it was obvious that there was no love lost between them."

"You saw them argue?" I said.

"I didn't hang around, and I'm not hanging around here, either. Let's go," he said again.

"You don't need me," I said. "You know where the dinghy is."

"Yeah. But I don't know if you're telling the truth about the outboard engine," said Randy. "And to be honest, you're beginning to piss me off."

The truth was that although I knew the dinghy was still there, it could be just a limp pile of rubber by now.

Quickly, I spun around, kicked the swing door open and darted out of the back office.

But Randy was faster.

He must have vaulted over the counter, because he caught me in the dark corridor and threw me to the floor.

I fought hard, kicking out with all my strength, but he overpowered me in seconds. I screamed blue murder, but no one seemed to hear me.

"Stop all this, Evie," Randy said wearily. "I like you. Just come with me to the dinghy, and then I'll let you go. I promise."

Defeated, I gave in.

Randy left the storm lantern behind and picked up a flashlight. Together, we left the hotel and descended the steep, narrow steps down to the causeway. The heavy dark clouds from earlier had passed to show the moon. I prayed that help would soon be on its way.

It was awkward trying to go down the steps side by side, but Randy didn't loosen his grip on my arm. We took the last step into the shadow of the bluff. For a moment I couldn't see the dinghy up on the ledge at all, and felt a wave of panic.

But Randy shone his flashlight and there it was. Still inflated, too! Though hopefully not sturdy enough to go far.

"This is where we say goodbye," said Randy. "Evie, I never meant for anyone to get hurt."

"You hurt Jerry," I said.

"I didn't touch Jerry." Randy shook his head. "That was an accident."

"Locking Louise in the burial chamber wasn't," I said.

"But you found her," said Randy simply.

"She was in love with you."

"All women love me, Evie. But Louise is a gold digger. She got what she deserved. Besides, she was becoming annoying with all her simpering neediness, and I abhor any form of drugs."

"Why are you telling me this?" I said.

"Because I'm not a bad person," he said. "I don't trade in stocks. I trade in greed. If people are desperate to take high risks, why should I care if they lose?"

"But what about those who dream of finding treasure or getting their movie made?" I said. "Those people who are willing to trust you with their life savings?"

Randy didn't answer. "Tell me one thing: How did Carrie find me?"

"Instagram hashtags," I said. "It seems that Carrie discovered Mister Tig had an account."

"But of course." Randy gave a wry grin. "I knew I shouldn't

have trusted that cat. Help me launch the dinghy and then you can go."

I'd be a fool to believe him and I didn't.

I saw my chance. I knew he wouldn't be able to hold me and move the dinghy, too.

The minute that Randy loosened his grip, I bolted for the steps. But Randy didn't follow.

Halfway up, I knew I was safe.

Panting, I reached the top and stepped out onto the flagstone terrace. The lights from the hotel were ablaze. I was badly shaken, but I was safe. Everything was going to be okay now.

"Evie," came a voice. "Thank God you're all right. I've been looking everywhere for you."

It was Sam.

Chapter Twenty-Four

Sam pulled me into his arms, and I let him. I was overwhelmed with relief. I felt emotionally and physically exhausted.

"Where's Dennis?" I said.

"Out looking for you," said Sam. "We split up. He went north."

"Thank God he's all right," I exclaimed.

"Got a pretty nasty blow to the back of his head and a bruised ego," said Sam. "But you know Dennis. He never seems to get upset. And yeah, I found him when I went down to the basement to switch the power back on—Jesus. You're shaking like a leaf. Are you sure you're okay?"

I pushed him away. "Fine. Honestly."

"Do you want to tell me what happened?" Sam asked.

I gave him the short version.

"Randy won't get far," I said. "He's taken Ollie's dinghy. It's got a slow puncture. He might make it across the causeway to Tregarrick—"

"But he could also come back." Sam looked worried. "It's just as well I didn't go with the others."

"Why didn't you?" I said.

"I had a bad feeling about leaving you guys," said Sam. "I had a hunch that Randy might still be on the island. If he's evaded capture for so long, he's smart enough to double back. The four girls had Cador and the police waiting on St. Mary's. Here, it was just you and Dennis."

"Well, you were right," I said. "And I'm glad you are here."

"Not quite how I expected a reunion with my old buddy to be, that's for sure," said Sam. He began to talk about the wreck in the sound, and the syndicate, but I wasn't listening. I was too freaked out about Randy. There were so many uninhabited rocky islets for him to hide and wait it out. Until Randy was caught, this was far from over.

"We need to tell the police about the dinghy," I said.

"We'll do all that at the hotel. Let's get inside." Sam put his arm around my shoulders as we crossed the flagstone terrace to the main entrance. I should have felt comforted by the lights blazing from the windows, but all I could think about was how Randy could very well get away.

"I can't believe that you didn't hear my screams," I said. "I really thought Randy was going to kill me."

"You can't hear a thing from the annex," said Sam. "I didn't even know that the power was out until I reached the terrace and the hotel was in darkness. When I couldn't find Dennis, either, I knew something was wrong. And I was right."

We entered reception. It was empty and felt hollow. I was glad of Sam's company.

"Did Dennis take the walkie-talkies?" I said. "We need to tell him that you found me."

Sam hesitated. "No. But we should take them. If Dennis isn't back at the annex, then we'll have to go out and look for him."

My heart sank. There was no way I wanted to be roaming the island in the dark. I also didn't want to be waiting in an empty hotel while Sam was out looking for Dennis, especially if Randy really was going to reappear like in some nightmare horror film.

Sam must have guessed by my expression. "Dennis suggested we rendezvous at the annex. It's not so exposed as the hotel."

"I have to get my mobile," I said. "I need to call Margot and I'm positive she'll have been trying to reach me. I left it in the Residents' Lounge."

"Go and get it. I'll call the police about the dinghy, pick up the walkie-talkies—where are they?"

"In the drawer under the counter in reception." I left Sam to make the call and went to look for my phone. I could have sworn I'd left it on the windowsill, but it wasn't there after all.

I returned just as Sam was putting the phone down. "All sorted. They're on it." He brandished the walkie-talkies and gave one to me. "Let's go."

Sam steered me out of the hotel. "Look. I think you should wait in my room. You've got the walkie-talkie. And to take your mind off things, you can look at the cutlass. The markings are really interesting."

I didn't answer. Looking at a bath full of muddy water was the last thing on my mind.

We reached the annex, went down the steps and entered the gloomy corridor. "Dennis!" Sam called out. "Hey! I found her! I've got Evie. She's okay."

There was no reply. The sight of the crime scene tape criss-crossed over Ollie's door gave me the creeps. A peculiar prickle ran up my spine. Something felt off. I suddenly didn't want to be down here with Sam anymore, but he'd already opened the door to his bedroom, stepped inside and flipped the light switch.

I hung back in the corridor. "What time did Dennis make for the rendezvous?"

Sam checked his watch. "On the half hour. We just missed the last one. Would you rather I stayed here and waited with you?"

I hesitated. Was I going crazy? Why did I feel so uneasy?

"No, I'll be fine," I said, and stepped into the bedroom. I noticed it had been tidied. The bed was made and clothes had been put away.

"Check the radio frequency," said Sam. So we did. "I'll be back as soon as I can. Hopefully, with Dennis." He pointed to the "Dive Truk Lagoon" poster above the chest of drawers. "You should come out there one day."

"I'm not great underwater," I said.

"A lot of people feel that way at first." Sam gestured to the low armchair in the corner. "Make yourself comfortable. The cutlass is in the bath."

I nodded but made no move to go and look. I'd already decided that the minute Sam left, I would go back to the flat. I didn't like it here.

Sam pointed to the shallow print tray on the chest of drawers. "Cutlery is in there. Protective gloves are on the side. Right,
I'm off. Are you sure you're going to be okay? Do you want
something to drink? Tea? Wine?"

"No, really, I'm fine." I showed him my walkie-talkie. "Got
this."

Sam left, leaving the door ajar. As I waited for his footsteps
to fade away, I took in the room and my eye caught a tall, narrow mailing tube propped in the corner. It had to be at least
three and a half feet, maybe four, in length. I recognized the
name Pegasus Couriers in the document sleeve stuck to the
side.

Curious, I took a closer look. For a wild moment I thought
it was the package that Ollie had picked up with mine and that
had been missing—especially as this one had also been mailed
from "Sam in F.S.M." to himself, exactly as Kevin had told me
when I'd followed up on Saturday. But that couldn't be right.
The tube was far too narrow to house a Bazooka water-blast
pistol. This one was poster-size.

I stepped back to think and scanned the room, my eyes
stopping on the "Dive Truk Lagoon" poster. I felt a shiver of
foreboding. There was something menacing about the ghostly
submarine in the image, surrounded by dark blue water. I moved
closer to study the small print underneath the tagline. It said
Underwater Heritage Site. Something told me that was important, but I couldn't figure out why.

Frustrated, I turned away, thinking I had given Sam long
enough to have left the annex, but then I saw something on the

nightstand next to the door. Under his neatly folded red-and-white striped tie was a paperback book with a red-and-cream cover, *The Complete Book of Emigrants in Bondage, 1614–1775*.

Wasn't this the book that Sam had talked about at dinner? The one that listed the names of the ships and the convicts who had sailed on them? I had expected a tattered hardback book since Sam had said this book was difficult to find, yet this copy seemed almost new. I flicked through it, searching for the *Isadora*.

When I saw the name of the ship listed in the index, I was surprised at how excited I felt. I turned to the page number, and a slip of paper fluttered to the floor. I couldn't be certain, but it looked like a receipt from Amazon.

Dropping down to pick it up, I saw a woman's gold earring peeping out from under the bed. As far as I knew, no one other than Sam and Ollie had used the staff accommodation since last October.

But it wasn't an earring.

It was a gold dental cap—just like Ollie's.

My stomach turned over.

Derek had said the blow to Ollie's face had been so severe that it had knocked out a tooth. With a start, I realized Ollie had been in here.

Just as fast, it registered that Dennis would never have gone out looking for me on the island without taking a walkie-talkie. I should have known that. He was meticulous to a fault.

This was a trap.

I spun around and bumped straight into Sam. I hadn't heard

him return, but now I realized he must have retraced his steps on tiptoe. Maybe he hadn't even left the building. He could have been watching me through the crack in the door all the time.

It took everything in my power to keep calm. I closed my fist over the gold cap and waved the book at him. "This is fascinating stuff," I said with forced gaiety. "I found the *Isadora* listed. I can see how easy it is to get caught up in this."

Sam stepped toward me, forcing me to back into the room. He kicked the door shut behind him.

"No luck finding Dennis, I assume?" I knew I was jabbering, but at the same time, I was weighing my options. A swift kick to Sam's manhood would be a start, but I needed him away from the door to do that.

"Dennis isn't coming," said Sam. "He's still locked in your darkroom." He held out his hand. "What have you got there, Evie?"

I thrust the book at him. "This, you mean?"

"Not that." His expression darkened and his eyes were cold. "In your other hand."

"I don't know what—" I gave a yelp of pain as Sam grabbed my wrist and prised Ollie's tooth out of my closed fist.

The gold cap fell to the floor. Without releasing my hand, Sam ducked down, scooped it up and stared at it.

"It's just an earring," I said.

Sam continued to stare at the tiny piece of gold in his hand until the truth dawned on him and he knew that I knew.

"Poor Ollie," whispered Sam. "He should have minded his own damn business. It wasn't addressed to him. He just had to look."

And then it hit me. Ollie had been killed right in this room. I felt as if my knees would buckle under, but I forced myself not to panic.

"I have no idea what you're talking about." It was a dumb thing to say, but I decided I'd play dumb. Surely the fact that Sam had suggested I wait in his room while he looked for Dennis meant that he hadn't figured out that I knew.

I could feel Sam's eyes on me. He gave a heavy sigh. "It really didn't have to end this way."

"I honestly don't have a clue about what you mean," I lied as my heart began to pound even harder.

Sam gave a bitter laugh. "I'd had a hunch, but I couldn't be sure. And I like you, Evie, but really? Why make such a big deal about the water pistol for my godson? Oh, and yeah—'Please use my darkroom, Randy,'" he mimicked. "'We can get a much better look at the artifacts in there.'"

"Sorry. Still not clear what you're getting at," I lied again.

"You want me to spell it out?" When I didn't answer, he added, "You knew what you would see under your magnifying glass. The details. The markings . . ." His voice trailed away and I followed his gaze over to the "Dive Truk Lagoon" poster and the *Underwater Heritage* tagline.

And then it all fell into place.

"It's not a seventeenth-century cutlass, is it?" I said quietly. "It's a twentieth-century Japanese sword."

"Clever you!" Sam smirked. "The correct name is Showato. Would you like a history lesson? All Japanese officers were required to wear a sword. But to supply such a large number of swords the traditional way during wartime was damn near impossible. They used other materials, quicker methods. The tang was stamped to indicate the sword was inferior. They're confiscated in Japan now, but trust me, elsewhere, they're a collector's dream."

I was stunned. "You found this in Truk Lagoon and smuggled it out?"

"It was from the *Fumizuki*," said Sam with pride. "A destroyer. Sunk by American aircraft on February 18, 1944."

"And the cutlery?" I asked.

"Circa 1942. U.S. military issue."

"And to smuggle it out . . . oh." I stopped mid-sentence as I understood the significance of the extra-long mailing tube.

It was the perfect size to transport a Japanese sword.

There was never any Bazooka water-blast pistol for Sam's godson.

No wonder Sam panicked when he found out that Ollie was going to Pegasus Couriers. It was me who had told Ollie that Sam's package was a water pistol, and Ollie, who had always wanted one, just couldn't help himself. He had to see it.

"He shouldn't have opened it," said Sam, as if reading my mind.

I was horrified. "But . . . you could have talked your way out of it," I protested.

"You think I didn't try that first?" Sam shook his head. "The little shit tried to blackmail me and when I refused, he turned nasty."

"He was just a kid!" I exclaimed.

"He was a manipulative bastard with a temper," said Sam.

I remembered the mark on Sam's jawline. "Ollie hit you, didn't he?"

"Yeah. You could say that," said Sam. "He came at me swinging the fire extinguisher."

"But . . . but how much money did Ollie want?" I was still grappling with this extraordinary turn of events.

"A thousand quid."

I looked at Sam in astonishment. "You killed Ollie for a thousand pounds?"

Sam didn't answer.

My heart began to race again. I was trapped in Sam's bedroom. Dennis was still locked in my darkroom. Patty had said she'd send the chopper as soon as she could. I had to stay calm and keep Sam talking. I had to play for time.

"I'm curious," I said. "Did you meet Ollie at the causeway?"

"Yep," said Sam. "He needed help with carrying all the stuff, so I obliged."

"But why didn't you come straight to the hotel?" I said. "Kim was waiting for the groceries for dinner that night."

"I didn't know the stuff was for Kim until she was asking me if I'd seen Ollie and that he had something for her," said Sam.

"So what did you do with the shopping?" *Other than a handful of cherry tomatoes*, I wanted to say.

"I threw the bag out of Ollie's bathroom window," said Sam. "There's a gap between the annex wall and the hillside."

"But I'm just not clear on something," I said. "When did you and Ollie have this . . . altercation?"

"You really want to know?" Sam didn't wait for my answer.

It was as if he wanted to tell me everything. "Let me think. Ollie got back to Tregarrick with the boat around six-fifteen. We went straight back to Ollie's room in the annex. He was in a filthy mood over Becky's dad and then, out of the blue, he suddenly wants to try out the water pistol."

"He'd already opened it?" I said.

"Yeah. When Ollie went to make a coffee in the kitchen, I saw that the tube had been tampered with," said Sam. "He must have done so on the boat coming back, but I just didn't know what he planned on doing with the information. He came here. We had a . . . discussion . . . and you know the rest."

I took a deep breath and forced myself to ask the question. "So . . . all this happened . . . before dinner?"

"Yep," said Sam. "It was surprisingly quick. Then I joined you all for dinner."

I was so shocked, it took me a moment to speak. "You left Ollie *dead* in your room all night?"

"In the bathroom, actually," said Sam.

I was still trying to come to grips with the horrible fact that Ollie had been in the annex the whole time. It would never have occurred to me to check Sam's room.

"Fortunately, I remembered you had a wheelbarrow," Sam went on.

"So it was you who went into my potting shed," I whispered.

"And the pair of us went for a little predawn jaunt to the Mermaid Lagoon."

I gasped. "You . . . you actually put Ollie's body into the wheelbarrow!"

Sam nodded. "The path to the lagoon is a bit steep, I admit," Sam went on. "But there's an overhang that—"

"You tipped Ollie out and he fell into the sea." I was horrified.

"I just miscalculated the riptide and currents in the sound. I thought he'd merrily join the Gulf Stream and be on his way to Mexico by now."

"And our boat? The *Sandpiper*? What did you do with that?" I asked.

"Oh, I dealt with that before dinner, too," said Sam. "While everyone was getting changed, I nipped back to the causeway. Took the boat around the point, shoved the throttle forward and jumped overboard." My expression seemed to amuse him. "What? You think Randy is the only good swimmer around here? I spend my life in the water for a living."

"But what about the spare boat key?" I said. "I saw it in Ollie's room after dinner. Then, in the morning, it was gone."

"Yeah, that was a mistake," said Sam. "You could say that I was in a bit of a rush to move the boat and when I got down to the causeway, I realized I had forgotten it. Luckily, there was another key in the glove box. The next morning, I was cleaning Ollie's room and tossed the spare out of the bathroom window."

"But you didn't clean up everything," I said. "You missed the receipt for the co-op."

He smirked. "No one's perfect."

I had to ask. "It was you who disconnected the ground rod, wasn't it?" I said quietly. "You had hoped that it would have been me who touched it, not Jerry."

"In all fairness, I didn't expect it to be fatal, and I'm pretty upset over Jerry even though he could be a pain," said Sam. "I just didn't want you using that darkroom."

"Because it would be obvious that those artifacts were not from the *Isadora* and Randy would know."

"Correct," said Sam. "I'm not going to jail, Evie. Have you any idea what they do to people like me?"

I had a good idea. Jails in the Western Pacific were notoriously bad, and once Sam's dealings on the black market came to light, his punishment would be swift and brutal.

He stood there watching my face. I tried to pretend I wasn't afraid of him, but as the extent of his treachery began to sink in, I was terrified. I *had* to keep Sam talking. I *had* to play for time. Even if he hadn't made that call to the police about the dinghy, I knew my sister would have been trying to reach me to make sure I was okay. Help would be coming. I had to believe that.

"You know I can't let you go, Evie," said Sam. "I'm truly sorry. I'll make it quick, though." In a flash he'd snatched up the red-and-white striped tie, snapped it free and wrapped it around my neck.

Desperately, I tried to pull it off, flinging myself from side to side.

"Don't fight me!" Sam panted as the noose grew tighter. "Just relax."

I saw the shallow print tray and managed to edge my way over. Lights began to dance behind my eyes, but I groped blindly into the solution, not caring if it would burn my hand.

I reached out, my fingers inches from the edge, and managed

to tip it over. I found the fork and, with lightning speed, plunged it into Sam's cheek.

He screamed, loosened his grip and fell backwards onto the bed.

I pitched forward and half crawled, half dragged myself into the bathroom and closed the door, fumbling for the dead bolt. It slid across and for a split second I felt safe. The pain in my throat was unbearable. Every breath hurt. I tried to steady my shaking hands, will my heart to slow down. *Help's coming*, I whispered to myself. It was then that I noticed the dark green duffle bag set against the bathtub on the floor. It was unzipped, but I could see clothing. Sam had been packing for his own getaway. He knew the island so well and there were so many places for him to hide.

I was struck by the sobering thought that, if I died, everyone would blame Randy.

For a moment there was no noise from the room beyond. It was deadly quiet, but I knew he was there.

Finally, a tap. "Evie, don't be silly," he said. "Come on, open the door."

I sat against it, hunched over, clasping my knees in abject terror. There was absolutely no escape. The frosted bathroom window was far too small for me to get out.

I stared at the murky bathwater. I did not know what solvent he had used, but I had touched the liquid from the print tray and still had all my fingers.

I braced myself for pain and plunged my hand into the water. I pulled out the sword, half expecting to see it clean and covered with Japanese markings, but it was still coated in crud.

The "cleaning solution" was just muddy water.

"Evie!" Sam bellowed. "Open this damn door!" He began to kick it. I watched, frozen in terror.

I only had one chance.

The panel began to splinter. I stood to one side, grasped one hand on the door handle and the other on the sword.

Swiftly, I undid the bolt and yanked the door open.

Caught off balance, Sam tumbled in and fell straight onto the blade. It went right through.

I didn't stop to see if he would live or die. I just dropped the sword and ran.

As I stumbled up the terrace steps, I was struck by dazzling lights and the comforting *wump, wump, wump* of a police chopper attempting to land on our terrace.

Crouching down beside the potting shed, I watched the long line of blooming flowers in my stone planters get shredded by the downdraught.

Margot was right. We really needed a helipad.

Chapter Twenty-Five

Margot was making my breakfast for the second morning in a row. She'd also cooked me lunch and supper, too, and had been fussing constantly.

"I'm not an invalid, you know," I said. "But I could get used to this."

"It's my way of showing how much I love you," said Margot. "And you are an invalid. You practically lost your hand." She pointed to my heavily bandaged paw.

"Perhaps I should get you one of those pinafores that Kim wears when she cleans," I teased. "Then you'll really look like a 1930s housewife."

Margot topped up my coffee and sat down herself. "Evie, I don't think I will ever get over the horror I felt when we got to Godolphin Court and Randy's room was empty. I thought . . . I thought you were . . ."

"Dead, I know you did," I said gently.

"And then when you came staggering into reception with

your hair all a mess and those marks on your throat and—" Her eyes filled with tears. "There was so much blood . . ."

"Most of it wasn't mine," I pointed out. "I didn't even know I'd grasped the blade of the sword first. Honestly, I'm fine."

Well, that was a bit of a stretch. Every bone in my body ached and I was covered in bruises.

"I can't believe that Sam was trafficking artifacts," Margot said. "Patty told me that he could have easily got ten grand for that Japanese sword. I know I go on about motive and all that, and that's a lot, but not enough to kill someone for."

"Sam was terrified of being jailed in Micronesia," I said. "Punishment is severe and the conditions are notoriously appalling."

"Of course." Margot nodded. "Do you remember that movie *Midnight Express*?"

"Yes, I do. It was horrible." I gave my sister an indulgent smile. "You and your movies."

"So why not just give Ollie the thousand pounds and be done with it?" Margot mused. "I mean, he could afford to, right? We know that Sam stood to inherit some money from his mother's estate."

"I thought the same. Sam told me that he tried to reason with Ollie, but Ollie wouldn't have any of it," I said. "And then they fought and it was too late. I also think he felt the net was closing in."

Margot raised a quizzical eyebrow. "How come?"

"He didn't expect Cador to come back to see the *Virago*," I said. "Cador would have known immediately that, even under all that crud, the artifacts Sam was trying to pass off as belonging to the *Isadora* were fakes."

"You should have seen Cador's face when he realized Randy wasn't there and you were in danger!" Margot said. "He insisted on coming in the police chopper with Patty. Rather sweet, actually." She checked her watch. "Speaking of Patty, she should be here any minute. She wants to see us."

"That sounds ominous," I said.

"I saw a different side of Patty when she realized that Randy had tricked us," said Margot. "She was frantic and kept blaming herself."

There was a tap on the door.

"It's open!" Margot called out.

Patty stepped inside, balancing a paper bag on top of a large rectangular box marked Pegasus Couriers. "Blueberry muffins," she said. "All the way from my kitchen. I always seem to be eating your food—now you can eat mine. And this, Evie, is for you."

It was my camera equipment. "But . . . where did you find it?" I demanded.

"Hidden under Sam's bed," said Patty. "I hope nothing is broken."

She joined us at the kitchen table while Margot got her a plate and poured her a cup of coffee.

I ate a second breakfast. The blueberry muffins were delicious.

"And speaking of finding things," said Patty. "When we did a sweep of the annex both inside and out, we discovered a mound of rotting vegetables in the gap outside Ollie's bathroom window along with a boat key marked Spare. Thank you, Evie, for telling us where to look."

"It adds new meaning to 'tossing the salad,'" Margot said with a grin.

"Tests also showed that the small fire extinguisher in the annex kitchen had blood on the pressure gauge that proved to be Ollie's," Patty went on. "Sam claimed that, in the scuffle, Ollie attacked him with it but fell and hit his face. That's how Ollie lost his tooth."

"There was something else I wanted to ask," I said. "Did you ever find out what Ollie was doing after he left the co-op with the groceries and before he departed St. Mary's harbor in the *Sandpiper*?"

"Ollie had a very long conversation with Stephanie on the phone," said Patty. "She told us he was furious with Becky's father. It turns out that Becky was very jealous of Ollie's friendship with his ex, but she had no reason to be. Even so, Ollie kept their conversations a secret because—and I quote from Stephanie—'he didn't want to rock the boat with Becky.'" Patty grinned. "I'm glad I'm not that age anymore. So much drama!"

"So there was nothing sordid and Sam had lied about overhearing an X-rated conversation," I said. "Didn't he think we'd check? I told you that his water-pistol idea was spur of the moment."

"Sam does have a godson, by the way," said Patty. "But his birthday is in June."

"That toy would never have fit into a mailing tube designed for a poster, which must have been what aroused Ollie's curiosity in the first place," I said. "And then Sam didn't secure the potting shed door properly after using my wheelbarrow, or close the bathroom window."

Patty nodded. "You'd be surprised at just how many stupid mistakes criminals usually make unless they are true professionals, like Randy Campbell—or should I say Noah Charles McClean?"

Margot and I exchanged looks. "Tell us everything," I said.

"Actually, Randy Campbell is just one of his many identities," Patty went on. "You've heard of a Ponzi scheme, I take it?"

"Yes," I said. "It's a fraudulent investment scam that generates returns for earlier investors with money taken from later investors."

Margot regarded me with surprise.

I grinned. "I looked up the official definition."

"I couldn't have said it better myself." Patty grinned, too. "Well, our Randy had been running a Ponzi scheme for almost a decade, which is an astonishing accomplishment. Most Ponzi schemes collapse after six months, or a year at most. We don't yet know the extent of how much he's swindled out of those poor sods who fell for his charms. We're thinking it's at least fifteen million pounds."

Fifteen million pounds!

"Poor Louise," I said. "Do you think she will ever see any of her money back?"

"It's unlikely, but that's out of my jurisdiction now," said

Patty. "What about your movie, Margot? I read *Lighthouse of Sorrow* at your recommendation, by the way. It's a good story. A tad depressing . . . does everyone have to die at the end?"

"As it turned out, the author, Ernest Potter, has been in a memory care home for the last six months and his nephew has power of attorney," said Margot. "He demanded an outrageous sum of money and, with Louise out of the picture now, it was easy to say no." Margot looked at me. "And honestly, I'm fine with that decision."

"How is Louise?" Patty asked.

"Bounced back as always," said Margot. "She's a survivor."

"Where did you pick Randy up, by the way?" I asked Patty.

"He only got as far as Tregarrick. When we arrested him—or should I say, rescued him, since the dinghy was underwater by that point—tucked in his rucksack was *another* hotel key. This was for the Bluebell Guesthouse on St. Mary's. Apparently he checked in there a week ago and kept the room for ten days. He'd registered as a Frank Abagnale—a name that is a complete mystery to me."

Margot laughed. "How unoriginal. Didn't you see the film *Catch Me If You Can* starring Leonardo DiCaprio?"

"And catch him we have," said Patty. "Locked in his room safe at the Bluebell Guesthouse were six passports under different identities, a laptop computer and a second mobile phone. We found out that *Frank* was booked on the Penzance to Dublin flight that would have departed yesterday morning."

"*Dublin?*" Margot was confused. "Why on earth would he want to go to Dublin?"

"It's known as the Dublin loop," said Patty. "There are a number of nonstop flights from Dublin to the U.S.A. Immigration is done in Dublin, so once Randy arrived in the States, he would have been free and clear."

"But what about Louise?" I asked.

"They were always going home separately," said Margot. "They would have traveled to Penzance together and from there, she would have returned to California and Randy—"

"Was heading to Boston," I declared.

"Yes. How did you guess?" Patty seemed impressed.

"He told us he was training for the Boston Marathon," I said. Margot nodded.

"Oh—and remember Randy's two truths and a lie?" said Patty. "He won two Ironmans, not three." Patty took a sip of coffee. "But his sister was right. Randy was not a killer. Sam, though . . ." She shook her head. "Just when you think you know someone."

Patty focused on finishing the crumbs on her plate. It was obvious that she was upset about Sam.

"People change," Margot said.

"He was so darn cute when he was sixteen." She forced a smile. "You should have seen him and Cador together, with their talk of wrecks and treasure. All my friends were crazy for them." Patty bit her lip and shook her head, as if to dispel the memory. "Sam has been smuggling artifacts out of Chuuk for a long time," she went on. "Always by mail and always to himself in a mailing tube. I had a chance to talk to him before he was deported. He told me that he never meant to hurt Ollie or you—especially Jerry." She went very quiet before adding, "One of the first homicide detectives I met on the job told me that everyone is capable of murder. *Everyone.* I guess that Sam just snapped."

"Speaking of being deported," said Margot. "Were you really going to report Louise to immigration?"

Patty looked blank.

"Louise's first marriage?"

"Oh, *that*." Patty laughed. "Actually, I didn't know anything about her first marriage. It was a bluff, but I knew that she was hiding something by the way she reacted to Sam's story about the woman who was deported for bigamy."

Margot gave a nod. "I told you so, Evie."

"But what about her prescription drugs?" I said. "The ecstasy?"

"I'm sure I don't know what you mean." Patty's eyes widened in mock innocence. "Everyone has secrets," she went on. "I always find that, by pretending I know, people can't help but give themselves away, and that's exactly what she did. And let's not forget Kevin Bacon and Bacon's Law."

"Hollywood Kevin Bacon?" I asked.

Margot groaned. "That theory has been going around forever. Apparently everyone is connected by six degrees of separation."

"And it's true," said Patty. "It was just a case of joining up the dots. I'd show you my mind map, but I think you can imagine it for yourselves. Ollie stealing the sapphire-and-diamond cross led us to searching his room—and, by accident, finding Sam's stolen artifacts. Ollie's need for money unfortunately provoked Sam to commit murder. Sam's determination to get money from Randy's imaginary fund—trying to scam a scammer, no less—set him at odds with his cousin Jerry, who had loaned him money. Kim's proficiency on Instagram alerted Carrie to Randy's whereabouts and the rest, as they say, is history."

"And speaking of Jerry?" I said. "His death doesn't quite fit Bacon's Law, does it?"

"Yes and no," said Patty. "Jerry was collateral damage."

"And me? Where do I fit in?" said Margot.

"Your book, of course. It all started with the *Lighthouse of Sorrow*," Patty said. "I'll be off now. I'll see you on Saturday. Vicar Bill is holding the sea tractor for me down at the causeway."

. . .

The open house was a resounding success. It was a perfect day with a cloudless blue sky, and the intoxicating scent of daffodils and narcissi with exotic names like golden Mary, Scilly white, golden spur, Soleil d'Or and cheerfulness filled the air.

In the background the jazz trio that Kim had booked played 1930s music. They had already agreed to perform twice a month in the hotel dining room. We'd also hired a handful of men and women to help with the catering and, thanks to Kim's skills as a seamstress, they were all dressed as 1930s waitstaff. This thirties theme was proving very popular. Many of our guests had got into the spirit and dressed in period, too—including Margot and me.

The art exhibition featuring local artists and crafts was working well and had produced far more sales than we'd expected.

We resolved to make it an annual event. I still couldn't believe we'd got it ready in time.

These past few days, Dennis, Kim, Cador, Margot and I had all worked like demons to get the hotel painted, the new carpet put down and the artwork on the walls. I asked Cador about his friendship with Sam, but all he said was that what had happened between them was so long ago and that the only history he was interested in was one that involved Spanish galleons. I was happy with putting Sam safely in the past, too.

As Margot and I stood in the Residents' Lounge next to the open doors that led to the terrace, where our guests were mingling, I couldn't help thinking how lucky we were. In spite of the devastating events of the past week, we'd done it. The hotel was now officially open and Margot and I were able to start our new life at last.

"Here's Cador looking his usual godlike self," said Margot.

We turned to greet him. I felt an unexpected jolt of pleasure as he smiled and headed toward us. Dressed in jeans and a white button-down shirt, he seemed relaxed and cheerful. In one hand was a glass of Holy Vale pinot noir.

Margot winked. "I'll leave you to it."

I suddenly felt nervous. "No. Stay."

"You are allowed to look at other men, you know," she said gently. "Robert wouldn't have wanted you to be a nun for the rest of your life." She left, muttering something about leaving the iron on.

"Was it something I said?" Cador gestured to Margot's departing back.

"Margot needed to check on the wine," I lied. "Wasn't today the day you were supposed to hear from your investors?"

"I did. About an hour ago." Cador beamed. "The company will be called Trident Explorers."

I raised my glass in a toast. "That's wonderful! Congratulations."

"It wasn't easy, though," said Cador. "One of the investors is all about names. He would prefer it if the treasure of the *Isadora* belonged to a king—or, at the very least, a nobleman. I told him I don't have any passenger names."

I gasped. "But I do!" I couldn't stop grinning. "Wait right here."

I hurried to the newly arranged bookshelves, where I'd added Sam's *The Complete Book of Emigrants in Bondage, 1614–1775* to the collection.

Handing the book to Cador, I said, "You can start with Jessica Tully-Paulette, or should I say Countess Tully-Paulette." I went on to tell Cador all about poor Jessica's fate and how she was deported on the *Isadora* for bigamy. Cador was ecstatic. He grabbed me by the shoulders and gave me a hug. I felt my face grow warm.

Kim, carrying her iPhone, came over to join us. She'd styled her hair close to her head and looked very chic in her Pic-Wic uniform.

"Can I take some photos for Mister Tig's Instagram account?" she said.

"I've been meaning to tell you how impressed I was with your hashtag skills," said Cador. "If it weren't for you, that Australian con man would still be free."

At that moment a black-and-white tuxedo cat came ambling toward us, tail held high.

"Me?" Kim feigned surprise. "I had nothing to do with it." She leaned down and scooped up Mister Tig. "It was this clever kitty."

"Ah yes, of course," said Cador. "How could I possibly forget? We must never, ever underestimate that cat."

Acknowledgments

One of the best things about finishing a book is having the opportunity to thank everyone who has played such a valuable part in the process. It is always the last thing I do and always takes me forever to do it. What if I forget to reveal what is fact and what is fiction, or leave someone special out?

Fact or Fiction:
Tregarrick Rock does not exist. It is a mash-up of Tresco, one of five inhabited islands in the Isles of Scilly, and the fabulous Art Deco Burgh Island Hotel at Bigbury-on-Sea in Devon. I encourage a visit to either. You won't be disappointed.

The *Virago* does not exist although dozens of other shipwrecks surrounding the islands do. For further reading I highly recommend *Built on Scilly: The History of Shipbuilding on the Isles of Scilly Between 1774 & 1891*, by Richard Larn O.B.E. and Roger Banfield.

George Goodchild (b. December 1, 1888-d. March 25, 1969), a prolific writer during the Golden Age of detective fiction, was very real. I was fortunate to meet his daughter, Diana Swayne (a vibrant 103), and granddaughter, Sandra Cooper, who have entrusted me with Goodchild's Imperial Model 60 typewriter. I can't type on it, but its very presence summons the creative muse.

With every book I write, I like to introduce an unusual skill or a profession I know nothing about. To that end I must thank my wonderful nephew, James "Jimmy" Beardsmore, of Beardsmore Veasey Electrical Contractors (BVEC), for educating me in all things electrical. I can now speak with authority on amps and ground rods. I also know how not to get electrocuted.

I am indebted to Detective Inspector Steve Davies, for his generosity in giving me an insight into what it means to be a real homicide detective in southwest England. Any inaccuracies in police procedure are entirely my own.

As always, I am grateful to Gill Knight, who provided the inspiration for the Island Sisters mysteries; to Rachel Young, who makes me feel so welcome when I visit Tresco; and to my beautiful sister, Lesley Dennison, who is nothing like Margot. The well-worn phrase "sisters by chance, best friends by choice" has never been truer.

My dad used to say, "Don't give up the day job," but in my twenty-two years of working for Mark Davis, CEO of Davis Elen Advertising in Los Angeles, I honestly don't want to. Thank you for continuing to be my biggest supporter.

A huge thank-you to my wonderful agent, Dominick Abel,

who has always been there for me day or night. Your candor and support are beyond measure.

I'd like to thank my incredible publishing team at Minotaur Books:

- To Hannah O'Grady, my dream editor, for her gift in making a story better, as well as her extraordinary patience.
- To Kaitlin Severini, my copy editor, whose sharp eye and attention to detail makes me look good.
- To Michelle McMillian, for the interior design of the book, and jacket designer Rowen Davis, for creating such a fabulous cover.
- To Rhys Davies, who transformed my scrappy sketch of Tregarrick Rock into an exquisite map.
- To the equally fabulous duo Senior Marketing Manager Allison Ziegler and Publicist Kayla Janas, whose support and enthusiasm for the Island Sisters is everything any author could hope for. I know I am one of many but you always make me feel special.

Heartfelt thanks go to my talented writer friends—Rhys Bowen, Elizabeth Duncan, Carolyn Hart, Clare Langley-Hawthorne, Jenn McKinlay, Andra St. Ivanyi, Alan Rose, Julian Unthank, Marty Wingate and Daryl Wood Gerber. I'm forever grateful to Claire Carmichael, my writing instructor at the UCLA Extension Writers' Program, where my journey to publication began.

To all my family, who put up with my bizarre behavior when I am in full-on writing mode. Thank you for not judging me.

To my daughter, Sarah, for keeping me organized and grounded, and to the canine gods for sending me Draco and Athena. There is a reason why the affectionate Hungarian Vizsla is called the Ultimate Velcro Dog.

I know I speak for all writers who thank YOU, the reader (with a special mention to Barbara Ballard), along with the incredible libraries, booksellers and online bloggers. Without your support none of our stories would be given life.

And finally, this book is dedicated to producer-writer Mark Durel who in all the years we've been friends and I've needed advice with my plot would say, "Send it over!" And a day later he'd call and say, "It's great but …what if?"

To all his "what ifs" I say thank you.